I0527865

# REIGN

## THE DRAAX SERIES
### BOOK ONE

## ELIZABETH KELLY

EK PUBLISHING INC.

Copyright © 2018 Elizabeth Kelly

Published by
*EK Publishing Inc.*

*ISBN-13: 978-1-988826-24-0*

This book is the copyrighted property of the author and may not be reproduced, scanned or distributed for commercial or non-commercial purposes. Quotes used in reviews are the exception. No alteration of content is allowed.

Your support and respect for the property of this author is appreciated.

This book is a work of fiction, and any resemblance to persons, living or dead, or places, events or locales is purely coincidental. The characters are productions of the author's imagination and used fictitiously.

Edited by
*L. Nunn Editing*

Cover art by
*The Final Wrap*

# REIGN

**One small mistake. Two lives changed forever.**

### Sabrina

I would do anything to save my sister's life. Which is why I'm about to be living on the alien planet of Draax. Giving up three years of my life on earth to be a nanny for the alien who healed my sister should be easy.

Only, I think there's been a mix up. This is a palace, not a farm.

I'm on an alien planet with a malfunctioning translator, a storm trapping me in a home I don't belong in, and a silver-eyed, sexy alien warrior who keeps touching me like I belong to him.

I have a bad feeling he thinks I'm here to have his baby.

### Quillan

As king, my people demand a queen and an heir to the throne. With females of our kind nearly extinct, breeding with the human females is our race's only chance at survival.

I have no desire to be mated for life, but from the

moment I see my future queen, I'm obsessed. I want the curvy human in my bed and by my side at the throne. Her soft kisses, fiery spirit and response to my touch ignite an unending need for her.

There's only one problem – she's breeding incompatible and cannot be my queen.

# CHAPTER 1

*Sabrina*

I noperable.

Incurable.

Two words that had torn through me like a meteorite through a jumpgate.

But two years later, my little sister had beaten cancer. All thanks to a sweet-tasting pink drink called gallberry juice.

I walked into Carrie's bedroom, smiled at my sister, and eased my chubby body onto the bed beside her. "How are you feeling?"

"Much better. I feel like a new person, Sabrina."

"Good." I studied Carrie's pale and thin face before handing her the glass I held. "Drink the last of it."

"I don't think I need to," Carrie said. "I feel much better, and it might be best to save some of the gallberry juice. It's so hard to get."

"You have to drink it all. It's exactly the amount needed to heal you completely. Drink."

Despite being twenty-three, Carrie drank with the obedience of an eager-to-please toddler. When she'd drained the glass, I took it back and set it on the nightstand. "Would you like to get out of bed?"

Carrie nodded, and I pulled back the bedcovers and helped her stand. Shaky and weak, she leaned on me, and we walked slowly past our parents' second-hand hologram screen and into the living area. Only five days ago, my sister was on the verge of death, and now she could get out of bed.

A miracle.

Not a real miracle.

A gallberry juice miracle.

I settled Carrie on the sofa and tucked a heated blanket around her.

"Sabrina?"

"Yes?" I was checking messages on my PAR phone. It was a third-generation model with almost nonexistent holographic capabilities, but it was all I could afford. I looked up when Carrie touched my arm. "What's wrong?"

"Do you have to go to the Draax planet?" She wasn't crying yet, but she was close.

"I can't renege on the contract. I don't look good in prison orange."

"It's a shame you have to give up three years of your life for me."

Her words were right, but the tone was off. Like all I was giving up was a trip to the moon. Hell, even people like us can afford *that* day trip. But it didn't matter. I would give up *fifty*-three years to the Draax if it meant Carrie would live.

I said something I needed to believe was true. "You'd do the same for me. Besides, you'll be fine. You have Josh."

"But I need you, too." Carrie's voice was a quarter coaxing and three-quarters demanding. "Seventy-five light years is so far away. What if I never see you again?"

"Don't be silly. It's an adventure." My tone was as brisk as a cold mountain wind. "I'll send you a hologram or email every day."

"I've heard the Draax aren't nice," Carrie said. "What if your new boss is mean to you?"

Mean to me? I should have been used to Carrie's child-like perception of the world, but that was my fault for sheltering her. Carrie had always been the fragile one.

"Why would he be?" I said. "I'm qualified and competent, and children frickin' love me. His kid will think I'm the bees' knees."

The old saying lured out a sliver of a smile. "But what if they try and keep you there for breeding?"

"They won't. I have a nanny-only contract."

"Their race is dying out. What if the Draax are lying? What if he puts you in chains? What if he forces you to breed?"

I laughed. It was erratic and irregular. Uncertainty coated it. "You have to stop believing everything you read on the InfoNet. The Draax are our allies in the United Space Coalition. The breeding program is voluntary. No one is ever forced."

Carrie continued to stare at me, and I leaned forward and took her hands in mine. "The agency is very reputable. He's a farmer without a wife. This is just another nanny job."

"It isn't just another nanny job." Her voice rose with a what-the-fuck vibe. "You'll be on a different planet in a different star system."

"The Idalia system is only one jumpgate away," I said.

"Maybe he'll let you visit me?"

"Maybe."

I doubted my new employer would allow me to visit. If

the rumours were true, the Draax were rather emotionless. He wouldn't care that I missed my sister.

It was the Draax race that came to our rescue when the planet was attacked by the Gokmards nearly forty years ago. The Gokmards were brutal killers, and their advanced technology destroyed our defense systems within a matter of weeks. We were on the verge of becoming slaves to the Gokmards when the Draax joined the war.

It had all happened before I was born, but I had watched the holograms of the war. The Gokmards had advanced weaponry, while the Draax fought with huge steel swords. By all accounts, the Gokmards should have destroyed the Draax easily. But the Draax were a warrior race. Their large green bodies were as big if not bigger than the Gokmards, and they fought viciously and killed without mercy. At the time, humans believed they had a supernatural ability to heal from the wounds they received during battle.

It wasn't until the war was over that the Draax revealed what allowed them to heal so quickly. The gallberry plant. The light pink plant was a miracle plant as far as humans were concerned. When harvested, the juice extracted from it healed everything from minor cuts to gunshot wounds to – I swallowed heavily – cancer.

"I hope he'll let you visit," Carrie said. "But what if your new employer is tricking you? Plenty of women have gone to the Draax planet for nanny jobs and been tricked into breeding with them."

Carrie had a valid fear. The Draax hadn't saved our planet from the Gokmards out of the goodness of their hearts. Despite being an alien race, their anatomy was remarkably similar to ours – if you ignored the green skin and the tails – and the Draax needed us. Females were rarely born on their planet. Females of mating age were becoming increasingly scarce, and desperate to save their dying race, the Draax had been searching for an alien race that could carry their young.

In exchange for not only saving us from the Gokmards but also supplying us with limited quantities of gallberry juice, the Draax wanted to start a breeding program with us. Earth's highest authorities had agreed quickly.

"He isn't like that," I said to Carrie. "He assured me by email that he had no interest in breeding with me. He only wants a nanny for his child. Besides, I'm not compatible for breeding purposes. It's one of the reasons he chose me to work for him."

Carrie gave me a doubtful look, and I squeezed her hand reassuringly. Only seventy percent of human females could successfully breed with the Draax males. Something about a particular type of gene that some women carried. I didn't know the specifics, and frankly, I didn't care. I wasn't breeding compatible and I was happy about that.

*Are you?* My inner voice whispered.

I flushed brightly. The breeding program the government had developed with the Draax was entirely voluntary for women. Not surprisingly, there weren't many volunteers. Proving themselves to be intelligent as well as capable warriors, rather than take the women by force, the Draax had simply begun to withhold the supply of gallberry juice that Earth had already started to depend on.

Desperate to save their loved ones from diseases, more and more women joined the breeding program. Once they had fulfilled the contract by giving their Draax mate a child, they were free to return to Earth. Many didn't, of course. What mother would want to leave their child? The Draax used their reluctance to leave their children to their advantage, and in the last thirty years, their numbers had begun to grow. Female children were still a rarity, but even that was changing. Thanks to humans, the Draax race was no longer on the verge of extinction.

"Why are you so red, Sabrina?" Carrie asked.

"No reason."

I was lying. I had never spoken to a Draax male, but I'd seen plenty of them. There were always tons of them here on Earth. They spent a lot of time trying to seduce women into breeding with them and joining them on their planet. It wasn't illegal as long as they didn't bribe them with gallberry juice. The use of gallberry juice was strictly regulated by the government and the agencies they had created. Of course, like everything illegal, there was a massive black-market operation for the sale of gallberry juice. Both humans and Draax were involved in it, and according to the government, it was becoming a significant problem.

I was blushing because just the thought of being in a Draax's bed brought a funny pulsing ache between my legs. Obviously, I'd never slept with one, but I knew the rumours as well as the next woman of the Draax's legendary skills in bed.

In fact, most humans believed that our women didn't return to Earth after fulfilling their breeding contract, not because of their bond with their children, but because of their bond with the Draax male they had bred with. Because they craved the pleasure the Draax males gave them.

Draax males were huge and exceptionally strong. I had watched more than one Draax porn hologram in the privacy of my bedroom. Their dicks were massive, and just the thought of trying to take one brought on that funny little ache between my legs and simultaneously scared the hell out of me. The women in the porn holograms never seemed to be frightened by the enormity of the cock they were taking, but they were professionals. I was about as far from a professional sex worker as you could get.

My cheeks now felt like they were on fire. I spent my time working and caring for my sister, and there was no time for dating. I was the only twenty-five-year-old virgin I knew, and it embarrassed me more than I would admit. I was anxious to get rid of my virginity – hell, I had more pent-up desire and lust than was healthy - but sleeping with a Draax male for my first time was a terrible idea.

I hadn't actually heard of a woman being split in two by a Draax dick, but it's not like they'd let that information get out to the general public, would they?

*You're being ridiculous, Sabrina!* My inner voice snapped. *Human females wouldn't still breed with them if the sex was hurting them.*

Sure, they would, I thought morosely. Desperate people did desperate things. If they needed the gallberry plant bad enough, they'd risk the chance of permanent vaginal damage by Draax dick. Hell, in less than a week, I'd be on a completely different planet looking after an alien kid because her father agreed to save my sister's life with gallberry juice.

*Yeah, and you would have bred with one if you were compatible.*

It was true. I applied for the breeding program first as there were more available positions than with the nanny program, which had cropped up in the last ten years. When I tested incompatible, I applied to the nanny program in desperation, not expecting to get chosen. To my surprise, an alien had chosen my application – a combination of my nanny experience, plain old luck, and his desire for a human female who he couldn't breed with.

I shook off the small trickle of hurt I felt. It was ridiculous to be hurt by a Draax's lack of interest in mating with me. It had nothing to do with my looks or the chubbiness of my body. I wasn't compatible for mating so a Draax would have no interest in me.

Unfortunately, I didn't have many prospects with males of my kind either. I was taller than most men cared for – why did so many men want short women? – and the extra forty pounds I carried wasn't appealing to them either.

Feeling sorry for myself and my inability to lose my virginity was stupid. I knew I could find a guy who was willing to overlook my chunky thighs and stomach for a wham, bam, thank you ma'am quickie before I left for the Draax planet, but I couldn't do it. I wasn't into casual sex, even if it meant I would be the world's oldest virgin when I finally returned to Earth.

*How do you know you're not into casual sex?* My inner voice pouted. *You might be. You could at least try it and see, for God's sake.*

"Sabrina? Are you still in there?" Carrie's finger poked me in the middle of the forehead.

"Yes. What did you say?"

"I asked about the…other thing," Carrie said. It was her turn to go red even though she'd had sex and was no innocent.

"The other thing isn't going to be an issue. I already told you he's not interested in me like that."

"But what if he is? What if he's interested, and he wants you to have sex with him and – and another?" Carrie's face went down in a little moue of disgust.

I tried to arrange my face to mimic hers. "I'm not going to have a threesome with my employer and another Draax male."

"But they like that sort of thing!" Carrie almost wailed. "You know they do."

My little sister wasn't wrong. Compared to humans, the Draax had a very free-spirited attitude when it came to sex. Their fondness for threesomes with a human female was well known, and there was plenty of pornographic hologram evidence to back it up. Although the research I did before I applied to the breeding program suggested that the Draax encouraged females to choose only one male when it came to marriage and breeding.

A little shiver went down my back. What would it be like to be with not one Draax but two? I wanted to be disgusted like my sister was, I wanted to pretend it was wrong and sick, but the heat in my belly and the sudden throbbing of my pussy wouldn't let me.

I almost laughed out loud. I'd never taken a single dick, and here I was fantasizing about two. What was wrong with me?"

"Sabrina? What are you thinking about? Your face is really red now," Carrie said.

"Nothing."

Carrie gave me an uncertain look but said, "Is he handsome?

I shrugged. "I have no idea. I've only seen pictures of his daughter. She has purple skin and is a pretty little thing. I'm sure I'll get along very well with her."

"What if he's handsome?"

I frowned at her. "What does it matter?"

"You might fall in love with him and stay on the planet forever. I'll never see you again." Carrie's face drew down into a pout. "I need you, Sabrina. Now that I'm better, Josh and I are considering having a family. I can't have a baby without you here to help me. You know I need you, right? Promise me you'll come back after the three years are up.

Promise me you won't be like other women and fall in love with one of the aliens."

I tried not to think bitter thoughts. Carrie didn't mean to be selfish. She didn't really want me to be alone forever, with my only purpose in life being to make hers easier. She was just young and immature, and she depended on Josh and me to care for her.

I squeezed her hand again. "Honey, that's not going to happen. Stop worrying, okay? Everything is going to be fine. I'll be back before you know it, and while I'm gone, we'll email every day and hologram chat at least once a week."

Carrie's lower lip trembled before she sniffed. "Yes, okay. Just please say that you'll come back to me. Please."

I leaned forward and hugged her. "I'll come back. I love you, honey."

"I love you too."

# CHAPTER 2

*Quillan*

"**M**y king." Teo bowed low as he entered my private quarters. I made an irritable snort before gesturing for him to sit down.

"What is it?" I stared out the window at the dark sky.

"Your new mate arrives tomorrow. Have you even looked at her file?"

"No." I stood and, my tail swishing angrily, stalked across my private quarters to the kitchen. I grabbed a gallberry juice from the cold storage unit and drank half of it in three large gulps. I didn't need it. I was in top form despite my sparring with Galan this morning, but I welcomed the rush of energy it gave me.

"You need to look at it," Teo said.

"Why?" I grumbled. "I don't care to know anything about her."

"She will be your mate, my king!" Teo said in exasperation.

"Only in words. You know I have no interest in a mate, Teo."

"Yes, but you do want to be a father," he said.

My advisor had a point. I did want to be a father – desperately, in fact. My paternal urges had kicked in nearly two moons ago. It was the only reason I had even agreed to a mate. Of course, if I wasn't king, I could breed and have children without the necessity of performing the mating ritual and binding myself to a female.

I drank the rest of the gallberry juice and tried not to noticeably shudder at the thought of being bound to a female. Not just a female, but a human female.

"Stop looking like that, my king," Teo said dryly as if he had read my mind. "Do you know how many of your men would gladly take your place for the chance to be bound to a human female?"

"Then perhaps I will trade places with them." My voice was sulky and not at all king-like.

Teo sighed. "I know it has been difficult for you since your brother died, Quill. You never expected to shoulder the burden of ruling. I wish I could help you with that, but you have no choice. The kingdom is yours now, and your people want you to have an heir. It makes them nervous that you do not."

"It will be a half-human heir," I said.

"Just as most of our children are now. Your people believe that a half-human heir is better than no heir at all," Teo said. "They are right."

"I do not see why I need to be mated."

Teo rolled his eyes. Only he would dare be so blatantly disrespectful to me. "It is custom for the king to have a queen. The human is a good choice for you. She is meek and quiet in personality and very strong and healthy. More importantly, she tests very high in compatibility for breeding. She will have no trouble carrying and bearing your young."

"Does she have other children?" I asked.

"No, my king. We thought it best that you marry a human woman who has no other children or family on Earth."

I had a sudden thought and gave Teo a horrified look. "She is not an innocent, is she?"

He shook his head, and I stared at him suspiciously. "Are you certain? I have no wish to deflower a virgin. Human females are difficult enough to fuck when they have experience taking cock."

Teo frowned at my crudeness, but I was speaking the truth. Before becoming king, I had made many trips to Earth and slept with plenty of human women. The number of them who chose to move to our planet and breed with us was still too low as far as I was concerned, but that didn't mean they didn't want to fuck us with no commitments required. It was ridiculously easy to bed human women, even without the lure of the gallberry plant or speaking their language. Simply buy them one of their foul-tasting drinks at the entertainment establishments they called bars, and they were yours for the taking.

None of the human females I'd fucked knew of my stature as royalty, and I always used the human's ridiculous looking but effective rubber contraception method before sleeping with them. I loved the softness and curves of human women as much as the next Draax did, but it was occasionally a lot of work to fuck them. It could take forever to get them wet enough for me to enter them, and even then, not a single one of the human females I'd fucked could take my cock in its entirety. Still, beggars could not be choosers, as the humans liked to say.

"I am certain." Teo's green skin was darkening as his irritation with me grew. "Read the file, Quill."

I nodded, but it was for show. I didn't care about the woman I would be mated to. As long as she was quiet, didn't question me and accepted both my cock and my rule over her, we would get along just fine.

"She realizes this is permanent, does she not?" I said. "That she will not be allowed to return to Earth even after she bears me a child."

"Yes. It was made very clear to her, and she accepted the terms of the agreement."

"Why?" Very few women willingly agreed to stay on the Draax planet when they first entered the breeding program. Of course, nearly a hundred percent of them changed their minds once they arrived. Most Draax men were eager to mate permanently and were excellent mates to their females. Females were precious on our planet, and they were treated as such.

Once a human female realized that they were reluctant to return to the human men who did not revere them the way they deserved. Of course, there was an exception to every rule, and I supposed that was me in this particular case. While I understood how precious females were, I lacked the yearning that other Draax males did to be mated to one. I wanted children, not a mate.

"Does it matter?" Teo asked. "We got lucky in finding a female who agreed to be mated permanently to a male she has never met. Do not question it."

"How much gallberry juice did she ask for?"

"Only a small amount. A human measurement of a gallon."

"Are you serious?"

"I am," Teo said.

14

"A gallon of gallberry juice in exchange for altering her life forever." I mulled that over briefly before asking, "Is she ugly? Small?"

I waited anxiously for Teo's response. So many human females were too thin. Galan had told me that most human males preferred their females bony. I would never understand that. What male didn't want a female with lush, heavy breasts to suck on and wide hips to grip during fucking? I had never thought to ask my best friend his preference, but the females Galan and I had shared over the years were always curvy.

"I do not know," Teo said. "The file has images of her. Look at it."

I just shrugged. "Does she speak Draax?"

"No, of course not. You know it's difficult for the humans to speak our language."

"Perfect," I muttered. "Mated to a woman who cannot even speak to me."

"I would think that would make you happy. You have no interest in speaking to her, remember?"

I glared at Teo. "I still need to communicate with her from time to time. I need to correct her if she is disrespectful or tell her how to raise my young properly."

"She will have a translator embedded just like every breeder," Teo said. "The ship should be here at dusk tomorrow. It would be good if you were there when it landed."

"No."

"It would show your people you are serious about being mated and producing an heir."

"No," I repeated as my green skin darkened. I scrubbed a hand through my thick black hair as my tail flicked back and forth. "You and Galan can meet her and bring her back to the palace. I will meet her then."

Teo didn't reply and I picked up my sword and made a few experimental swings with it. "Did you ready guest quarters for her?"

"Yes, but she should be sharing your private quarters."

I gave Teo a look of horror. "No. She is not allowed in here, Teo. Do you hear me?"

A shudder went down my back, and my tail drooped to the ground at the thought of another person living with me. As king, I was around others constantly. My personal quarters were my sanctuary, and I only allowed Teo and Galan to join me here for extended periods. I would not extend that courtesy to my new queen.

"It will be hard to mate with her if she is not in your bed," Teo said.

"Fine. She can mate with me and then return to her bed," I acquiesced.

"Those who work in the palace will tell others you do not share a bed with your mate."

"I do not care."

"You have always been stubborn," Teo said with a low sigh.

I grinned at him before flicking my tail out and smacking his thigh with it. "You enjoy my stubbornness, old friend. It makes your job more exciting."

A gust of wind rattled the windows. I moved to the closest one and stared at the setting sun. "A storm is coming."

"Yes. The elders predict it will last at least a moon length."

I groaned loudly. A moon of being confined to the palace. I would go mad.

"It will give you plenty of time to breed your new mate," Teo said. "If you are diligent in your duties, perhaps she will carry your young before the storm ends."

"Hmmph," I snorted as Teo stood with a slight groan. He rubbed at his back.

"Take some gallberry juice with you," I said.

He shrugged. "It does not help like it used to, my king."

A little spike of fear went through me. I shook it off and grabbed two bottles of the juice to hand to him. Teo was aging, but he still had many years left.

"Drink both," I demanded.

"Yes, my king."

I hesitated and then hugged him roughly. "Thank you, Teo."

He returned my hug. "For what, Quill?"

"Everything," I said with a grin. "I will see you in the morning, all right?"

"Yes. Good night."

"Good night, old friend."

When he left, I retired to my bedroom and stretched out on the bed. I stared at the space next to me. That spot would have a warm female by this time tomorrow. Despite my apprehension, my cock stirred in my pants. I had not fucked a female since becoming king nearly a sun cycle ago, and I was growing tired of my own hand.

I thought briefly about looking at my soon-to-be mate's file but turned on my side and closed my eyes instead. Hopefully, she wouldn't be ugly or small, but it didn't matter that much if she was. I would just close my eyes when I was fucking her.

If she was ugly or we weren't compatible in bed, I only needed her to give me one heir. After that, she could do whatever she wanted, and I would slake my needs with other females I found more appealing.

"You are slowing down, Quill."

I bared my teeth at Galan and attacked with renewed vigor. He parried each of my blows, our swords gleaming in the light as we sparred. My best friend and I had always been even in match when it came to battle, but Galan was right. I had slowed down a little. My duties as king prevented me from sparring as often as I'd like, and I was downright forbidden to engage in battle.

We backed away from each other, both breathing heavily. "Perhaps you would like to take over the king's duties while I return to my former position as head of the guard?"

Galan laughed. "Definitely not, Quill. You know I would be a terrible king."

I lowered my sword and stretched my other arm above my head, loosening the tight muscles. "I fear I am not much better."

"You are a good king," Galan said.

"No, I am a good warrior. I was meant to lead my people in battle, not from the throne."

Galan gave me a sympathetic look. "The guard misses you as well."

I shook off my melancholy. It didn't matter that I had never wanted to be king. It only mattered that I was. "Ignore me. I have a duty to my people, and I am proud to do it. I am just feeling sorry for myself. Come, let us begin again."

"I cannot." Galan hung his sword on the wall. "I am leaving to pick up your mate."

I grunted disinterestedly before hanging my sword next to Galan's.

"Are you sure you do not want to come with us?" Galan asked.

"Positive."

"Quill…"

I clapped Galan on the back. "Speak your mind, Galan."

"Will you ask me to join you?"

I shrugged carelessly. "Of course. If the female is willing, that is. But why would she not be?" I grinned at Galan. "Human females always find two cocks better than one. Why would you even ask? You know you are always welcome to join me."

"You are king now, Quill, and she will be your mate, not some random female we seduce into fucking. You will be trying to actively breed her, remember? Your people do not want a bastard child in line for the throne."

"She is my mate only by ritual. And as far as the breeding – we have plenty of the human's," I paused as I tried to remember the word, "rubbers here at the castle. You can use them."

Galan made a face. "I hate them."

"As do I, but they are sometimes a necessity. Listen, if the female is willing, then we will both fuck her. Simple."

"Simple," Galan repeated with a doubtful expression.

"Yes." I clapped him on the back again. "Why must you make things so complicated, my friend? Now, go and collect your future queen and try not to fuck her before you return to the palace."

Galan laughed. "Yes, my king."

*Sabrina*

"SABRINA, WAKE UP."

I blinked rapidly and stared at the blonde woman in the lab coat hovering over me.

"Where am I?" I stared groggily at the unfamiliar white walls.

"The International Space Station." The woman walked to the cot next to me and shook the woman lying on it.

"Evelyn, open your eyes, please," she said loudly as I sat up and rubbed my forehead.

The events of the last twenty-four hours rushed over me, and I ignored my immediate rush of homesickness. My old life on Earth ended yesterday afternoon when I boarded the ship that carried me to the International Space Station. It was late when we'd finally docked, and the other woman on the ship and I were ushered to a room with a dozen narrow cots. Thanks to a combination of nerves and grief over leaving my sister, I hadn't slept at all the previous night, and I was exhausted. I'd fallen asleep almost the moment my head hit the pillow.

Now, I smiled tentatively at the woman sitting up in the bed next to me. We looked strikingly similar with our chubby bodies and dark hair. Although, she was about twenty pounds lighter than me, and she had green eyes rather than blue. I also didn't sport the large, purple bruise on her shoulder where her top had slipped.

The woman gave me a nervous look and pulled the shirt up to cover the bruise. A little embarrassed to be caught staring, I said, "Hi, I'm Sabrina. I didn't get the chance to introduce myself yesterday. It was pretty loud on the ship."

She smiled at me and said in a soft voice, "I'm Evelyn. It's nice to meet you."

"Nice to meet you, too." I glanced at the empty cots around us. "Not many volunteers on this trip, huh?"

"Are you in the breeding program?" Evelyn asked tentatively.

I shook my head. "No. I have a job as a nanny. You?"

"Breeding program." A look of fear crossed Evelyn's face, and I reached across and touched her arm.

"You okay?"

"Yes. Just, uh, a little nervous."

"Understandable, but I hear the Draax treat their females very well."

She gave me another scared little smile, and I reached out and squeezed her arm. Her timid nature reminded me of Carrie and made me feel connected to her in a small way. "I'm sure it will be fine."

"Yes," she said, but I could hear the fear in her voice.

Before I could reassure her again, the woman who had woken us came bustling back into the room. I studied Evelyn's fabric-covered shoulder for a moment. "Hey. Do you have any gallberry juice she can have?"

The woman scowled at me. "Of course not. Don't be ridiculous." She had a harried and distracted vibe, and she yanked a giant syringe from the left pocket of her lab jacket as she approached me.

"Whoa," I held up my hands, "what is that for?"

"It's your identification chip," she said impatiently. "It has all of your details as well as the details of the Draax male you're breeding with."

"Not breeding," I said in alarm, "nannying."

"Yes, yes," the woman said irritably. "Lift your sleeve."

I lifted my sleeve and tried not to flinch when she injected me in the upper arm with the syringe. It stung, and she wiped it with a cotton ball before taking another syringe from her right pocket and moving to Evelyn.

"Arm, please," she said as the flag emblem on her lab jacket glowed brightly. "Oh for…"

She sighed and slapped her hand against it as Evelyn pushed up her sleeve.

"Yes, what is it?"

A man appeared in a hologram behind Evelyn. "Are they ready for transport? A storm is brewing on Draax, and we want to get them there and drop them off before it gets too bad and we end up stranded."

"I'm just chipping them now, and then I need to put the translators in," the woman said.

"Well, get a move on it," the man said irritably. "We're leaving in ten."

"Shut up, Gary." The woman slapped the emblem again. Gary disappeared, and she injected Evelyn with the syringe.

"There," she said. "If you get lost, they can scan you and know who you belong to."

"Oh, perfect," I said, "we've been microchipped like stray dogs."

The woman scowled at me as Evelyn gave me a horrified look. I grinned at her as the woman in the lab coat said, "You might want to watch your mouth when you're on Draax. They like the women they sleep with to be submissive and quiet."

"Well, it's a good job I'm nannying and not fucking then," I said.

Evelyn's mouth dropped open as the woman made a loud snort of irritation. She stood, rummaged in the inside pocket of her lab coat, and removed two small gun-like contraptions.

"What are those?" I asked.

"The translators. One is embedded in your skull here," she pointed to just behind Evelyn's right ear, "it'll translate the Draax language into English for you instantly when they speak to you. The other one is injected here," she touched the spot above the hollow of Evelyn's throat, "and it will translate your English to Draaxan when you speak."

"Right," I said. When I applied for the program, they gave me a little information packet. It explained how the translators worked, and I was relieved I wouldn't have to take a crash course in Draaxan at the time. Of course, watching the woman press what looked like a silver gun to Evelyn's skull made me wonder if learning the language might not have been the way to go.

"Is it going to hurt?" Evelyn asked in her soft voice.

"It's not going to feel like kisses, sweetheart," the woman said.

Evelyn flinched, her face drawing down with pain when the woman pulled the trigger on the gun.

"Lift your head," the woman said as she reached for the second device. Without ceremony, she injected the second translator into Evelyn's throat. A trickle of blood slipped down her throat, and the woman held a piece of gauze against the entry point. "Apply pressure for a few minutes."

She left Evelyn pressing the gauze to both her throat and behind her ear, and approached me. As she readied the translator guns, she said, "So, don't panic if these don't work immediately. Sometimes, the chips can take a day or two to start working and translating properly."

I stared at her as she pressed the gun behind my ear. "A day or two? Seriously? We'll be on a strange planet where we won't speak or understand the language for forty-eight hours, and you're just mentioning it – ow! Fuck, that hurt!"

I rubbed at the spot behind my ear and glared at the woman.

"Lift your head," she said.

I lifted my head grudgingly and winced when there was another sharp pain in my throat. Already, I could feel blood seeping into my hair, and I took the gauze from her with a scowl before pressing it against my head and throat.

"Seriously?" I said. "A day or two? Why didn't you implant the damn things before we left Earth then?"

"Not my department." The woman pointed to the far door. "That's the bathroom. You've got five minutes, and then I'll be back to take you to the ship."

---

As we hurtled toward the ground, I held the bottom of my seat on the ship in a death grip. Across from me, Evelyn was the colour of a Draax male, and she had already vomited twice into the little plastic bags tucked into the side of the seats.

"It'll be okay," I shouted at her over the wailing noise of the wind.

She nodded and closed her eyes as I leaned forward and strained to see past the pilots. I wished immediately that I hadn't. It was pitch black outside of the ship's windshield, and as I watched, hail the size of golf balls began to ping off the windshield and metal hull of the ship. The sound was deafening, and I clapped my hands over my ears as the pilots hollered instructions at each other through their headsets. The ship dipped and then dropped with terror-inducing speed. I clung grimly to my seat and tried not to pee my pants as Evelyn made a soft shriek of fear.

"Almost there, ladies!" The pilot shouted.

Why the hell was he laughing?

Oh God, I was going to die.

I really should have emptied my browser history on my tablet. Maybe I'd get lucky, and like me, it would be splattered across the countryside on impact, and no one would see the Draax porn I'd downloaded.

There was another sharp drop that made my stomach

heave up into my throat. I swallowed down terror-induced bile as we hit solid ground with a teeth-rattling thud. If I hadn't been strapped into the seat, even my oversized ass would have gone flying.

As the pilots slowed to a stop, hail continued to ping off the ship, making it impossible to hear anything. I smiled reassuringly at Evelyn as the outside doors opened. A blast of cold air whipped the dark strands that had escaped my braid around my face. I squinted at the two Draax males who boarded the ship.

I'd never been this close to a Draax male before, and I stared wide-eyed at the one who unbuckled my seatbelt and helped me to my feet. He said something I couldn't hear past the sound of the hail. The second male helped Evelyn to her feet and brought her over to me as three more Draax squeezed into the ship. They were all well over six feet tall and had broad chests, narrow hips and short black hair. I tried not to stare at the tails I could see waving back and forth behind them. Without speaking, Evelyn and I put our arms around each other and huddled together as the five Draax males stared at us.

One of the males was obviously older. His body was bent with age, his black hair graying, and he wasn't as muscular as the others. He said something into the ear of the one standing next to him, and the Draax shrugged. The old man pulled a thin silver box from his cloak before approaching us. We allowed him to pull us apart, and Evelyn didn't resist when he pushed up her sleeve and scanned her right arm. The screen lit up, and he read the information before pressing a button and making it disappear. He scanned my arm, reading the information that appeared before nodding and pointing to me. The Draax who had unbuckled me, took my arm and led me toward the door.

Oh good, the stray dog microchip worked.

"Wait!" I shook myself free and hugged Evelyn impulsively. She winced and made a soundless gasp of pain before returning my hug.

"It was nice to meet you, Evelyn," I shouted into her ear over the sound of the hail. "Take care of yourself, okay?"

"You too!" she shouted back.

The Draax took my arm again and gently tugged me to the door. I couldn't understand them, so they probably couldn't understand me either, but I tried anyway. "So, uh, are you my new employer?"

He cocked his head at me and said something that was lost in the sound of the storm. He was rather handsome for a green-skinned alien, and I felt a little tickle of heat deep in my lower belly when he put his hand around my bare arm. I stared at those long fingers, more heat burning in my stomach, before raising my gaze to his. My breath caught in my throat. The alien had gorgeous copper-coloured eyes, and as he scanned my face, they slowly darkened. He pulled me a little closer until I could feel the heat of his body.

"I really hope you're my employer," I said. "Because I just might rethink my whole 'no fucking the boss' stance if you are."

I blushed as soon as the words were out of my mouth. What was I doing? What if the translators had started working the minute I said that? If this surprisingly hot alien were my employer, I'd be mortified. Hell, I'd be mortified no matter what. I wasn't here for breeding.

The alien leaned down and studied my cheeks before tracing his fingers over them. His touch lit up my nerve endings. He was close enough to me now that I heard the low groan that escaped his mouth when I licked my lips. My own groan slipped out when he brushed his thumb along my lower lip.

The older Draax spoke sharply to him, and the alien straightened. The skin on his cheeks was darkening, and I figured that was his version of a blush as he gave the older Draax an apologetic smile.

I squeaked in surprise when the Draax picked me up. "Holy shit, you're strong."

He cradled me against his massive chest as the other Draax draped a cloak over him. It covered both of us completely. As he raised the hood to cover his head, I had one final glimpse of Evelyn smiling nervously at the two remaining Draax standing in front of her. I wondered if one of them was the Draax she would be breeding with and hoped desperately that he was sweet to her. She looked like she would bolt and run at the slightest sign of irritation.

The Draax stepped out into the hail, and I squealed and buried my face against his thick throat to protect it. He jogged through the storm to a large silver land vehicle. He dumped me in the back seat and climbed into the driver's seat. I sat up and looked around as the older man sat beside me. The third Draax was carrying my trunk over his shoulder, and he tossed it into the cargo space behind us before climbing into the passenger seat and slamming the door.

The sound of the hail was not as deafening, but my ears were still ringing. As the vehicle moved forward with a jolt, the old man said something, but I barely noticed. I was staring in delight at the Draax who was driving. The vehicle reminded me very much of the old Earth vehicles. They were powered by gas and people actually steered them themselves. The gas-powered cars were obsolete long before I was born, and I had only seen the old vehicles behind thick protective glass in museums. I watched in fascination as the Draax gripped the steering wheel with his big hands and squinted out the windshield as he drove through the storm. I wondered again if he was my new employer. It wasn't the Draax sitting beside me, he was much too old to have a child as young as the one in the picture, but the other two looked young and healthy.

There was a tap on my arm, and I turned to see the older Draax staring at me. He said something that was complete gibberish to me, and I shook my head. "My translator isn't working."

He pointed to the spot behind my ear and the base of my throat with a questioning look. I nodded and said, "But they're not working. Translators not working yet."

He scowled and rolled his eyes. Although he couldn't understand me, I was pretty confident he had figured out what I was saying. I settled back in my seat as he pulled the silver box from his pocket again and studied the screen.

I wanted to ask them how long it would be to get to my new home, but there was no point in asking them if they didn't understand me. I stared out the vehicle window and hoped like hell that my translator would start working soon.

# CHAPTER 3

*Quillan*

I tapped my foot against the cold stone floor. The storm was worsening by the moment, and I regretted not going with Teo, Galan, and Faro to pick up the human female. Galan could handle the vehicle during the storm, but I was still worried.

I paced back and forth in the great hall of the palace. Various employees hurried in and out. I nodded to each of them when they made small bows before hurrying on their way. The palace was always full of people, and I wondered if I shouldn't wait for my new mate in the guest quarters. Our first meeting might be best done in private in case she was ugly. My people didn't need to see my disappointment. It would make them fearful that I would not fulfill my duty as king and produce an heir.

Before I could message Teo and tell him to meet me in the guest quarters, the front doors opened, and the three of them staggered in from the wind. Faro strained to close the doors behind them as Teo pushed back his hood and bowed.

"Good evening, my king."

"Teo, are you all right?" I asked.

"Yes. But the storm has descended earlier than we thought. I am afraid the vehicle took a beating from the hail. We will not be going anywhere for the next moon."

"I do not care about that." I gripped Teo's arm and looked him over. "You are certain the hail did not injure you?"

"Yes."

"Good." I breathed a sigh of relief before peering around him. "Where is she?"

"Here, my king," Teo said.

He turned to Galan and pulled his cloak off with a flourish. Galan was cradling the female against his chest, and her face was buried in his neck. Her dark hair hung to the middle of her back in a thick plait, and I stared at the soft curves of her body. My cock twitched, and I felt an uncharacteristic thread of anger toward my best friend as I stared at the way his hand gripped her thick thigh.

It was hard to tell with how she rested in Galan's arms, but she looked a little thinner than I liked. But I wouldn't know for sure until she was standing. Her arms were wrapped tightly around Galan's neck, and an involuntary growl of irritation escaped my throat. She shouldn't be clinging to Galan. She was my mate, not his.

"Show me your face," I said.

"Her translator is not working yet, my king," Teo said.

My sigh of frustration turned into a sharp inhale when the little female lifted her head and turned her face to me. Krono help me, she was beautiful. I studied her pale skin, so different from the purple of the females of my race but still oddly appealing. Her eyes were a light blue, and they widened when I studied her full lips. Her round little cheeks flushed red with colour, and I watched the red creep down her neck. Did that delightful flush of red cover her entire body? I suddenly, desperately wanted to find out.

"Put her down," I barked at Galan.

He glanced at Teo before carefully setting the little human on her feet. She was taller than most human females but short compared to my nearly seven feet. Still, she was delightfully curvy with heavy breasts that I couldn't wait to cup in my hands. What colour were her nipples, I wondered. How big would they get when I sucked on them?

I wanted to take her back to my private quarters and find out.

I realized she was staring up at me with a look of apprehension. She hadn't curtsied or bowed, and I frowned at her. Did humans not know how to greet royalty properly? She stared at me like she didn't care that I was the king.

My frown deepened, and the little human stepped back before staring anxiously at Galan. She actually pressed her body against him, like she thought he would protect her. Fresh irritation flickered through me. She was mine to protect.

"Come to me." My voice was harsher than I intended. She hesitated and glanced at Galan again when I held my hand out.

Galan gave her a gentle push forward, and she made an adorable little squeak when I took her hand and pulled her into my embrace. I studied her face before leaning down and burying my face into her neck. Krono, she smelled good. I inhaled again as my hand dipped down to grip her full ass.

She squeaked again and tried to wiggle out of my grip. I scowled and wrapped my hand around her thick braid before tugging her head back. She was staring at me anxiously, and I smiled before brushing my lips against her cheek. Had I ever felt skin that soft?

"Do not be afraid," I told her. "This is what you are here for, remember? I will breed you tonight, and you will see you have nothing to fear."

I traced my thumb over her trembling bottom lip as Teo said, "Perhaps you should give her an evening to rest, my king."

"No," I said. "I want her now."

"Her translator is not working yet," Teo reminded me. "You know it often takes a day or two before -"

"She does not need to understand what I am saying to fuck me."

"At least let her eat and have a hot bath. Her stomach grumbled on the ride here, and it was freezing out. I fear the humans cannot hold their heat as well as we do," Teo said.

"Fine." I ran my thumb over her lips again. "But first, I want to taste her."

She was talking to me and making hard, jabbing motions with her tiny hands. I couldn't understand a word, but I liked the sound of her soft voice. Still, I didn't want to listen, I wanted to taste, so I dipped my head and pressed my mouth against hers. Her lips closed abruptly, and I pushed my tongue at the seam of them until she parted them again with a low noise in the back of her throat. I wanted to kiss her hard, wanted to show her who she now belonged to, but her entire body was vibrating against mine, and her little hands were gripping my arms with fear, not desire.

I kept my mouth gentle, ignoring the fact that Teo, Galan and Faro were standing behind us, and urged her tongue into my mouth. I sucked on her tongue and growled with satisfaction when her pelvis bucked against me. I put my arm around her waist and lifted her – she weighed next to nothing – until her pussy was notched against my thickening cock. I rubbed her against my cock, and she made a sweet little moan that lit my blood on fire. I deepened the kiss as I cupped one heavy breast with my other hand and kneaded it. Her back arched, and I could suddenly smell her arousal. She was wet for me already, and it sent an answering surge of lust through my large body. I couldn't wait to fuck her.

I was just about to pin her up against the wall and yank her pants down so I could sink my cock into her pussy, when Teo cleared his throat. I had entirely forgotten about the three men, and I pulled my mouth away from my mate's as she made a small whimper of need.

"Shh, my mate." I set her down and stroked her hair. "You will have my cock soon. I promise. Teo, take her to the guest quarters, ensure she is fed, and has a bath. I will be there in an hour."

"Yes, my king."

Teo and the other two bowed, but my mate just stared at me with a dazed look.

Her refusal to bow or curtsey was actually kind of cute, and I pressed another quick kiss against her mouth before pushing her toward Teo. "Go on, mate."

---

### Sabrina

I STARED AT THE WOMAN IN THE MIRROR. I TOUCHED MY RED, swollen lips and the woman in the mirror touched her red, swollen lips. Behind me, steam rolled up from the tub in lazy swirls. The bathroom was starting to become downright muggy.

"What just happened?" I whispered.

The woman in the mirror stared silently at me, and I turned abruptly and stripped off my clothes before unbraiding my hair and climbing into the tub. I was freezing cold, and the hot water felt amazing. I took a deep breath and slipped completely under the water, staring at the wavering ceiling as I listened to my heart beating in my ears. My head ached dully from where the translator was inserted, and so did my throat. I held my breath until my lungs were screaming at me and then sat up and gasped for air as the water streamed over my body.

I sank into the tub until just my head stuck out of the water and stared at the ceiling. Okay, something had obviously gone terribly wrong. I didn't need a working translator to know that. For one, I was in a giant house that reminded me of a damn palace rather than a farmhouse. For another, there was no sign of the little girl I was supposed to be nannying.

*It's late*, my inner voice said. *She's probably in bed.*

"Oh yeah, maybe," I said in a loud and decidedly hysterical voice. "That's a perfectly reasonable explanation. Of course, it doesn't explain why the biggest fucking Draax male I've ever seen manhandled me in front of three other Draax. What was that about, huh?"

My inner voice remained silent, and I groaned and slapped my hand against my forehead. Fuck. I knew exactly what had happened, and just because I didn't want to say it out loud didn't mean it wasn't true.

I took a deep breath and said, "There was a mix up. That stupid woman injected me with the wrong goddamn microchip. They scanned it at the ship and it said I was Evelyn. He thinks I'm Evelyn, and he thinks I'm going to breed with him. Fuck me sideways."

*If you're not careful, he probably will*, my inner voice said cheerfully.

I groaned again. Okay, I needed to think about how I

would fix this. The translator wasn't working and probably wouldn't work until tomorrow. I might be naïve to sex, but I was pretty certain that the big green guy with the incredibly gorgeous silver eyes, who had touched me like I belonged to him, was planning on trying to have sex with me tonight. I needed to figure out how to tell him it was a case of mistaken identity before that happened.

*Why?*

Why? Because I wasn't Evelyn! Because I wasn't compatible for breeding! Because the guy's dick had felt about twelve inches long when he rubbed it against me, and I'd never had a normal size dick anywhere near my hoo-hah, let alone a monster dick.

If I didn't want to be dicked to death, I needed to figure out how to communicate with the big guy and quick.

"Maybe I could draw him a picture," I said before laughing.

Draw him a picture of what? A dick with a big X across it? I had a feeling that wouldn't be enough to deter him. For the first time in my life, it was very clear that a man wanted me, and I had no idea how to tell him I didn't reciprocate his feelings.

*Uh, except you kind of do. Or have you forgotten the way you tried to hump him in front of his friends? You certainly weren't trying to stop him when he kissed you, when he grabbed your ass and your tits.*

"Shut up!" I muttered. "It took me by surprise, that's all."

*Bullshit. You wanted him. You were so wet for him from one little kiss that you were practically swimming in your panties.*

I ignored my inner voice. Just because his touch had turned me on a little didn't mean I needed to give up my V-card to him. I sat up and studied the tiled wall beside the tub. There was a panel in the wall with three green buttons, and I studied it before pushing the closest one experimentally. A stream of sweet-smelling soap shot out of a hole beneath the button. I pushed the button again, holding the facecloth draped over the side of the tub to catch the soap before quickly washing my body. When I rubbed the cloth between my legs, the dull ache between my legs intensified, and I hesitated before dropping the cloth. I rinsed the soap away before touching my clit. It was swollen and protruding from between my pussy lips, and I felt a moment of embarrassment before I rubbed it briskly. The guy turned me on, so what? He was a good kisser, and any woman would get a little turned on when a guy looked at her like he looked at me.

It felt a little awkward to be masturbating, but I needed to do something. Maybe if I took the edge off, I wouldn't be so tempted to let the alien take me to his bed. I closed my eyes and thought about how it had felt when the Draax had kissed me. The way he tugged on my bottom lip, the feel of his mouth sucking on my tongue.

I moaned softly, my hips arching up as I grew closer and closer. I wasn't going to last very long. In fact, I was about three seconds away from coming when there was a knock on the door, and it opened.

I screamed and scrambled into a sitting position, throwing my arms over my naked tits as the very alien I was masturbating over grinned at me. He started to step into the room, and I shook my head vigorously and shouted, "No! No, I need privacy! Go on! Shoo, big alien! Shoo!"

I waved my arm at him, keeping the other one clamped across my breasts as he scowled. He took another step into the room, and I glared at him and increased my waving. "No! Go on! I'll be right out!"

I sighed with relief when he retreated and shut the door.

The minute it was closed, I jumped out of the tub and snatched the towel from the hook on the wall. I dried my body hurriedly as I wrapped my hair in a smaller towel, turban-style. My trunk of clothing and personal items was in the bedroom, and there wasn't a robe in the bathroom. I wrapped the bath towel around my ample body and tucked the edge in securely. Unfortunately, the Draax seemed to have smaller than average towels. While it fit around my chub, it barely covered my ass and crotch, and I would have to walk very carefully to the bedroom. I opened the bathroom door and peeked out. The alien was standing by the table in the small kitchen, and I barely noticed the platter of food on the table. My attention was taken by the smoldering look on his face as he stared at my cleavage before studying my bare legs. My pussy ached pleasantly, and I could practically feel my nipples standing to attention.

"Oh no," I said under my breath. "Nope, this is not a good idea."

I held my hand up. "Stay there, please. I'll be right back."

I walked carefully toward the bedroom, holding my hand over my barely-covered ass to keep the towel from rising. I had gone half a dozen steps when his long, surprisingly strong tail wrapped around my waist and dragged me back.

"Wait! I'm not who you think I am!" I held desperately to the hem of the towel as he lifted me in his arms. He brought me back to the table instead of carrying me to the bedroom. Jesus, was that disappointment I was feeling? I didn't want him to carry me off to the bedroom like some barbarian and have his dirty way with me. Did I?

*Yes, please.*

*You're not helping!* I snapped at my inner voice.

My disappointment disappeared when the big alien sat down and plopped me onto his lap like I was a little kid. The towel had hiked up, and even though the front of my crotch was still covered, my bare ass and the bottom of my pussy were resting directly on his lap. I blushed and tried to stand. He held me tightly and kissed my bare shoulder, smiling when it brought goose bumps skittering to life on my skin before he tugged the towel away from my hair. He combed his fingers through my long locks, and I winced when he brushed against the spot where the useless translator was embedded.

He frowned and parted my hair to stare at the spot before tipping my head up and studying the base of my neck. I had a small scab at the injection site, and he kissed it tenderly before smiling at me.

I pulled at the hem of my towel before trying to tighten it around my chest. "Um, do you think I could get dressed? Or maybe sit in that chair over there?"

I tried to slide off his lap and his smile turned into a frown. He held me on his lap with one hard hand on my hip as he stared at the spot on my throat again. Without speaking, he reached across the table and picked up a glass. It was filled to the brim with pink liquid, and I took it with shaking hands when he handed it to me.

It was gallberry juice. I could tell from the colour and the smell. I gave him a hesitant look. Gallberry juice was like pure gold on earth, and I had never tasted it before. Having an entire glass for small sore spots on my head and throat felt like a waste.

"Um, I don't need this." I tried to set the glass down.

He scowled again and pushed the glass toward me before making a drinking motion. I licked my lips and sipped cautiously at the liquid. It was delicious, sweet and thick and reminded me a little of strawberries. I drank it more eagerly as he made a soft sound of approval. I drank over half of it before stopping to take a breath.

"Oh my God, that's so good." My head and throat no longer hurt, and the weariness lingering in my body was completely gone. I felt like I could run a damn marathon.

"I feel so much better," I said as I stared at the glass. I set it down before I was tempted to drink more. That shit could get addictive real quick. The alien frowned and handed the glass to me. I shrugged and finished it off. Who was I to argue if he wanted to share his magic healing juice.

"So, uh, my name is Sabrina." I touched my chest. "Not Evelyn. Sabrina. There's been a mix up, and I'm not who you think I am. I'm Sabrina." I touched my chest again.

The alien stared at me before touching my chest. "Sabrina."

God, his low and gravelly voice saying my name did things to my insides. I ignored the quaking and nodded. "That's right. I'm Sabrina."

We were making progress. The alien would know his new breeding female's name, so now he knew I wasn't her. "There's been a mistake. I'm Sabrina Green." I shook my head. "Not Evelyn."

"Sabrina Green," he said again before touching his chest. "Quill."

"Quill," I repeated. "That's, um, a cool name, but maybe you want to find your friends and tell them I'm not Evelyn. Explain the mix up?"

He ignored me and reached for the platter of food. He held out what looked like beef, and I tried to take it from his fingers. He shook his head, and I leaned back as he tried to feed me. "I can feed myself."

He made a growling noise and held the food out of reach when I tried to take it from him. I glared at him and reached for the platter of food on the table. He put one big arm around me, pinning my arms to my sides with ease, and I sighed in frustration.

"I really would prefer to feed myself."

He just held out the food, and I rolled my eyes before opening my mouth. He placed it on my tongue, and I waited until he withdrew his fingers before closing my mouth. I chewed tentatively at the food. It was delicious, spicy with a hint of pepper, and I didn't object when he fed me more. I was suddenly ravenously hungry and enthusiastically tried everything he gave me off the platter.

I ate way more than usual, but I hadn't eaten all day and was starving. Still, when I finally stopped eating and shook my head, he gave me an irritated look and tried to feed me one more piece of sweet, juicy yellow food that reminded me of watermelon.

"No, I'm full," I said. "But thank you."

He stared at his fingers. They were sticky with juice, and I pressed my lips together when he touched the pads of his fingers against them. It was obvious what he wanted, and I shook my head when he poked at my mouth. He arched his eyebrow at me and waited patiently.

After a few minutes, I gave in and opened my mouth. Quill slipped his first two fingers into my mouth, and I licked them clean as he watched. When they were clean, I tried to move my head back, and he shook his head and cupped the back of my skull. He said something that I didn't understand, but I had no trouble interpreting the hot look of need in his eyes. It set off a pang of pure desire in my belly, and I shifted on his lap before sucking on his fingers.

He made a low sound of approval and watched as I sucked hard on his fingers. I'd never done anything remotely like this before. My sexual experience was limited to a few over-the-shirt grope sessions with a boy in high school and time alone in my bedroom getting myself off, but the way his cock hardened under my ass made me suck enthusiastically.

I moaned a little in disappointment when he pulled his fingers free of my mouth, but he threaded his hand in my hair and pulled my head back so he could kiss me. I sucked at his tongue when he pushed it between my lips, and his hand tightened in my hair before he reached down and untucked my towel.

I grabbed at it as it fell to my lap, but he pushed my flailing hands aside and cupped my breast before squeezing lightly. I could feel the power in his hand, but I didn't feel any fear that he would hurt me. He pulled his mouth away and stared down at my breasts. His silver eyes were darkening, turning an equally appealing slate grey, and I caught my breath when his thumb swept over my nipple. It hardened immediately, and he made another sound of approval before capturing it between his thumb and finger and pulling.

I moaned, and he paused, studying my face before pinching my nipple. I gasped with a combination of pleasure and pain, and he smiled, revealing his straight white teeth, before kissing me again. His hand continued to caress and squeeze both my breasts, and I was helpless to stop from arching my back.

I was so turned on I couldn't think straight, and I had forgotten all the reasons why I shouldn't let the alien fuck me. In fact, I thought a little hysterically as his hand unfolded the towel from around my waist to expose my pussy, I might go a bit crazy if I didn't find some relief. I had never felt this type of pulsing, all-encompassing need before, and it didn't seem to matter that I barely knew him. He wanted me, and God help me, I wanted him too.

His big warm hand pushed at my thighs, and I widened

them eagerly so he could cup my pussy. He made a noise of surprise, and I flushed bright red when he pulled his hand from between my thighs and stared at his fingers. They were soaked with moisture, an embarrassing amount, actually, and I tried to yank the towel around me as he studied his fingers.

"Oh God, this is embarrassing," I muttered. I could feel my damn juices dripping down my thighs, and when he set me on my feet and stood, there was a giant wet spot on his pants.

"Oh no," I moaned as my face turned bright red. The guy hadn't even touched my pussy, and I had ruined his damn pants. "I'm so sorry. I – oh my gosh!"

The giant alien pulled my towel away and lifted me over his shoulder like I weighed nothing. He caressed my ass with his big hand before dipping his fingers between my thighs.

"Oh! Ohhh!" I moaned as his fingers brushed across my clit. He carried me into the bedroom and dropped me on the bed. He stripped off his shirt and pants, and I stared at his dick. My mouth dropped open, and he grinned when I shook my head and tried to squirm off the bed.

"Nope," I said. "Uh uh – no way. This has been fun, but there is no way in hell I'm putting that monster in me."

I squealed when his big hands grabbed my ankles, and he dragged me back onto the bed and pulled my legs apart. He studied my dripping wet pussy, and I blushed when a smug grin crossed his features before he knelt between my thighs.

Despite my protests, excitement coursed through me when he rested the head of his cock against my entrance. Jesus, was I really going to do this?

*Why not? You can't get pregnant with an alien baby, and you don't want to be a virgin anymore, remember? Tomorrow, when the translator kicks in, you can explain the mix up, and they can find out where Evelyn is and bring her here. You don't have to mention that you fucked her guy, and besides, she won't care. It's not like she's in love with him.*

My inner voice was oddly persuasive, and I didn't object when Quill pushed my thighs apart even wider to fit his large body more snugly between them. Instead, I said, "Um, so this is my first time. Maybe we could take it slow?"

He cocked his head before leaning down and kissing me. I moaned and returned his kiss as he rubbed the head of his cock up and down my pussy. It brushed against my clit, and I gasped with pleasure. "Please, Quill! Please do that again!"

I tried not to moan in disappointment when instead, he guided his cock back to my entrance. I squeezed his arms and smiled at him. "Slow, okay?"

He said something in his deep voice and shoved his cock in with one hard thrust. Pain lanced through my lower body, and I screamed. He froze, and his eyes widened in horror. He stared down at me, and I whimpered when he abruptly pulled out. He stared at his cock, at the streak of red that covered it, before he made a low guttural sound and jumped off the bed.

He ran his hands through his short black hair as his tail swished in agitation. He paced back and forth before stopping and staring at me. I was nearly crying with embarrassment, and I yanked the blanket over me to hide my nakedness. My lower body was throbbing with pain, and I was utterly humiliated, but the look of shame on his face made me reach out tentatively for him.

"Quill?" I whispered. "Quill, I – I'm sorry?"

He pulled away from my touch, and I watched silently as he quickly dressed. Without looking at me, he stormed out of the bedroom. I heard the apartment door slam shut, and I burst into tears and curled up on the bed. Fuck, I had messed up so badly. I was on an alien planet with no way to contact another human for help, and I couldn't even leave. Not with the storm that was raging. I would die within the hour in weather like that.

*Maybe he'll kill you. Did you ever think of that? Maybe you should take your chances with the storm.*

Fear mixed with the pain in my belly, and I stared at the ceiling. Quill wouldn't kill me, would he? I really had no idea, and I swallowed down my sobs of fear. Without the translator working, I couldn't even beg for my life. Oh God, I was in so much trouble.

# CHAPTER 4

*Quillan*

Old Teo nearly fell out of his chair when I stormed into his quarters. He dropped the mug of gallberry tea he was drinking and stared wide-eyed at me. "Quill? What is wrong?"

"She is a virgin!" I shouted as I stormed back and forth in front of him. "She is innocent! You swore to me she was not, Teo!"

"I – she was not – is not," Teo stammered. "My king, I can assure you that your new mate is not an innocent."

For a moment, I was tempted to drop my pants and show Teo the evidence of her virginity that was drying on my cock. I controlled the urge and said, "I can assure *you*, Teo, that she is a virgin. Or rather – was."

I groaned and sank onto the small couch. What had I done? The little human was so wet and aroused for me that I was certain she could take my cock easily. I hadn't even tried to make sure she was ready before I fucked her.

I muttered a curse and stared at Teo. "I hurt her. I – I did not know she was an innocent, and when I took her, I hurt her badly." The sound of her scream still echoed in my head, and I flinched when Teo touched my shoulder.

"I am sure it is not as bad as you think, Quill. Even I could see the little human wanted you earlier. I am sure she was more," he paused, "prepared than you think. And I am sorry, I do not mean to argue with you, but there is no way she can be a virgin. Perhaps she is just," he gave me a delicate look, "tighter than the average human?"

"No." Another sick pulse of guilt went through me. "Sabrina was a virgin. I swear to Krono she was."

"Who is Sabrina?" Teo was giving me a puzzled look, and I scowled at him.

"What do you mean, who is Sabrina? Sabrina – my new mate. The non-virgin, virgin!"

"You mean Evelyn," Teo said slowly.

I stared at him like he'd gone mad. "No, I mean Sabrina."

"Her name is Evelyn, not Sabrina."

"She said her name was Sabrina. She pointed to her chest and said Sabrina." I thought back, and my mouth dropped open. "She said Sabrina, but she also said Evelyn."

"She said both names?" Teo's voice was as confused sounding as I felt.

"Yes. She pointed to her chest and said Sabrina, then shook her head and said Evelyn. She did that a few times and..."

I gave Teo a look of horror. "Bring up her file. Bring it up right now!"

The old Draax tottered back to his chair and grabbed his phone. He pushed a button, and the image sprang to life in the air in front of me. Using my finger, I scrolled through the pages of the document. The picture of my mate was at the very end, and as her face popped up, I staggered back.

The woman staring at me looked similar to the woman in the guest quarters, but it wasn't her. The woman in the file had green eyes and was thinner. Her dark hair was a little shorter as well.

"Who is that?" Teo said as he studied the picture.

"That is Evelyn, my mate," I said.

"No, that is the other female human from the ship." Now, it was his turn to give me a look of horror. "I scanned her chip, my king. I swear by Krono's hand that I scanned the chip. It said Evelyn Fisher."

"I believe you," I said. "Obviously, the humans implanted them incorrectly."

I paced back and forth again. "What in Krono's name do I do now?"

"It is fine," Teo said. "I will contact the humans and find out who the other female was and where she was going. Your mate is with this Draax male. We will simply contact him, inform him of the mix up and make the switch."

"Have you forgotten about the storm?" I said. "We will have lost our connection by tomorrow morning if we have not already."

Teo sighed. "We will just have to keep the woman here at the palace until the storm ends. Then, we will fix the human error. In the meantime, the female can stay in the guest quarters."

"I hurt her," I said. "What do we do about that?"

"I will take her some gallberry juice to help ease her discomfort. When the translators are working, we will explain the situation, and you can apologize."

"I will take the juice to her," I said.

Teo frowned. "I do not believe that is a good idea, my king. If you hurt her like you said you did, she may be frightened of you now."

My stomach churned, and my tail drooped to the floor. Why it bothered me that some random human female would be afraid of me, I had no idea. She wasn't my mate. She was not this Evelyn Fisher. She was Sabrina, and she was not meant for me.

"I am going with you," I said. "I want to make sure that she drinks all of the gallberry juice. She was hesitant to drink the entire glass earlier."

"Yes, my king," Teo said.

---

WHEN TEO AND I ENTERED, THE LITTLE HUMAN STOOD IN THE farthest spot from the door. She wore the tight and stretchy pants that were so popular with the females and a bulky top that hid the beautiful swell of her breasts. Guilt flooded through me when she pressed her body against the wall and began to babble in her language. I held up one hand and made soothing sounds as Teo and I approached her like she was a skittish grundleswat.

"Shh, little human," I said in a low voice. "Shh. I will not hurt you again. I promise."

She froze when I stopped in front of her. Tears were drying on her cheeks, and I had the strangest urge to pull her into my arms and hold her against my body. I was being ridiculous. If I did that, she would go from scared to terrified.

Instead, I held out the glass of gallberry juice toward her. "Drink, little human."

She stared at the glass, and I nudged it a little closer. Her hand trembling badly, she took it from me, making sure her fingers didn't touch mine. She spilled a little of the juice and made a moaning cry of fear when it splashed on the floor.

"It is fine, little human," I said. "It is fine. Drink." I made a drinking motion, and she downed the glass of juice, wiping her mouth with the back of her hand. Teo held out his hand and she gave the glass back to him as she stared at me.

"Better?" I said.

She obviously didn't understand me, and ignoring Teo's low grunt of disapproval, I stepped closer. I had to touch her, had to somehow make her understand that I felt bad for what I had done. She moaned and pressed herself against the wall, her lovely blue eyes wide with fear. Moving slowly, I pressed my hand against her lower belly and rubbed gently.

"I am sorry," I said. "I am sorry I hurt you, little human."

I continued to rub her belly until she relaxed a little. She was still trembling, but she no longer looked like she was going to drop dead of fear. I smiled at her and stroked her belly once more before forcing myself to drop my hand and step back.

"I am sorry," I said again.

She stared at me and said something in her sweet little voice.

"Sabrina," I said.

She nodded, and I glanced at Teo. "Sabrina," I repeated before shaking my head, "not Evelyn."

There was a tiny flicker of relief in her eyes, and she licked those full lips. My gaze dropped to her mouth, and she pressed herself against the wall again, folding her arms protectively against her torso.

I flinched and immediately stepped back. Krono, I had really made a mess of things.

"We should go," Teo said. "Perhaps the translators will work by tomorrow, and we can communicate with her."

"Maybe I should stay with her tonight," I said. "She is afraid and -"

"That is not a good idea," Teo said. "She is frightened of you, my king."

I knew he was right but said, "I could stay out here. If I do not go into the bedroom, it should be fine. She will know I am here if she needs me."

"Quill," Teo said, "this female is not your mate. It would be best if you had little to do with her."

I sighed in frustration. Teo was right, even if I didn't want to admit it. Once the translators were working, I would apologize to the little human, make her understand that I never meant to hurt her, and then I would not go near her again. The storm would end in a moon's time, and I would never see her again anyway.

"You are right, Teo. Come, we will leave her alone and let her rest."

We backed away toward the door. Sabrina watched us with a look of confusion, and Teo gave her a little wave as we opened the door. "Good night, human."

She waved back hesitantly, and I followed Teo out of her quarters and shut the door.

---

*Sabrina*

IT WAS MID-MORNING WHEN THERE WAS A KNOCK ON MY DOOR. It took me forever to fall asleep last night. When I finally fell asleep, I dreamed about the large green alien, his low voice whispering in my ear as his hand rubbed my stomach.

I'd risen early and, after a few minutes of studying the shower, figured out how it worked. It had multiple showerheads, and I especially enjoyed the blast of hot air that surrounded me when I shut the water off. I had explored the apartment, a little surprised by how many things were similar to Earth. I wondered if they had mimicked our styles or if it was just a coincidence that so much of their furniture and decorations were identical to ours.

I couldn't find any food in the kitchen, but wasn't particularly hungry. The visit from Quill and the old Draax last night had convinced me they wouldn't kill me. They wouldn't have wasted a second entire glass of gallberry juice on me if they were, but I was still afraid of what would happen next. I was also terribly homesick for Earth, and I missed Carrie and Josh with a fierce yearning that surprised me.

I touched my lower stomach just above my pubic bone. I'd still been sore when Quill returned last night, but the gallberry juice had taken care of it quickly. I shivered as I remembered how Quill rubbed my lower belly so gently. I couldn't understand his words, but I had the feeling that he was trying to apologize for earlier.

Now, I took a deep breath and watched as the old Draax stepped into the apartment.

"Hello, human," he said in perfect English. "Can you understand me this morning?"

"Yes!" I said excitely. "Can you understand me?"

"I can." A slight grin crossed his face. "Thank Krono. That did not take as long as I thought it would. My name is Teo."

"Yeah, nice to meet you, Teo. Listen, there's been a huge mistake. I'm not Evelyn – I'm Sabrina Green."

"Yes, we figured that out last night after the king left your quarters," Teo said. "We are sorry for the mistake. Your chip scanned as Evelyn."

"The idiot woman at the Space Station injected me with the wrong chip. I didn't realize it until I got here, and Quill..."

I stared at Teo. "What do you mean the king?"

"Quillan is the king of the western province of Draax," Teo said. "Evelyn has been chosen to be his mate and to bear his young."

"He's royalty." My voice was uncharacteristically quiet. Well, that explained the bowing the others kept doing.

My eyes widened. I had sat on the lap of the king of Draax. I had let a king kiss me, touch my tits, and take my virginity. Holy fuck.

"Human? Are you all right?" Teo asked anxiously. "Your face is very white."

"Just a little shocked." I groped for a kitchen chair. I sank into it and stared up at Teo. "I didn't know he was the king. I didn't mean to be disrespectful. I was supposed to be a nanny for a farmer. Uh, people here don't get beheaded for disrespecting the king, do they?"

Teo blinked at me before laughing. "No, strange human, they do not. The king understands that you were not aware of who he was. Although you are expected to curtsey when he is in your presence."

"Right." I had no idea how to curtsey, but I could fake it. My shock was fading a little, and anger was setting in. "So, you know that shit like this wouldn't happen if you guys had translators implanted in you, right? Why the hell don't you?"

"The translators are for human use only," Teo said. "Implanting translators in us is a waste of resources. If we believe there is a good reason for a human to speak to us, we implant them with a translator. The system works well."

"I think I'm proof that it doesn't," I said in exasperation.

"Technically, human error caused this," Teo said. "They implanted the ID chips incorrectly."

"Yes, but if you'd had a translator implanted in your head, I could have told you that I wasn't Evelyn, and you wouldn't have needed the ID chip."

Teo just shrugged, and I didn't know whether to laugh or cry at his arrogance. I decided to move on. What was done was done. "So, now what?"

"We will contact Earth and find the name of the farmer you are nannying for. Evelyn is with him, and we will simply right the wrong by exchanging you and Evelyn."

"Okay, good," I said. "Uh, will I see Quill, I mean, His Majesty, before I go?"

Teo blinked at me. "I am sure you will at some point. The storm has cut off all communication with Earth and even with others just outside of the palace."

"It's still going?" My apartment had no windows, and I didn't have a clue about the weather.

"Of course," Teo said. "The storm will last at least a moon."

"How long is a moon in Earth time?" I had an awful feeling in the pit of my stomach.

"A month, give or take a few days," he replied.

"A month? The storm will last a month?"

"Yes."

"But I promised my sister I would email or hologram her daily."

"I'm sorry," he replied. "That is impossible while the storm rages."

I sucked in a deep breath and rubbed at my forehead as I tried to quell my panic. Carrie would be fine. She was completely healed, and she had Josh. She would be fine.

"Human?"

"Yes?"

"I want you to know that the king did not mean to hurt you last night when he -"

I cleared my throat as my face turned red. "Uh, yes, I know. He believed I was there to breed with him."

"Yes, he did." Teo paused and then forged ahead. "Did he finish last night?"

I stared blankly at him. "Finish what?"

Teo's light green skin darkened, and his tail swished nervously behind him. "Did he deposit his seed within you?"

My mouth dropped open, and Teo said hurriedly, "I only ask because I need to know if there is the possibility that you will carry his young."

"Oh," I said, "Oh, uh, no, he didn't finish. But I'm not breeding compatible anyway."

Relief crossed his face, and I tried not to take it personally. "Good. The king had a matter to attend to this morning, but I will inform him that your translator is now working. He will visit later this afternoon to apologize for last night's mistake."

I cringed. I never really thought that losing my virginity would be referred to as a mistake, but I also never thought I would lose it to a king and that it would hurt like a thousand bees were stinging my lady parts at once. I shuddered at the memory of the stabbing pain. Christ, why had I ever thought having sex with a Draax male for my first time was a good idea?

*You weren't thinking. Quill had you so worked up that you weren't even thinking straight. You wanted to come, girl, and you didn't care how big his cock was.*

My inner voice had a point, but the good news or the bad news, depending on how you looked at it, was that I didn't have to worry about losing control like that again. I was never going near another dick again – Draax or human. I was destined for spinsterhood now, and that suited me just fine.

Teo was moving toward the door, and I said, "Um, is there

somewhere I can go for food? Do the servants here have a communal kitchen or something?"

He stared at me blankly for a moment before shaking his head. "There is a communal eating area, but you are to stay in your quarters."

"Why?"

"You are an unmated female, and many men in the palace are looking for a mate."

Fear stabbed through me, and Teo must have seen the look on my face because he said, "The males here would never hurt you, human. I promise you. But if you were to become attached to one and mate with him, the Draax who has employed you would be out a nanny. You would be breaking your trade with him, and that is an offense on Earth, is it not? You could go to, oh, what are they called..."

"Prisons," I said. "I can be sent to prison for breaking the trade agreement. Listen, I'm not going to. I don't care how charming your males are, I have no interest in breeding with any of them. They won't want me anyway – I'm breeding incompatible."

He shrugged. "Some of our males do not want young ones. They only want a mate."

"Really?" I gave him a look of surprise.

"Yes, and we will not force them to raise young if they do not desire to," he said. "Anyway, I see your point, but I must insist that you remain in your quarters until the storm ends. We will have food brought to you."

"I can't stay in this apartment for a month by myself. I'll go crazy!"

"We will bring you books and other earth forms of entertainment," he said. "Now, I will have Galan bring you some breakfast, all right? You met him last night."

"Sure," I said.

He paused at the door. "Remember, do not leave your quarters."

"Yeah, I heard you the first time."

He stared uncertainly at me and left the apartment.

---

### Quillan

"My king." Faro bowed low before giving me a questioning look.

"Have you seen Galan?" I asked. "I have been looking for him all morning."

"I believe he is still with the human," Faro said. "He took her breakfast this morning, and I have not seen him since."

A weird burning feeling developed in my stomach, and my skin felt itchy and tight. "Why is he with my mate?"

Faro blinked at me. "My king, Teo told us of the mistake with the humans. Your true mate is on a farm, is she not?"

I shook my head in irritation. "I mean, what is Galan doing with the human?"

"I do not know," Faro said. "Perhaps he is trying to convince her to mate with him?"

The burning intensified, and Faro stepped back in the hallway as my skin darkened to a forest green. I was suddenly filled with a rage so great I was nearly blinded by it. I turned and stalked away. I was at the far end of the palace, and it took me almost twenty minutes to reach her quarters. I tore open the door and stomped inside, ready to tear Galan off the little human.

"My king?" Galan was sitting at the kitchen table with the human. "What is wrong?"

"What are you doing in here?" I snapped at him.

"Visiting with the human. Teo asked me to bring her breakfast and keep her company." He gave me a curious look as I glared at him. My tail was flicking back and forth, and Galan eyed it before standing and bowing. "I will leave you alone with the human."

"No." The little human stood up, rubbing her hands over her thighs. "No, I don't want to be alone with him."

Galan frowned at her as fresh guilt flooded through me. "Do not speak so disrespectfully to the king, Sabrina."

Another little burn in my belly when Galan said her name.

"Leave us, Galan," I said abruptly.

He bowed and left. Sabrina backed up until her delightful ass bumped against the counter.

"Your translator works now," I said.

"Yes."

I stared at the glass of gallberry juice on the table. Sabrina had eaten her breakfast if her empty plate was any indication, but she hadn't drunk any of her juice.

"Sit down and drink your juice," I said.

"I don't want it," she replied.

"You will do as I say." I cringed inside. The human was afraid of me, and acting this way would not help reassure her. But Krono, knowing that Galan was here alone with her all morning was driving me crazy.

"I'm not injured," she said. I blinked at the note of stubbornness in her voice. The human was afraid of me but not so scared that she wouldn't defy me.

I sighed and said, "You must drink your juice every day regardless of whether you feel ill or are injured."

"Why?" she asked.

I snorted irritably. "Because it is good for you. Drink it, human!"

"Fine!" She dropped into the chair and drank the entire glass in four large gulps before slamming the glass on the table. "Better?"

"Yes."

"God, are you always this bossy?" She stiffened when I sat down across from her but didn't try to leave the kitchen. I decided this was progress.

"I am your king, and you will do as I say."

"I'm human, not Draax," she said. "You're not my king."

My mouth dropped open. Were all human women this infuriating? What had happened to the frightened little human of last night?

"Why are you no longer afraid of me?" I said.

"Because I know last night was an accident."

"I am sorry for what happened," I said stiffly. "It was not my intention to hurt you, and if I had known you were not my intended mate or that you were innocent, I would never have fucked you."

She winced. "Yes, I know."

There was silence, and I said, "Why did you allow me to fuck you?"

She turned bright red, and I had to force myself not to stare at her upper chest to see if it was moving down her body. She was wearing the stretchy pants again, but her upper body was covered with a blue shirt that clung to her breasts and showed a healthy amount of cleavage.

"I got carried away with the moment," she said finally. "I made a mistake, too. I'm sorry I acted like such a baby last night. I was afraid, but I'm not anymore."

I scowled unhappily. Why did it make my gut burn to hear her say it was a mistake to fuck me?

"If you're not afraid of me, why do you not wish to be left alone with me?" I asked.

Another brighter flush in her cheeks. "I just – never mind, it doesn't matter."

"Tell me," I said.

"No," she replied.

I wanted to turn her over my knee and spank her for her defiance, but instead, I said, "I spoke with Teo. He told me he explained the error to you." He had failed to mention that he sent Galan to spend the morning with her.

"Yes, I figured it out last night, but I didn't know how to make you understand."

"As soon as the storm ends, Teo will find out who the Draax male is, and we will exchange you for Evelyn."

"Right," she said. "Listen, speaking of the storm, I don't want to stay in the apartment alone the whole time."

I shrugged. "You have no choice. We cannot risk you becoming attached to one of my men and mating with them."

"I'm not going to," she said. "I could go to prison for not holding up my end of the trade agreement. Besides, I'm not interested in mating with anyone ever again. Ever."

This time, the guilt made me feel sick to my stomach. "Human, what happened last night is not how it is during fucking. If I had known you were innocent, I would have taken more time to prepare you. I would not have entered you so roughly, nor would I have forced you to take so much of my cock at once. A female's first time does hurt, but not in the manner in which you suffered. The next time you mate, it will not hurt."

"Thanks for the pep talk, but I'm not risking it," she said.

"Human -"

"I don't want to discuss this with you," she said. "Can I leave the apartment or not?"

"No."

She glared at me, and her tiny hand balled into a fist. "You could give me a chaperone."

"What is a chaperone?" I frowned at the unfamiliar word.

"It's a," she waved her hand in the air, "someone who keeps an eye on me to make sure I don't get in trouble. Maybe Galan could be my chaperone. I like him."

I snarled and leaned forward. "You are not to let Galan fuck you."

She blinked at me. "I just told you I'm not interested in that. I want to explore the palace a little. I'll go crazy if I have to stay here by myself. I'm a social person, do you understand that?"

I shrugged and stood up. The human's scent was intoxicating, and I couldn't stop my gaze from dipping to her cleavage. I needed to leave before I tried to touch her. "No. You will stay in your quarters."

"You can't keep me prisoner!" she shouted at me.

Krono, the little human was adorable when she was angry. I hurried to the door and said, "You will do as I say, little human."

"My name is Sabrina!" she snarled as I opened the door and slipped into the hallway. I shut the door and walked quickly to my quarters as I adjusted my half-hard cock. I needed a cold shower.

# CHAPTER 5

*Sabrina*

"Yep, that's the winner." I held the paper plane to the light and admired its design.

In the six hours since Quill stalked out, I had explored every inch of the apartment. Drawers were opened, cupboards were inspected, and books were investigated. The books were written in Draaxan, but I had entertainment once I ripped out the pages. I hadn't made origami animals since my early teens, but the art of folding, creasing, and bending the paper was easy to fall back into. I felt guilty about destroying the books, but that's what they got for leaving me alone.

Once the high of origami creation dwindled, I moved on to paper airplanes. The living room floor was littered with the corpses of failed designs, but I had high hopes for this one. The key was a slightly longer nose and a little junk in the caboose. I creased the nose to a sharper point, held it over my head, and let the paper plane fulfill its destiny. The door to my little apartment opened. The plane crashed into a broad, cotton-covered chest and joined its fallen brethren on the floor.

Galan stood in the doorway, and heat invaded my body faster than the Gokmards raiding a planet.

"Hello again, Galan."

He studied the graveyard of paper planes. "Hello, Sabrina. I brought your meal."

He was carrying another plate of food and a glass of the gallberry juice. My mouth watered. Great, I was addicted to the pink stuff.

"Thanks. Will you join me?" The raised pitch of my voice betrayed the casual vibe I wanted.

His gaze slipped to the closed door. I gave him a pleading look and sat at the table. "Please? I'm so bored."

Galan approached the table, and I watched in fascination as the end of his tail wrapped around the back of the chair. I studied the tuft of black hair on the end of it. Their tails were surprisingly long, and their look reminded me of a lion's tail. He used his tail to pull the chair back as he set the tray of food and juice on the table and his butt on the chair.

Holy shit. Would I ever get used to the tails?

"What does bored mean?" Galan's voice drew my scrutiny from his tail.

"Um, it's when you have nothing to do, and you're just hanging around feeling, well…bored," I said. "God, that's a terrible explanation. I'm dying to do something, anything. Even wash dishes."

"Ah." His face was as blank as Carrie's when I tried to explain how to program the AutoBroom.

"Great, now I've bored you. It's funny how only a few English words aren't the same in Draaxan. Most of the words are easily translatable."

"True. When we needed an alien race to help us breed, we searched for ones like us. Eat, please."

I stared at the food on my plate. I hadn't eaten earlier. My anger with Quill had made my appetite disappear like a havoc cruiser in hyperdrive. The plate was piled with that pepper flavoured, I-think-it's-meat-God-I-hope-it's-meat, meat. The rich, spicy smell made my stomach throw up a hallelujah. I recognized the yellow chunks as the fruit-like food from the night before, but the Smurf-blue rice piled next to it was new. I poked at the blue rice with my fork while Galan watched with interest.

"What is this?" I held out a forkful of the blue rice.

"Orechoke."

I returned the orechoke to my plate and shook it off my fork. "Don't suppose you have fries on your planet, huh?"

"The orechoke is healthier than fries."

"You know what fries are?"

"I have spent time on your planet." Galan's gaze dipped to my cleavage for only a moment, but more heat invaded my belly.

"What are these?" He pointed to the three rows of paper animals.

"It's called origami," I said. "It's a hobby on earth. You fold paper to make animals."

He picked up the paper rabbit that was closest to him. I thought he would scold me for ruining the books, but he studied the rabbit before smiling. "I like this origami."

"You can have that one."

"Thank you, Sabrina." He made it disappear into the pocket of his pants.

"Yeah, don't mention it." I popped a chunk of the sweet yellow fruit-like stuff into my mouth and chewed. "You said you searched for other races. How many did you check out?"

"Not many, and humans were by far the closest. Anatomy and technology."

"And decorating choices," I said.

"Right." His voice was polite, but his face was confused. Confused as a cat caught in a time tunnel.

"Never mind." I ate more food while I contemplated the pink-make-my-mouth-drool juice just within reach.

"You are a rather weak species, though." His tone was pragmatic, not apologetic. "It almost stopped my people from choosing humans."

"So, why did you?" My hand inched toward the gallberry juice. I really shouldn't, but God, I craved it.

"Drink. It's good for you." Galan was feeding my addiction. "We knew you were about to become slaves to the Gokmard race. We knew you would be desperate for help. We knew we could defeat the Gokmards."

His tail movement was a slow, smooth, sensual distraction. "And according to my grandfather, we were scratching for a fight."

"I think you mean itching for a fight." My laughter didn't bother him.

The Draax were very blunt, and I was digging it. Galan picked up another origami animal –a crane - and traced its creases and bends while I ate the rest of my meal. My earlier belief that the Draax were emotionless had disappeared. I had certainly learned that wasn't true in the last twenty-four hours. The range of emotions I had seen from Quill – amusement, irritation, anger, regret – was a testament to their emotional capabilities.

*Don't forget lust. You saw plenty of lust from him.*

My pussy throbbed at the memory of Quill's hard mouth and warm hands. I scowled at my crotch and scolded it silently. *Stop that! It might have felt good initially, but don't forget the agonizing pain at the end.*

"Sabrina?"

"Yes? I'm sorry, what did you say?"

"I said it was easy to convince your governments to help us when their race was on the verge of being enslaved."

"Yeah, I bet it was." I took a big drink of the gallberry juice. "So, what do you do?"

"What do I do?" he repeated.

"Like, for work," I said. "I know Quill is the king and I think Teo is his second-hand man?"

"He is his advisor, yes," Galan said.

"Right. But what do you do?"

"I am the head of the king's guard," he said with a hint of pride.

"Wow. That's cool. So, have you seen a lot of battle?"

"I have seen my fair share." He didn't elaborate, and his green skin had begun to darken, and the end of his tail was thumping against the legs of his chair. I was already figuring out they were signs of agitation or discomfort for the Draax.

"Does Quill fight in your, uh, battles?" I asked.

"He did. He used to be the head of the king's guard before me. He was, and still is, one of our fiercest warriors," Galan said.

"How long has Quill been the king?" I asked.

"Not long. After his father died, Quill's older brother was declared king."

"What happened to his brother?" I had a bad feeling in the pit of my stomach.

"He is dead," Galan said bluntly. "Finish your meal, please."

I knew well enough when someone was changing the

subject. I ate a few more bites before asking, "Do you have any females in the palace?"

He shook his head. "No. Only you."

"You're kidding," I said.

"I am not," he said. "There are human females in the western province, quite a few actually, but none that live in the palace."

"Oh," I said. "You should consider trying to find some females who want to breed with, uh, you guys at the palace. Your new queen will be lonely when she arrives and would probably like some female friends."

"I will speak to the king about it," Galan replied.

"So," I took another drink of juice before saying casually, "if you're not busy, do you think you could take me for a walk outside the apartment? I'd love to get some exercise and see a bit of the palace."

"Teo has informed me you are not allowed to leave your quarters," Galan said.

*Dammit.*

"Oh, I'm not allowed to leave alone," I said. "But I'm sure Teo would be fine with it if I had someone with me."

Quill had explicitly said I couldn't leave even with a chaperone, but maybe Teo didn't know that.

"I will ask him," Galan said. "If he says yes, I will take you for a walk tomorrow after breakfast."

"Great, just like a dog on a leash," I said.

"What?" he asked.

"Nothing." I was being an ungrateful brat, and I made myself smile at Galan. "Thank you, Galan. I really appreciate that."

"You are welcome, human."

Galan was big and broad like Quill, although the king was a few inches taller than him. His gaze flicked down my body, stopping at my tits, and there was that little thread of lust again in my belly. God, what was happening to me? Normal women didn't get the hots for two men.

*Does it matter? You've become a self-proclaimed nun, remember?* My inner voice said smugly.

I crossed my arms across my chest and Galan immediately raised his gaze to mine. His copper eyes had darkened, but he gave me a look of embarrassment before awkwardly drumming his fingers on the top of the table.

"So, uh -"

"Sabrina, would you -"

We both stopped, and Galan said, "Sorry."

"It's fine. What were you going to ask me?"

"I was going to ask if you were interested in joining the breeding program." His tail thumped against the chair.

"Oh, uh, I already have a nanny contract."

"I realize that," he replied. "But when it is finished, you could join the breeding program and stay on Draax. Our planet is beautiful during the warm season, and you could have as much gallberry juice as you wanted."

My mouth watered again. They knew how to push the juice. I'd give them that.

"I'm not interested in breeding with a Draax male," I said.

He sighed and leaned forward. "Sabrina, I know what happened with Quill was very frightening and painful, but I can assure you that -"

"You know what happened?"

He nodded. "Of course. Teo told me."

"Oh my God," I moaned. "That's so embarrassing. Did he tell everyone?"

"I do not believe so," Galan said.

"He shouldn't have told you!" I said.

"Why?"

"Because it's private."

He shrugged. "I will not share it with anyone else."

"Great, thanks," I muttered.

"As I was saying, I know it was painful and frightening, but if you were to agree to breed with me," his gaze flickered to my chest again, "I promise it will be different. I will not hurt you."

"I'm incompatible for breeding." I waited for his disappointment, but he smiled at me.

"I have no wish for young ones. So, you are the perfect mate for me."

*Shit.*

"If you want, I will bring you to orgasm with my hand right now," Galan said. "To show you that it can be pleasurable. We could even try fucking a couple of times before you leave to be a nanny. If you enjoy being fucked by me, we can keep in touch while you are working, and I will claim you as my mate when you are finished with your trade agreement."

My stomach was churning with embarrassment, but under it was that tiny thread of lust. I didn't want to be attracted to either Galan or Quill but, God help me, I was. What if what Galan was saying was true? What if being with him didn't hurt? Maybe his dick was smaller. It might be worth finding out. He was handsome and seemed kind, and he was attracted to me.

*Quill's attracted to you, too.*

That was true. I'd say one thing for the Draax – they did wonders for a girl's self-esteem.

*You want Quill.*

No, dammit. I didn't want anyone. I wanted to be left alone. I'd tried sex, but it wasn't for me. No big deal.

Galan was still waiting patiently for my reply. I smiled weakly at him. "Um, that's nice of you to offer, but no, thank you. I don't want to stay on Draax. I have family back on Earth, and I miss them already."

Galan nodded. "I understand, but I would be willing to let you visit them occasionally. Please consider my offer. Draax is more beautiful than Earth, I assure you, and Draax males are very skilled at fucking."

I snorted, I couldn't help it, and he said earnestly, "We are, Sabrina. What happened with my king was an unfortunate mistake. I know he feels terrible for hurting you and wishes he could change what happened that night. Most women are eager to fuck the king. He is very good at making females come."

He paused and then said with a small grin, "Not as good as me, of course, but good enough."

I laughed and drank the rest of my gallberry juice. "Of course. And how exactly do you know he's good at it, anyway?"

"We have been best friends since we were very young," Galan said.

"Okay," I said. "What does that have to do with... oh! You and the king like to tag team a girl. I get it now."

My cheeks were flaming red, and Galan leaned forward and studied me. "Is being with two Draax something you want, Sabrina?"

*Yes! Oh God, yes!*

*Shut up*, I ordered my inner voice.

"Is it?" Galan's voice had lowered, and I shivered when he reached out and caught my hand. He stroked my palm with the tips of his rough fingers.

"I already slept with Quill," I whispered. "It – it hurts too much."

He squeezed my fingers. "He did not mean to hurt you."

"I know," I said.

"If you are interested in two Draax, I can find another to help me please you."

I stared into his eyes as that thread of lust grew stronger. "I don't think – who?"

He smiled, and I blushed again. "When we were boys, there were three. Quill, Galan, and Krey. The king's son, the farmer's boy, and the orphan. Krey is off planet, but when the storm ends," his fingers brushed the palm of my hand again, "he will return."

"Have you and Krey, uh...."

"Pleasured a woman together?" Galan said.

I nodded, my cheeks burning, and Galan leaned a little closer. "Yes, little human. In the past, we have pleased a woman together."

He lifted my hand to his mouth and pressed a kiss in the center of my palm. I shivered all over as my nipples tightened and moisture dampened my panties.

"I will show you pleasure now, and when the storm ends and Krey returns, we will both show you pleasure."

"I – I'll be gone from here when the storm ends," I whispered.

He kissed my palm again. "Your employer will give you days here and there to do what you want."

Despite my earlier pledge that I was never having sex again, my body was blissfully ignoring it. It was practically screaming at me to take Galan up on his offer. I bit my bottom lip. As stupid as this was, considering that I had vowed never to let him near me again, my real reason for my hesitation was Quill. He had deliberately told me not to let Galan fuck me. He wouldn't like it if I slept with Galan and Krey - even if they were his best friends.

"I appreciate the offer, but I'm not interested in mating with anyone," I said.

He gave me a disappointed look but let go of my hand. "All right. I will leave you for the evening. Good night, Sabrina."

"Will you ask Teo about going for a walk tomorrow?" I asked.

"Of course," he said. "Sleep well, Sabrina."

---

## Quillan

I GRUNTED IMPATIENTLY AND SWUNG MY SWORD IN WIDE ARCS while waiting for Galan to show up to spar. Yesterday, after informing the little human that she couldn't leave her quarters, I spent the rest of the day with Roden, our head gardener for the west, going over his plans for the new crops we would plant during the warm season. I usually enjoyed this sort of thing. I'd spent many hours as a child in the palace garden with my mother, planting, weeding, and harvesting, but I seemed to have no patience for anything. I tried to hide my irritation but by dinner, I retreated to my quarters and refused to see even Teo.

I'd gone to bed late and slept terribly. I couldn't stop thinking about the human female and how I'd hurt her. Her scream still echoed in my head, no matter how hard I tried to block it out. I deserved to hear it, I thought angrily. I had hurt her, and there was nothing I could do about it, and it was driving me crazy. If she would let me near her, let me show her that I could be gentle, then perhaps I could find a measure of peace.

It was almost mid morning, and Galan still hadn't appeared. Scowling, I left the sparring room and headed toward Galan's quarters. I turned left and stalked down the hallway. I would take a shortcut through the garden, I decided, before taking another left and entering the garden. I could smell the sweet scent of the gallberry plant and the mixture of scents of the dozens and dozens of other plants that grew in the garden.

The scent eased my irritation, and I slowed along the stone walkway between the plants. The palace garden was beautiful, even in the cold months. I glanced up at the ceiling. In the warm months, the glass ceiling opened to allow fresh air and light from our star keo. Now, the ceiling was closed tight, and a heavy layer of snow covered the thick glass. But Roden had turned on the artificial light, and with the light, the sound of the birds who made the garden their home in the winter and the abundance of plants, being in the garden was like experiencing the warm months of our planet. When it was cold but not storming, we would open the garden to the public so they could sit and enjoy the warmth. It was a tradition my father had started and my brother and I continued.

"Is that a rose bush?"

I stopped, my entire body stiffening at her soft voice. What was she doing in the garden? When Galan's voice murmured in reply, anger replaced my shock, and I stomped down the pathway and turned right.

Sabrina stood at the end of the path. Just ahead of her around the corner was the waterfall, and she cocked her head and spoke loudly to be heard over the sound of the water. "Did you take the rose bushes from Earth, or do they grow on your planet too?"

"They grow on our planet as -"

"Galan!"

Galan turned at my angry shout, the smile on his face fading when I stormed up to them.

"My king? What is wrong?"

"We were supposed to be sparring this morning, and you disobeyed my orders!"

"Forgive me. I promised Sabrina I would show her the garden, but I lost track of time," he said. "Wait, what orders did I disobey?"

"The human was to stay in her quarters," I snarled.

"The little human asked if I would be her ch-chaperone," he stumbled a little over the unfamiliar word, "so I asked Teo if I could take her for a walk today, and he said yes."

My jaw dropped, and I stared at Sabrina. To my surprise, she didn't look ashamed of her behaviour. She grinned at me rather smugly.

"You would deliberately mislead both Teo and Galan?" I said.

"Damn right, I would." She lifted her chin and gave me a defiant look. "It's not right for you to keep me a prisoner."

"It is for your safety," I said through gritted teeth.

"No, it's because you think I won't be able to keep my hands off one of your men, even though I could go to prison for breaking my trade agreement and even though I told you I wasn't interested in mating with anyone."

She planted her hands on her full hips and glared at me. "You know you really need to work on your listening skills. You'd think as king, you'd be better at hearing what people say."

Galan's mouth dropped open, and he stared in shock at the little female before staring at me. I barely noticed. I was too busy glaring at the human.

"I'm not a good listener?" I growled. "Who is wandering the garden after being told specifically to stay in her quarters?"

"That's not because I'm not a good listener," she shouted.

Her face was bright red, and she made an angry little noise when my gaze dropped to her heaving chest. "Hey! Eyes up here!"

My gaze snapped to her face, and she said, "I'm a perfectly fine listener. I just chose not to follow your ridiculous request to stay in my apartment."

"It was not a request. It was a command, and as your king, you will do what I say."

"You are not my king."

"Oh, Krono," Galan said in a worried voice.

I glared at her. "You live in my province, and you are under my roof. I am your king, and you will do as I say, or I will…"

"You'll what?"

"I will…"

She stared wild-eyed at me. Krono help me, the only thing I could think to do to her was take her back to my private quarters and bury my face between those smooth thighs. She was furious with me, but I bet once I started licking her little pussy that anger would turn to lust in a heartbeat.

"You'll what?" she repeated.

When I didn't reply, she said, "You know, you need to learn to control your temper. I've met your future mate, and she's sweet and very nervous. You'll scare the hell out of her when you have these temper tantrums."

"I am not having a temper tantrum!" I shouted, even though I had no idea what a temper tantrum was.

"Of course you're not," she said sarcastically.

"For the sake of Krono!" I took four deep breaths and turned to Galan. "Return her to her apartment and meet me in the sparring room."

"Yes, my king." He bowed, and I stared expectantly at Sabrina.

Instead of curtseying, she stuck her tiny, delicate and oh-so-sweet-tasting tongue out at me.

I threw my hands up and stomped away.

---

WHEN GALAN RETURNED TO THE SPARRING ROOM TEN minutes later, I stood in the middle, holding my sword tightly. I indicated for him to raise his sword and he shook his head.

"No, my king."

"Do as I command," I snapped.

He shook his head again. "I will not. We should not spar when you are so angry with me."

I opened my mouth to say I wasn't angry and then shut it with a snap. I was angry with him. I shouldn't have been, Sabrina had tricked him, but I hated that not only was she enjoying his company, but he was attracted to her.

I lowered my sword and said, "You are attracted to her."

"I am," Galan said. "But she does not share my enthusiasm."

Relief flooded through me, and I immediately felt guilty. The little human did not belong to me, and Galan was my best friend. He deserved to be happy, and if the human made him happy, I should step aside and allow him to fuck her.

So why couldn't I say that to him?

I stared at Galan, and he laughed. "My king, you are beginning to wear your emotions on your face, much like the humans."

"I am not."

"You are," Galan replied. "Forgive me, Quill. If I had

75

known you still wanted her, I would never have approached her about becoming my mate."

"You asked her to be your mate?" I stared at him in surprise.

He nodded. "Well, I told her she could finish her employment as a nanny first and then asked if she would consider being my mate. I even offered to let her try Krey and me together when he returns home."

"What did she say?" My gut was doing that weird burning thing again.

"About being my mate? Or allowing Krey and me to pleasure her together?"

"Both!"

"She said no to both. She is not interested in sleeping with a Draax male ever again."

His voice had no tone of accusation, but my shoulders slumped, and the end of my tail hit the floor with a loud thump. "I did not mean to hurt her, Galan."

"I know, my king," Galan said.

"I want to fix it, want to show her that fucking can be pleasurable, but she refuses, and I do not know how to change her mind. She is so stubborn." Now, my tail flicked rapidly.

Galan laughed. "She does seem to be a bit temperamental. Truthfully, I am a little glad that she turned down my offer. I do not think I would enjoy such a volatile mate."

I opened my mouth to agree and instead said, "She is just very strong-willed."

"That she is, and, surprisingly, you seem to enjoy it," Galan said.

"I thought I would want a more docile mate, but I do not mind Sabrina's wildness," I said grudgingly. I didn't want to admit to Galan that her fiery spirit and refusal to follow my orders mindlessly made me as hard as a rock.

"She is right in that it is not fair to keep her locked in her quarters," Galan said. "A moon is a long time to be by herself."

"I know," I said. "But I think keeping her from the other males is best."

"Because you want her for yourself?"

"No, because I... because I do not want to cause tension among the others."

"If you make it clear that she is yours, there will be no tension," Galan said.

"She is not mine, remember?" Saying the words put me on edge.

"Not permanently. But you can claim her for the moon she is here. Just because you do not make her your mate does not mean you cannot claim her at all."

Galan was right. They wouldn't go near her if the men thought Sabrina was mine. Of course, it would only work if she let me touch her, and that wasn't...

My eyes widened as I was hit with a sudden thought. Krono, would it work? It might. She was desperate to be out of her quarters, and this was a way to give her what she wanted and give me what I wanted, too. I could show her that fucking was pleasurable, and perhaps the sound of her scream would finally stop ringing in my head.

"Quill? What is it?"

"You are right, Galan," I said. "She cannot stay locked up in her quarters for the storm. I will go to her now and offer her a deal to give us what we both want."

I left the sparring room before he could reply. I was nearly vibrating with excitement, and I hurried to Sabrina's quarters, barely noticing the people who stopped to bow as I passed them. I knocked but didn't wait for her answer, just opened the door and walked in. Sabrina was sitting on the couch, and she jumped up and gave me an exaggerated and exceedingly clumsy curtsey before dropping back onto the couch.

"My king," she said.

I ignored her sarcastic tone, even though it made my cock twitch against my pants, and joined her in the living room.

"What can I do for you, my king?" she said in a sweetly fake voice.

I folded my hands behind my back and said, "You are right, Sabrina. I should not keep you a prisoner in your quarters."

Her mouth dropped open, and she quickly closed it when I grinned at her. "I -yes, of course I'm right."

"I will allow you to leave your quarters every day with me as a chaperone. In fact, I will take you back to the garden this evening after dinner."

She stared at me with narrowed eyes. "What's the catch?"

I grinned. My little human was a clever one. "I will allow you to explore the garden tonight in exchange for kissing me."

"Wh-what?"

"If you would like to explore the gardens, you will be required to kiss me."

"Are you crazy? Is that it? You're crazy, right?" she sputtered.

I said nothing, just kept my hands folded behind my back and waited. Outwardly, I looked calm and patient, but my stomach was a jumbled ball of nerves. If she did not agree to my deal, I would never be able to fix what I'd done to her.

The minutes ticked by as I fought to keep my tail still. I had a feeling that the little human had already figured out our tails were an excellent way to gauge our emotions. Indeed, her gaze kept flickering to where my tail rested against the floor.

"Just one kiss?" she finally said.

"No. Kissing," I replied.

"For how long?"

"An hour."

"Fifteen minutes."

"Forty-five minutes," I said, trying not to laugh.

"Twenty."

"Forty."

Twenty-five," she said.

"Thirty."

"Fine. Half an hour of kissing, and you'll let me explore the gardens."

"For half an hour," I said.

"What? That's not long enough."

I shrugged. "If you kiss me for an hour, I'll allow you to explore the garden for an hour."

"Bastard," she muttered.

I grinned. The Earth's cuss words were always amusing to me.

"Just kissing, though. Right?" Her boldness had been replaced by apprehension.

"Yes," I said soothingly. "Only kissing, little human. Nothing more."

She took a deep breath. "Okay. Half an hour of kissing for half an hour in the garden."

"We have a deal then?" I held out my hand in the traditional Earth custom of agreement.

She studied my hand before giving it a quick shake. "Yes. We have a deal."

# CHAPTER 6

*Sabrina*

When Quill arrived at my quarters just after dinner, I was ready. I had brushed my teeth – that just seemed like common courtesy – but I had scrubbed my face clean of the makeup I was wearing earlier, and I made sure to wear an old pair of jeans and my biggest and thickest sweatshirt. I didn't want him to think I was excited about kissing him because I wasn't. Not at all. The butterflies in my stomach were because I was excited about returning to the garden. The garden was super cool. The kissing was just something I had to endure to enjoy the garden.

As Quill looked me up and down, I tried not to blush. I was feeling a little ashamed of my behaviour earlier. I had hollered at royalty and stuck my tongue out at him. Was I five years old? I accused him of having temper tantrums, but I had stuck my tongue out at him and been about five seconds away from stamping my feet like a toddler.

*Just keep it together*, I told myself.

I was surprised when Quill approached the kitchen table

and studied the rows of origami animals perched on it. I joined him, and when he picked up one of the cranes, I plucked it from his hand.

He frowned at me. "I would like that, little human."

I just shrugged, and his green skin darkened. "You gave Galan one. I saw it."

"Galan is my friend." I swept up the other paper animals before he could take them.

I waited for him to order me to give him one. Instead, his face was almost hurt as he stared at the origami. I immediately felt guilty. Why was I acting so childish?

I held out the crane. "Here."

Satisfaction crossed his face, and he stared at the crane in his palm before looking at the other ones I still held.

"What?"

"I want that one as well." He pointed to the rabbit.

"You already have one."

"I want two." His voice was adorably stubborn.

I handed over the bunny, and he grinned triumphantly at me. "Thank you, little human." He tucked both into his pocket.

I placed the other ones on the table as Quill held his hand out to me.

"No," I said. "No touching."

I expected him to be irritated, but he just smiled. "It is important that the other males know you belong to me, human."

"I don't belong to you," I said.

"While living here at the palace, you belong to me. They do not need to know that we are not," he paused, "mating. They only need to..."

"Believe that we're having sex."

"Yes. It will keep them away from you."

"Teo said the males here wouldn't hurt me."

"They will not," he said reassuringly. "But they will be relentless in trying to convince you to mate with them if they think you are available."

"Okay," I said slowly. "That kind of makes sense."

I studied his hand before grasping it. He squeezed it and led me out of my quarters and into the hallway. They were wide enough that we could walk side-by-side. His hand tightened on mine when we met the first male in the hallway. The Draax bowed, then straightened and gave me an intense look that was part curiosity and part longing.

I twitched when Quill's tail lashed out and curved around my waist, pulling me closer until my hip brushed his thick thigh. The Draax immediately stared at the floor and murmured, "Good evening, my king."

"Good evening, Bitta," Quill said. To my surprise, he introduced me. "This is Sabrina."

"Hi, Bitta. It's nice to meet you." I held out my free hand.

Bitta reached to shake my hand. Quill made a weird noise that was somewhere between a growl and a cooing noise. Bitta dropped his hand without touching mine and smiled politely.

"Good evening, Sabrina. It is nice to meet you as well."

He bowed again before carrying on down the hallway. I stared at Quill's tail, which was still wrapped around my waist. He released me and said, "Draax males use their tails around the waist of their female to show other males she belongs to him."

"Cute." I rolled my eyes.

Still holding my hand, he led me toward the garden. It was slow going. Every male we met in the hallway – and there were many – stopped and bowed to Quill. We went through the same song and dance we did with Bitta with every other male. Quill would introduce me and wrap his tail around my waist. The Draax would get the message and quickly move on. I stopped trying to shake their hands after the fifth one. Quill made that same weird growly noise every time another male even came close to touching me.

"What's with the growling?" I finally asked. Despite having been to the garden just this morning, I was still hopelessly lost in the maze of hallways. Quill's home was impossibly large, and I felt like we had passed at least a hundred doors. Of course, I had a terrible sense of direction. Even if given free rein in the palace, I would need a guide to return to my apartment.

"What growling?" he asked.

"You growl whenever I try to shake someone's hand."

"I do not."

"You do."

"Do you have to argue with me over everything?" he asked.

I shrugged. "If you're clearly wrong, then yes."

He laughed. "You believe I am wrong about everything."

"Not everything."

"Name something you agree with me on," he challenged.

"Uh... gallberry juice is very good for me."

He laughed again, and a funny little shiver went down my spine. He had a nice laugh. We were finally at the garden, and I shook free of his hand and walked down the path quickly. If I only had half an hour, I wanted to see the waterfall.

I got to the first fork in the stone walkway and stopped. "Um, which way to the waterfall?"

"Left," Quill said behind me.

I turned left, and he called out directions until I turned the corner and came face to face with the waterfall. My jaw dropped as I stared up at it. The wall behind the waterfall was made of smooth stone and water poured from the top to splash down the rock and into a small clear pond below it.

I grinned widely. Small was a relative term, I supposed. I guessed the pond to be about seven feet in diameter, but when I peered into it, I couldn't see the bottom despite the water's clarity.

"How deep is it?" I asked.

"In Earth units of measurement, probably about ten feet," Quill said.

"Do you swim in it?"

He shook his head. "No, we use the pool when we want to swim."

"You have a pool? In the palace?"

He nodded, and I gave him an excited look. "Can I use the pool?"

I loved to swim. It was my favourite thing in the world, and I could barely contain my eagerness. Quill studied me for a moment before nodding again.

"Of course, little human."

"Thank you!" I walked around the pond, studying the flowers that grew at the edge of it. I didn't recognize most of them but saw a rose bush, a few black-eyed Susans, and peonies.

"Do you get some of the flowers from Earth?" I asked.

"Yes. Your food is difficult to grow in our soil, but your flowers flourish. The Draax love to garden, so the opportunity to bring in new plant life was hard to resist," Quill said.

"That's kind of funny."

"Why?"

"Well, because you're so big and tough and like to fight. You know?"

"Do human males who like to fight not like to garden?" Quill asked.

"Not usually," I said.

"Interesting. The Draax are taught at a young age to respect the plants that provide us with so much. Nourishment, beauty, and healing."

The gallberry plant," I said. Just thinking about the juice made my mouth water. I don't know if he saw the look on my face or if it was just a coincidence, but Quill pulled a flask from his pants pocket.

"Yes. The gallberry plant is vital to us." He unscrewed the flask and held it out to me.

I could smell the scent of gallberries, and I licked my lips. "Uh, I'd better not."

"Why not?" He scowled at me.

"Well, because I don't want to drink all of your supply of gallberry juice when there isn't anything wrong with me, and I think it's kind of addictive," I said. "I don't want to get methed out on gallberry juice."

"Methed out?"

"Never mind," I said.

He gave the flask an impatient little shake. "We have more than enough gallberry juice, and it is no more addictive than that dark, bitter liquid you humans seem to find so appealing."

"Are you sure?" I said. "Because I love coffee, but I already like the juice way more. I almost can't stop thinking about it sometimes."

"It is because your body is craving its natural healing abilities."

"I'm not sick," I said.

"You may think you are not, but obviously, your body is not fully well," Quill replied. "If you drink the juice and then begin to crave it the way you describe, it usually means you are ill."

"Really?"

He nodded, and I took the flask from him, drank two large swallows, and handed it back. He took his own drink before making it disappear back into his pocket.

"Thank you."

"You're welcome."

He sat on a wide wooden bench next to the pond and watched silently as I studied more plants before kneeling and trailing my hand through the water. It was ice cold, and I shivered before drying my hand on my jeans. I was studying the large pink plant that grew near the waterfall's base when Quill said, "It has been half an hour, human."

The butterflies immediately flickered to life in my stomach, and I gave Quill a hesitant look. He held his hand out. "Come, Sabrina."

I didn't want to. Not because I was afraid, but because just the idea of kissing Quill was making me feel too warm and - oh dear God – was my crotch starting to dampen?

I took a glance at the front of my jeans, half-expecting to see a damp spot spreading across my crotch. There was nothing, but hell, if my panties weren't starting to feel wet. What was wrong with me?

"Sabrina," Quill prompted gently.

I moved toward him. I made a deal with him and wouldn't back out. It was just kissing. Kissing was fine. Despite the way my pussy was starting to throb, I wouldn't be tempted by just kissing to let Quill go any further.

I was done with sex. I didn't need it and didn't want it. I knew that without a doubt. It was just taking my body a little longer to get with the program, and I couldn't blame it. Up until the actual intercourse, everything Quill did to me was extremely pleasant.

*Pleasant?* My inner voice snorted. *It was fucking hot, and you know it, girl. Stop thinking so much and give Quill the chance to fix what happened.*

Nope, no way, never gonna happen. I was standing next to Quill now, and I gave him a hesitant look as he continued to sit.

"Um, are you going to stand or…"

He shook his head and patted his lap. "Sit on my lap, Sabrina."

"You said just kissing." I was immediately alarmed.

"And I will keep my word." He rested his big hands on the bench. "Sit down, little human."

I bit my bottom lip before perching sideways on his thick thighs. My butt was pressing against his dick, but there was no hardness poking into me, and I relaxed slightly. I was at eye level with Quill and was suddenly grateful to the alien. Sitting on his lap and being on top at least gave me the illusion of being in control, especially with his hands still resting on the bench. It made me feel more confident and less worried that it would be more than just kissing.

"Are you ready, human?" He asked.

I nodded, and he smiled. "Close your eyes."

I closed my eyes and tried not to jump when he brushed his mouth against mine. His lips were warm and firm, and, God, he smelled so good. I returned his kisses tentatively at first, but it didn't take long before I was parting my lips. He ignored my silent invitation and continued to brush his lips across mine. I leaned forward, pressing my upper body against his and squeezing his arms with my hands. He sucked on my bottom lip, and then my top lip and I licked across the seam of his lips. He didn't open his mouth, and I moaned in frustration before pulling back.

"Please, Quill."

"What is it that you want, little human?"

"I want real kisses."

He smiled, and I blushed, but his amusement didn't stop me from licking at his lips again. This time, he opened his mouth, and I pushed my tongue into his mouth. He sucked hard on it, and my hips arched uselessly. As he finally slipped his tongue into my mouth and explored it with gentle licks, I tugged at his arms. His hands were still resting on the bench and it was irritating me. He was supposed to touch me when he kissed me. That's what normal couples did.

I moaned happily when he put one big hand on my hip, and the other cupped the back of my skull. He angled his mouth over mine, kissing me more deeply as I willingly surrendered. I felt drugged from his kisses – shit, this was better than gallberry juice – and I relaxed against him like a kitten as he kissed me repeatedly. His hand at my hip wasn't moving, but I liked the heat of his hand that I could feel even through the denim of my jeans. I touched his broad chest with the tips of my fingers, tracing the soft fabric of his shirt.

Did he have hair on his chest? Despite having seen him naked, I honestly couldn't remember. Even thinking about that day in my apartment and how it ended in pain should have cooled my lust. Oddly, it didn't. He had touched me that day – he had cupped my breasts and rubbed my nipples, and it had felt so good. My nipples were tightening against my bra just thinking about it. My skin felt too hot and tight, and I regretted wearing such a thick sweatshirt.

At the time, I'd thought it was a good idea to try to hide my breasts, but now I realized how stupid that was. If I was wearing a tighter shirt, Quill might be tempted to touch them through my shirt, at least. He sucked at my tongue again, and I arched my back, hoping he would take the hint. His hands didn't move, and I arched again.

Dammit, why wouldn't he touch me? He wanted me – I could feel his hard cock under my ass, so why wouldn't he...

He had an erection.

I froze against him, and he immediately pulled back. "What is wrong, Sabrina?"

"N-nothing."

"I will not hurt you."

"I know."

I could feel inappropriate laughter bubbling up in my chest. He thought I was afraid when I was trying desperately not to grind my ass against his dick.

He kissed me again, back to those light, not nearly enough, brushes of his mouth against mine. I dug my fingers into his chest in frustration.

"More," I muttered against his mouth.

He slipped his tongue into my mouth, and I couldn't help it, I rubbed my ass against his cock. He groaned, his pelvis arching up just the tiniest bit in response. It was the first indication of need from him since we'd started kissing, and it sent wetness gushing to my core. I ground my ass against him again. This time, he arched enough that I would have fallen from his lap if it wasn't for his big hand on my hip.

His kisses abruptly turned hard and demanding, the hand on my hip digging into my soft flesh as he forced my mouth wide and took what was his. I gasped with pleasure, my entire body shuddering against his as hot need coiled in my belly.

With a harsh groan, he pulled away from me and nearly pushed me off his lap before standing.

"Don't stop!" The soft little cry had tumbled from my mouth before I could stop it. I blushed in embarrassment and stared at the ground. My legs shook, I was sweaty and hot, and my heart raced like a frightened rabbit.

"It grows late," he said gruffly as I stared at the stone below my feet. "Come, human. I will return you to your quarters."

He took my hand, and we walked silently back to my quarters. When we were standing outside the door, there was a moment of awkward silence. I cleared my throat and said, "Thank you for taking me to the garden tonight. I enjoyed it very much."

"You are welcome, human."

Quill's voice was hoarse, and I couldn't resist peeking at the front of his pants. Even though we had stopped kissing nearly five minutes ago, the bulge of his erection was still very noticeable against the fabric of his pants. It gave me a weird combination of pride and lust to see the evidence of his need for me.

"I must go," Quill said. "I have an early morning."

"Okay, right," I said. "Good night."

He paused and said, "I will take you for a tour of the rest of the palace tomorrow evening."

"In exchange for more kissing?" Jesus, did I have to sound so eager?

He stared blankly at me before nodding. "Yes. In exchange for kissing."

"Okay, sure. Great." Oh God, I sounded like a sex maniac. "I mean, yeah, I guess if that's what I need to do to get out of my damn apartment. But just kissing and nothing else…right?"

"Just kissing," he agreed.

Did he have to agree so quickly to just kissing? I expected him to negotiate a better deal. A tour of the entire palace was something I really wanted, so hell, I would have agreed to let him feel me up a little for it. It was like he didn't even want to touch my boobs anymore. Which was

90

perfectly fine with me, so why was I feeling such disappointment?

"Good night, Sabrina." Quill opened my door and practically pushed me inside.

"Good night, Quill. Thank you ag -"

The door shut in my face, and I slumped against it before rubbing my hand across my forehead. What was happening to me?

---

*Quillan*

I HURRIED INTO MY PRIVATE QUARTERS. MY COCK WAS throbbing, and the pressure of my pants had turned painful. I slammed the door shut and tore at the buttons on my pants, releasing my cock. Groaning, I gripped it and rubbed briskly. My palm slid across the shaft as I closed my eyes and pictured Sabrina's full lips. She'd tasted so sweet with just a hint of mint. The soft little sounds she made when I kissed her, the fullness of her hip under my hand and Krono – the way she rubbed her ass against my dick. Not fucking her in that moment was an act of sheer willpower.

With a harsh shout, I arched my back, my hand yanking furiously at my dick as I climaxed. My seed landed on the floor, and I continued to stroke my dick until my shuddering had stopped and my breathing had slowed to a regular rate. I studied the mess on the floor before sighing and grabbing a cloth from the kitchen to clean the floor.

As I scrubbed, I tried to ignore the fact that I was way too fascinated by the little human who didn't belong to me. Her enthusiasm over the garden pleased me, and I was much too eager to show her the rest of the palace. If it hadn't been for

Sabrina, I wouldn't have even thought of bargaining with her for the chance to see my home. I wanted to fix the mistake I'd made with her, and I was already fucking it up.

I tossed the cloth in the disposal and headed to my bed. It was early, but I had a feeling it would take a very long time for me to fall asleep.

---

"My king?"

"What is it, Teo?" I didn't turn around but instead stared out the window at the storm blowing across my land.

"You have been in your private quarters all morning."

"I am aware."

During the warm months, my days were filled with meetings with everyone from palace staff to diplomatic representatives from other races, to my own people. It was a constant drudgery that I could not escape from, and I tried not to feel resentful. My people needed me. It was not their fault that my brother – who had always been much better at dealing with these types of matters – had died. Nor was it their fault that I yearned for the life I had before.

The cold months provided a reprieve, especially during a storm. No one dared to leave their homes during the fierce storms, and other races could not land ships. Usually, I enjoyed the opportunity to have some freedom, but today, I wished bitterly that I had something to occupy my mind. I couldn't stop thinking about the little human, which was driving me crazy. As I suspected, it took me hours to fall asleep last night, and even then, my dreams were plagued by the sound of Sabrina's scream.

"Is there something wrong?"

"No."

"Are you certain?"

"Yes, Teo. I am certain. What can I help you with?"

"You have not eaten breakfast, and it is now lunch."

"I am not hungry."

I turned to see him holding a tray of food in his hands. "I do not want that."

"It is not for you, my king," Teo said. "I am taking the human her lunch as Galan is busy. Your quarters were on my way and I thought I would check in on you."

I frowned at him. "Galan is still taking her meals to her?"

"Yes. She enjoys his company," Teo said.

"I will take Sabrina her lunch." I took the tray from him. "I know you are busy."

"My king, do not grow attached to the human."

I ignored his warning and left my private quarters. I nodded distractedly to the males I passed as I carried the tray toward Sabrina's quarters. I knocked on the door and glowered at her when she opened it and said, "Galan! I'm so happy you're…"

She gave me a suspicious look before backing up. "What are you doing here?"

"Bringing your lunch," I said.

"Where's Galan?"

I pushed past her and set the tray on the table as she shut the door. "You prefer Galan's company to mine?"

My stomach burned as she said, "Galan doesn't make me…do stuff. He's just nice for the sake of being nice. What exactly will I have to do to get my lunch?"

Her arms were crossed over her torso, and her shirt was stretched across her breasts. I could see the outline of her nipples against the fabric, and lust swept through me. Krono,

I wanted her. I hadn't planned on making her do anything for lunch, but I smiled at her and said, "You will sit on my lap while you eat lunch."

I expected her to protest, and I would give in when she did. The human barely ate enough food as it was. I wouldn't withhold nourishment from her.

"I'm too heavy to sit on your lap for that long," she said.

I laughed so hard that her cheeks turned a delightful pink. "What's so funny?"

"You are too thin, human."

Her mouth dropped open, and she studied her curvy body. "I – no, I'm not."

"You are," I said. "Draax males like their mates to be bigger."

"Plenty of skinny girls have mated with Draax males."

I shrugged. "We prefer bigger females, but it is not all about looks. Are human males so shallow that they will not mate with a female because she is too thin?"

"Some of them are," she said. "But it's usually the opposite on Earth. They don't have sex with a woman because she's too big. They like their mates to be thin."

"Is that why you eat so little?"

"I eat enough," she said.

"No, you do not."

"Yes, I do."

"No, you do not."

"Yes, I do."

I rolled my eyes as irritation mixed with lust flooded through me. "Enough. Make your choice, human."

She glared at me. "I seriously have to sit on your lap just to get some food?"

"Yes."

"Caveman." She wrinkled her nose at me. "No touching while I'm sitting on your lap."

I nodded in agreement and sat down on the chair. She approached me with much less caution than yesterday, and I tried to appear calm as she sat sideways on my lap. Her ass pressed against my groin, and it took all my willpower not to caress her thighs through her thin pants.

She picked up the glass of gallberry juice and took a few swallows before eating a bite of food. "What kind of meat is this?"

Trying to ignore my urge to cup her breasts, I said, "Grundleswat."

"Grundle, what?"

"Grundleswat. Tan coloured creature that lives in the forest and eats grass," I said. "Like deer in your world."

"Oh. It tastes like cow."

"We do not have an equivalent to cow. We do not domesticate any animal to raise for meat. We eat only what we hunt."

"You know a lot about Earth."

"It was a big part of my childhood studies," I replied.

"That makes sense." She ate more grundleswat. "Considering that you needed us to save your people, you would want to learn whatever you could about us."

"You needed us as well," I reminded her. "You would all be slaves of the Gokmards without us."

"True. If you learn about Earth in school, why don't you know how to speak our language?"

I shrugged. "We have the translators, so it was not necessary. Although I do know a few words in your language."

"Like what?" She popped a slice of bacuri root into her mouth. "Wait, before you answer that – what is this called?"

"Bacuri root. It is similar to your carrot."

She studied the bright green round slices before eating another. "It does kind of taste like carrot. What about this?"

"Orechoke," I said. "It is a grain that we grow."

"I like it. It has a nutty flavour to it. And this?"

"Warracot. A fruit that grows on trees."

"It's my favourite," she said as she eyed the yellow fruit. "It reminds me of watermelon on Earth."

"It is my favourite, too," I said. "We are trying to grow watermelon on our planet."

"Really?"

"Yes. Our soils are not similar, but Roden is working on a formula that will allow your food to grow in our soil."

"Are you worried we'll figure out how to grow gallberry plants in our soil?" she asked.

"No."

"Why not?"

"The gallberry plant can only grow on our planet. The gallberry requires our atmosphere to flourish even if our soils were the same."

She cocked her head at me. "Our air is the same as your air…isn't it? I mean, humans can breathe here, so it must be similar, right?"

"Yes. But the gallberry plant cannot and will not grow in your atmosphere. I will have Roden explain it in greater detail if you wish."

"No, that's okay. I believe you. Who's Roden?" She ate another piece of grundleswat.

My stomach growled. Being around the little human had soothed my restlessness, and my hunger had returned. "He is the head gardener for the western province."

"You're hungry," she said as my stomach growled again.

"I have not eaten yet."

"You should have said something," she scolded. "There's plenty of food here for both of us."

I didn't object when she stabbed a piece of grundleswat and held it in front of my mouth. "Eat."

I ate the meat as she scooped up some orechoke and held it out. I took the forkful of grain and smiled a little as she ate her own forkful. Sharing food and utensils with the little human should not please me so much.

"What Earth words do you know?" she asked as she handed the fork to me. "Help yourself, I'm getting full."

I ate some bacuri root and the rest of the grundleswat as she used her fingers to pick up chunks of warracot and ate them delicately.

"Only the curse words and your slang for mating," I replied. "Our race has integrated many of them into our language over the last forty years."

She laughed. "Of course."

I shrugged. "Human females like it when I tell them their pussies are tight or their tits taste good."

She coloured immediately. "Don't be rude."

"I am being honest, not rude."

"How many human women have you slept with?" she asked.

I was suddenly uncomfortable with the conversation. "I do not know."

"That many?" She raised her eyebrows at me, and I could feel my skin darkening with embarrassment.

"I do not keep track. Why?"

"Galan made it sound like you've slept with a lot of human women."

I was going to kill Galan at our sparring later.

"He has slept with many as well," I said defensively.

"I'm sorry," she said. "I'm being very judgemental."

97

"What does that mean?"

"It means that I'm measuring your character and who you are based on how many women you have slept with. In other words, I'm slut shaming, and that's a pretty awful thing for me to do."

My tail swished back and forth. I knew what the word slut meant in the human language, and I supposed it described me well enough. But knowing that the little human thought I was one made me feel ashamed for some reason. Sabrina touched my shoulder.

"I'm sorry, Quill. Honestly, I don't care how many women you've slept with. I was just a little worried that I might catch something from you. Some infections are sexually transmitted on my planet, and I know you weren't, uh, in me for very long, but we didn't use protection and -"

"You will not get any sexual infections from me. I know what you speak of, and such a thing does not exist on our planet, nor are they passed on to us by humans. Even if they were, the gallberry juice would heal us of them."

"Right," she said. "Sorry. I should have thought of that."

I stared moodily at her, and she held out a chunk of warracot. "If I give you a piece of this, will you stop staring at me like I kicked you in the junk?"

Without speaking, I dipped my head forward and took the warracot from her with only my mouth. She shuddered, and my cock twitched when her ass pressed against my groin for a heart stopping moment.

"Thank you," I said.

"Y-you're welcome," she whispered. "Do you, um, want more?"

"Yes." I held tightly to the fork, but she didn't even try to take it from me. Instead, she picked up another piece of the sweet fruit and held it in front of my mouth. I tucked the fruit into my cheek before licking the juice from her first two fingers. She moaned, and the sound went straight to my dick. It hardened immediately, and I sucked on both her fingers before releasing them and eating the piece of warracot as she stared at my mouth.

"Kiss me, sadora," I said.

I cringed inwardly. Sadora was a pet name that Draax males commonly used with their mates. I had never said it before and had no idea what possessed me to say it now. The human didn't notice the nickname or my discomfort. She was still staring at my mouth and licked her bottom lip before cupping my face and pressing her lips against mine.

I opened my mouth immediately and sucked on her tongue when she slipped it into my mouth. She tasted sweet like the warracot, and I couldn't resist gripping one firm thigh as she pressed her warm body against mine and kissed me eagerly.

Her hands threaded through my hair as my tail wrapped around her waist. Her ass pressed rhythmically against my crotch as we kissed, and I didn't think she was aware of the soft moans she made as I explored every inch of her warm mouth.

Krono, she tasted so good. I couldn't get enough of my wild and stubborn little sadora.

Her low gasp made me realize that I was cupping one breast and squeezing firmly. She arched into my hand, but I immediately released her and unsnapped my tail from around her waist. I tore my mouth away, and she made a cry of dismay before trying to kiss me again.

"Stop, sadora!" I rasped.

She gave me a stricken look and slid from my lap. "Oh God, I – I'm sorry."

"No, I am sorry. I should not have touched you the way I did," I said. "Forgive me."

"I – of course, yes." She studied the floor at her feet.

"I have to go. I am sparring with Galan and do not want to be late."

I headed toward the door, adjusting my throbbing cock when my back was turned to her. Her soft voice stopped me as I was reaching for the handle.

"Can I go with you?"

I shook my head. "It is not a good idea, little human."

"Please?" she said. "I'll be quiet and not get in the way. It could be a part of the tour you're giving me."

I should have refused. Being around the human and not being allowed to touch her or fuck her was pure torture. But I couldn't resist the pleading in her voice nor the chance to spend more time with her.

"Yes," I said abruptly. "But you cannot speak while we are sparring. We need to concentrate."

"I won't. I promise."

She followed me out of her quarters and shut the door. She reached for my hand, and I shook my head. Embarrassment flashed across her face and she muttered an apology as she dropped her hand.

I wanted to tell her that the only reason I didn't take her hand was because I didn't trust myself to not simply pick her up and carry her to my private quarters if I even touched any part of her. But that would not help win her trust and give me the chance to fix my mistake, so I ignored my urge.

Not that it mattered. The moment the first male appeared in the hallway, my tail whipped around her waist like it had a mind of its own and pulled her close to me. My hand crept to the back of her neck and stayed there as I led her toward the sparring room. The palace was busier during the day, and we passed many Draax males.

I kept my tail around her and my hand on the back of her neck in a possessive grip as I greeted each of them. She didn't object to either my hand or my tail and gave each Draax we passed a friendly smile and murmured greeting. I kept a quick pace and she was flushed and panting a bit when we finally reached our destination. I pulled the flask of gallberry juice from my pocket and handed it to her.

"Drink."

"Thank you." She drank her fill and returned it to me. I took my own swallow as that familiar flush of energy infused my body. I pushed open the door to the sparring room. Galan was standing with his back to me. He had already stripped down to just his pants, and I didn't like the way Sabrina was staring at the large muscles of his back.

With my hand still gripping her neck, I leaned down and whispered into her ear. "You are not to fuck Galan."

"I know," she said. "You've already mentioned that. God."

"Then stop staring at him like you wish to fuck him," I said peevishly.

She glared at me. "I'm not!"

I released her neck but kept my tail wrapped around her waist as Galan turned at the sound of the human's voice. "Sabrina! I did not know you would be here."

"Hi, Galan. Your king here agreed to let me watch you fight." She pulled at my tail, and I growled at her.

"Stop growling," she said. "You're squeezing me too tightly."

I released her reluctantly and stripped off my shirt. The burning in my gut eased a little when her gaze travelled over my naked chest, and a flush rose in her cheeks. Mollified, I tossed my shirt at her. "Hold this for me, human."

"I'm not your slave," she said, but she took my shirt and walked to the bench that ran along the far wall. She sat down and made a 'get on with it' gesture that made Galan laugh.

I chose a sword from the many affixed to the wall and faced Galan. He grinned at me and raised his sword before bowing.

I returned his bow and raised my sword. "Begin."

# CHAPTER 7

*Sabrina*

I should never have asked Quill to let me accompany him
when he sparred. What the hell was I thinking? I wasn't
thinking that was the problem. I was all hopped up on gallberry juice, warracot, and that damn green alien's kisses.
Why did he have to kiss so well? Why did he have to be kind
of funny, and well-spoken?

More importantly – why did I suddenly want to spend
every waking minute with him? Oh God, I was in trouble.

Big trouble.

Spread my legs and let the big, green alien bang me,
trouble.

I clutched Quill's shirt and watched as he and Galan
sparred. They'd been fighting for nearly forty minutes with
no signs of slowing down. I was alarmed at first. They used
real swords and attacked each other without regard for
safety, but my alarm disappeared as the fight continued.
Now, I was currently watching in a haze of lust so damn
thick I was surprised that Quill couldn't see it.

It was his fault, I thought. I watched the large muscles in his back ripple as he twisted and turned and swung his sword. He was half-naked and sweaty, and no one his size – man or alien - should have been that graceful. He was an incredible swordsman, and if the other Draax were even half as good as he was, I could see how they defeated the Gokmards, even with their advanced technology.

Watching the two Draax warriors fight gave me a weird tingling in my pants. I leaned my head against the wall, closed my eyes and concentrated on taking deep and even breaths. I would breathe the lust right out of me, I decided. It was not surprising that I was lusting after Quill. His body was beautiful, and those silver eyes were rather striking. All the Draax males were attractive, it's partially why they were so successful in convincing our women to stay on their planet and keep breeding with them. Hell, even Galan made me a little tingly in my girlie parts.

I blew out my breath in a harsh rush. Okay, so I was attracted to both of them. Quill was a fantastic kisser, Galan was sweet and sexy, and both Draax wanted me. And now that I knew they'd had threesomes with a woman before, I couldn't get the mental image out of my head.

It didn't help that they were sparring in front of me – both sweaty and grunting and the muscles in their upper bodies standing out in a delicious display of virile masculinity. It didn't even seem to matter that Quill was incredibly irritating. I wanted him. But there were three very clear reasons for not sleeping with Quill.

One – he had no genuine interest in me. I was incompatible for breeding, and he needed an heir. Two – in a month, he'd be fucking his real mate Evelyn. She seemed sweet and quiet and probably wouldn't annoy him like I did. I ignored the jealousy burning in my belly at the thought of Quill kissing her the way he kissed me. Three…

Fuck, what was the third reason? I tried to think past the throbbing in my pelvis. The third reason danced just beyond my reach. I banged my head against the wall in exasperation and winced. Right – pain. Sex with Quill hurt like a bitch.

*It was an accident!* My inner voice sounded decidedly frustrated. *He didn't mean to hurt you, and if you would give him a chance, he'd show you how much better it could be.*

"What's wrong, human?"

I opened my eyes and tried not to lick my lips. Quill was crouching in front of me, and I stared at his naked chest. A trickle of sweat was dripping down his neck, and I had the ridiculous urge to lean forward and lick it away. Holy hell, his body was incredible. His green skin glowed, and his arms were thick with muscle. His upper chest was hairless, but a thin line of dark hair arrowed down from his belly button and disappeared beneath his pants.

"Sabrina."

Quill's voice was hoarse, and I dragged my gaze away from his v-line visible above his waistband and stared at him. His eyes were the colour of dark granite, and I caught my breath as my nipples hardened and moisture flooded my pussy.

"For the love of Krono, do not look at me that way," he whispered harshly.

"I – I'm sorry."

He stood abruptly, and my eyes widened. His crotch was directly in front of my face, and the bulge of his erection was obvious. I licked my lips, and Quill groaned loudly. His hand reached for my head, and, for a moment, I was entirely sure he would pull my face into his crotch. At the last second, he dropped his hand, grabbed his shirt and stumbled away.

"Quill?" My voice was high and breathless, and I winced when he turned and stalked to the far wall. He rested his forehead against it, his back heaving as he took deep breaths.

"My king?" Galan said.

"Return the human to her quarters." Quill's voice was ragged.

"No," I protested. "You – you said you would give me a tour of the palace."

"Do not argue with me," Quill snapped without looking at me. "Galan, for the mercy of Krono, take the human to her quarters."

"Yes, my king." Galan bowed and walked over to me before wrapping his hand around my arm and hauling me to my feet. He was still shirtless, but he hurried me to the door anyway.

"Galan, wait," I said. "I want to speak to Quill."

"No, the king does not wish to speak to you. Come, Sabrina. Do not argue."

Hurt soared in me, and I swallowed down the lump that had appeared in my throat. I absolutely would not cry over the fact that Quill suddenly wanted nothing to do with me.

---

I SPENT THE AFTERNOON ALONE IN MY QUARTERS AND ATE dinner alone. Galan brought food to me but refused to stay. I picked listlessly at my food. It tasted like sawdust, and I finally pushed it aside before drinking my gallberry juice. Even that failed to cheer me up, and I paced restlessly in the small living area as the time ticked by. I was almost tempted to leave my quarters to find someone who could tell me where to find Quill. I had pissed him off, and I wanted to know why.

There was a knock on the door, and I ran over and yanked it open. Quill stood in the hallway, and he gave me a short nod. "Are you ready for your tour, human?"

"Is that all you have to say?" I said. "If you think we aren't going to talk about what happened this afternoon, you're wrong, Quill."

"Nothing happened."

"Bullshit. Why were you angry with me?"

"I was not angry."

"You were," I argued. "Tell me why."

"I was not angry," he said. "My behaviour was rude, and I am sorry for that. But I was not angry. Now, are we going on the palace tour, or shall I leave you to yourself for the evening?"

"No!"

He raised his eyebrows at my emphatic reply, and I said, "I mean, I would still like to go on the tour, please and thank you."

"Good. Follow me."

I shut the door, and we walked side-by-side in the hallway. The palace was quieter in the evening, but I still found it strange when, after half an hour, we hadn't passed a single Draax. It was puzzling and a little irritating, if I was being truthful. With no other males around, Quill didn't touch me with his tail or hand. In fact, he kept a respectable distance from me. I guess I had grown used to having his tail around my waist whenever we left my quarters. I was surprised at how much I missed the feel of it.

"Where is everyone?" I finally asked as Quill led me out of the kitchen. It was giant sized and chocked full of food and strange looking appliances. But even it was eerily empty.

"There is a gathering this evening," Quill replied.

"What kind of gathering?"

"A life celebration gathering. On Earth, you would call it a birthday party," he said.

"Whose birthday is it?" I asked.

"Teo's."

I stopped in the hallway. "Why are you not at the gathering? Teo's your friend, isn't he?"

"One of my closest, but I promised you a tour. When we are finished, I will join them."

I shook my head. "No, we can end the tour now. I would never have agreed to go if I knew I was keeping you from your friend's birthday party."

"It is fine, human."

"It isn't fine," I said. "Take me back to my quarters. We can finish the tour another time."

I started in what I thought was the general direction of my quarters. I didn't want Quill to see the disappointment on my face. I didn't want him to miss Teo's party, but I hated spending the rest of the evening alone. I hadn't lived alone for years, and not only was I missing my sister, but I was bored out of my mind.

*Is it just that, or are you disappointed that you won't get to kiss him?*

Nope. That wasn't it. Not at all.

"You could accompany me."

I froze and whirled around to stare at Quill. "Really?"

"Yes, but I would require something in exchange." His gaze flickered to my breasts.

"Wh-what did you have in mind?"

"More than just kissing, little human." His voice dripped over me like warm honey, and need blossomed in my belly.

His tail flicked out to snake around my waist. It tugged, and I walked toward him, stopping when I was only inches from his hard body.

"If I allow you to attend the gathering, you will allow me to touch you when it is over," he said.

"Where?" I couldn't seem to speak above a whisper.

"Here." His fingers stroked along my collarbone. "Here." His hands cupped my upper arms. "This spot right here." He traced my stomach and my ribs. "And here."

I moaned when his thumbs grazed across both my nipples.

"You will take off your shirt and this," he tugged on the strap of my bra through my t-shirt, "and let me touch, kiss, and lick."

He bent down until his mouth was hovering just above mine. "Do we have an agreement, human?"

"J-just the top half?" I whispered.

He nodded. His breath was warm on my lips and I couldn't stop from parting them in silent invitation. He hesitated and then brushed his mouth against mine.

"Please," I moaned.

"Do we have an agreement?" he repeated.

"Yes." I leaned forward to kiss him again, stumbling and nearly falling when he straightened and stepped back.

His tail kept me from falling, and he gave me a polite smile. "Are you all right, human?"

"Uh, yes. Thanks." My cheeks were on fire, and I stared in confusion at the floor as Quill released me.

"Come, human. The gathering awaits."

---

*Quillan*

I FLICKED MY TAIL AROUND SABRINA'S WAIST THE MOMENT WE joined the others at the gathering. She hovered close to me, looking nervous and uncertain as I approached where Teo was sitting. The gathering was being held in the garden, and he was reclining on a large cushion with his back resting against the stone wall behind him.

"My king!" He started to rise, and I shook my head.

"Sit, old friend. It is your day." I bowed to him, and he flushed with pleasure before raising his glass of gallberry wine. "To my king and his generosity on this, the day of my birth!"

The Draax roared their approval and raised their glasses before drinking.

"Hello, human!" Teo said. "Welcome to my life gathering."

"Thank you, Teo. Um, happy birthday. Thank you for letting me crash your party," Sabrina said.

"What does this crashing of a party mean?" Teo asked.

I sat on the empty cushion beside him and urged Sabrina to sit between my legs. She hesitated before sinking gracefully onto the cushion. She sat upright and didn't lean against me, but I kept my tail around her waist and rested my hand on the back of her neck as more Draax gathered around us. They were staring at her with curiosity, but both my status and my obvious possession of her kept them from even glancing at her lush body.

"It means attending a party even though you weren't invited," Sabrina said.

"Oh." Teo thought for a moment. "Well, a female as beautiful as you are is welcome to crash my party anytime!"

He raised his glass and shouted, "What say you?"

"Katalan!" the Draax shouted, and I grinned as they all drank enthusiastically.

Sabrina stared at Teo in surprise, and I pulled her against my chest before murmuring into her ear. "Ignore him. He has had too much gallberry wine."

"There's a wine version?" She gave me a look of pure delight as I tried to ignore the soft fullness of her ass pressing against my dick.

"Yes."

"Can I try it?"

I signalled to the Draax carrying a tray of wine glasses. He hurried over, and I shook my head when he tried to hand me two glasses. "One is enough."

"Of course, my king."

Sabrina sat up straight and twisted her upper body to face me. Before she could take the glass, I held it to her lips. She took a sip, and I pulled the glass away before she could drink more. Her cheeks flushed immediately, and she shivered all over. "Oh my God. That's amazing."

"It is very potent," I said. "You are so little that a few sips and you would be as drunk as Teo."

"One more sip?" she wheedled.

I laughed and allowed her one more before drinking the rest of it myself. "No more, little human."

She pouted, but even the two small sips had relaxed her enough that she rested against my chest without my urging. I rubbed her thigh and flicked my tail against her hip as she watched the Draax laugh and talk around us.

"What does katalan mean?" she asked.

"Long life," I replied.

"Oh."

She settled even more firmly against my chest, and I stroked her long, dark hair. It was silky soft, and I tried not to picture the way it would look draped across my thighs as she sucked on my cock.

My dick pushed against her hip, but she didn't seem to notice. She was still watching the others with bright interest, and I tried to concentrate on something other than the warm, soft woman sitting between my thighs.

---

"So, Sabina -"

"It's Sabrina." I gave Jarka an irritable look.

His green skin darkened with embarrassment, and his tail flicked back and forth. "Forgive me, Sabrina."

"It's fine, Jarka." She elbowed me lightly in the ribs. "Everyone makes mistakes. What is your question?"

It was nearly four hours later, and Teo was asleep and snoring loudly on the cushion beside us. He wasn't the only one. The gallberry wine had flowed freely, and most of the Draax had either staggered off to their beds or fallen asleep in the soft grass of the garden. Only about ten Draax were still awake and gathered around Sabrina and me. The little human had been very friendly and kind to them, and they were starting to ply her with questions about her life on Earth.

"What illness did you have that made you conduct trade with the farmer to be his nanny?" Jarka asked.

"I wasn't sick," Sabrina said. "My younger sister had liver cancer. She only had a few months to live, so I went through an agency and was tested for the breeding program. When I proved incompatible, I applied for the nanny program."

"You gave up everything for your sister?" Jarka said in surprise.

"I – well, it's only for three years," Sabrina said.

"Three years is a long time," Faro said.

"She was dying," Sabrina said almost defensively.

"I do not mean to offend," Faro said. "The human females I have talked to did not seem inclined to help others."

"Talk?" Jarka said. "I would have thought they were too busy sucking your dick to talk."

The Draax roared with laughter as Sabrina's face turned red.

"There is a female in our presence," I said.

Their laughter died immediately, and Jarka made a short bow. "Forgive me, my queen. I mean – Sabrina."

"It's fine," she said with a hesitant look at me.

I realized with a jolt that Jarka's slip of the tongue had not even registered. It seemed somehow fitting that they referred to Sabrina as queen. My hand tightened on her thigh. Krono, what was wrong with me? Sabrina was not my queen. My mate was a woman named Evelyn, and, unlike Sabrina, she could bear my young.

"Quill? What's wrong?" she murmured.

"Nothing." I relaxed my grip on her leg. Sabrina meant nothing to me. I simply wished to show her that sex could be pleasurable. When I had done that, my odd obsession with her would end.

"When your term as nanny ends, will you find a mate here on our planet?" Faro asked.

"No. I'm incompatible for breeding, remember?" Sabrina replied.

"There are many on our planet who have no wish for young," Jarka said. "Galan is looking for a mate only. Is that not right, Galan?"

He turned to my best friend, who nodded and took another sip of gallberry wine.

"You see. You could easily find a mate here, human. You are very pretty," Jarka said earnestly.

"Um, thank you," Sabrina said. "But I want to return to earth. I miss Carrie and Josh very much and -"

"Who is Josh?" My tail flicked angrily.

"He's my sister's husband, uh, mate," she said.

I relaxed and took a drink from the glass of gallberry juice before handing it to her. "Drink more juice."

She drank obediently before returning the glass to me.

"Teo says you met our king's future mate," Faro said. "What was she like?"

"Well, I only met her briefly," Sabrina said. "But she seemed very sweet. Quiet and a little timid."

"That's good," Jarka said. "The king likes his females quiet and submissive. She will make him the perfect mate."

"Be quiet, Jarka," I said harshly.

He blinked at me. "Forgive me, my king."

I ignored him and studied Sabrina. Her face was pale, and she was staring at her hands knotted together in her lap.

"What is wrong, little human?" I said in a low voice.

"Nothing." She gave me a strained smile. "Nothing's wrong."

She turned to Jarka before I could question her further and said, "What do you do in the palace, Jarka?"

---

*Sabrina*

As Quill opened the door to my quarters and ushered me inside, I tried not to show my nervousness. I had agreed to allow Quill to touch my breasts, and I would follow through with it, simple as that. I smiled at him as he led me to the couch.

"Thank you for taking me to the party. I had a lovely time."

"You are welcome, little human." Quill sat down on the couch and patted his lap. "Straddle me."

"Right." For some reason, I thought maybe we would talk some more, but that was stupid. Quill wasn't interested in talking.

I straddled his knees a bit gingerly. Despite his talk about how thin I was, I still worried I would be too heavy. Plus, I didn't want to get too close to his dick. Feeling how hard he was for me did weird things to my insides. My plan backfired when Quill immediately pulled me forward until my crotch was snug against his, and my stomach rested against his flat abdomen.

"Better," he said. "Lift your arms, human."

I tried to tell myself the butterflies in my stomach were from nerves and not lust as I lifted my arms, and Quill pulled my shirt over my head. But the look of desire on Quill's face when he stared at my tits sent an answering call through my entire body. I twitched when, instead of removing my bra, Quill cupped the back of my neck and kissed me. I returned his kisses, moaning with delight when he nipped my upper lip before sucking on it. I was growing as addicted to his kisses as I was to his damn gallberry juice. One big hand splayed across my lower back, rubbing the soft skin as I kissed him with a frantic kind of need that should have been embarrassing but wasn't.

When his hand moved to the back of my bra and unhooked it, I helped him pull the straps down my arms. He tossed my bra on the floor and immediately cupped both my breasts.

"Oh," I whispered when he rubbed his thumbs across my nipples. They hardened under his touch and he pulled on them until they were dark red and aching.

"Quill, please." I arched my back. I needed something, what, I didn't know exactly, and I rubbed my pussy against his dick as he bent his dark head. He kissed my collarbone and traced it with his tongue before pressing kisses against the top of my breasts.

"Lower," I begged.

He grinned up at me, and I threaded my hands in his thick hair and tried to push his mouth toward my nipple. When he only licked around my nipple before kissing between my breasts, I made a whine of disappointment.

"Shh, sadora," he said in his deep voice. "I will give you what you need in a moment."

"No, now," I demanded.

He laughed and threaded one hand through my dark hair, tugging on it until my head was back and my throat exposed. He kissed the column of my throat, licking and sucking at my skin as I rubbed my pelvis frantically against his.

"Such a bossy little human," he whispered into my ear.

I froze. Quill liked submissive women.

"What is wrong?" he asked immediately. "Have I hurt you?"

"No, of course not," I said. "I – you like submissive women, not bossy ones."

He studied me for a moment before pressing a kiss against my jawline. "I like you just the way you are. Do not pretend to be something you are not."

"A-are you sure? Oh God, that feels good!"

Quill was pinching and pulling at my nipple again, and his low laughter sent warmth to my belly.

"I am sure, sadora."

"Then give me what I want." I pushed his head down.

He laughed again, and I couldn't stop my loud cry of pleasure when his hot mouth closed around my nipple. He sucked hard before tugging on it with his teeth, and it sent an arrow of pleasure straight to my pussy.

I wondered if a woman could come just from having her

nipples sucked on as Quill cupped both my breasts together. I arched repeatedly, holding onto his thick arms for balance as he licked and sucked at my aching nipples.

"Do you like this, sadora?" he murmured.

"Yes!" I cried. "Yes, Quill! I need more!"

He immediately pushed me onto my back on the couch. His hard body was wedged beside me, with one thick thigh between my legs. I squeezed his thigh with my legs as he kissed me deeply. One hand threaded through my hair, holding me still for his kisses as his other hand played with my breasts, toying and pulling on the nipples. I moaned and gasped and pleaded as I rubbed my crotch against the hard length of his thigh. When his hand slipped under my pants and into my panties, I froze like a frightened deer.

"It is all right," he whispered against my mouth. "I am only going to make you feel good. I promise."

"Quill, I – I don't want to have sex." I waited for his anger, waited for him to call me a tease or a slut, but he just nodded.

"I know. I am only going to touch your sweet pussy with my hand. Tell me if you do not like it, and I will stop."

"I'm sorry," I whispered.

"You have nothing to be sorry about." He nuzzled my throat before sucking on my earlobe. "I will not hurt you, my sadora. I promise."

He smiled at me, and I put my arms around him when he kissed me again. His warm tongue stroked against mine. He tasted like the gallberry juice he'd been drinking, and I sucked at his tongue as my fingers dug into the fabric of his shirt. For a moment, I wished he was naked, wished I could feel his warm skin directly against mine. The thought was lost at the first touch of his fingers against my swollen clit.

I jerked in his arms and cried out. He stopped rubbing my

clit and pressed a soft kiss against my mouth. "Should I stop, sadora?"

"Fuck, no!" I sounded like a spoiled little brat, and I winced. "I'm sorry, that was rude."

He laughed and licked my bottom lip as his fingertips circled my clit with a gentle motion that made me arch into his hand.

"Oh please," I begged.

"Do you want more?"

"I do," I panted. "I really, really do."

He rubbed firmly. How did he know how to touch me in the exact way I liked? Already, I was on the verge of my climax.

"You are so wet for me," he whispered into my ear.

I blushed, and he kissed me. "It pleases me, sadora."

"Quill, I'm close," I gasped out.

"I know."

I screamed in pure pleasure when he pinched my clit. It sent me flying over the edge, and I climaxed with an intensity I'd never felt before. My pussy clenched uselessly around nothing, and I dug my nails into Quill's back as he rubbed lightly at my clit and kissed my throat. I was shaking and twitching uncontrollably, and I pulled on Quill's wrist when he rubbed my pussy again.

"Enough, please," I gasped. "Too – too sensitive."

He slipped his hand out of my pants. His fingers were dripping, and I had enough sense to be embarrassed when he wiped them on his shirt. He caught the look on my face and said, "It pleases me, sadora. Remember?"

"Yes," I whispered.

He stroked my round tummy and pressed kisses against my upper chest as I slowly came down from the high of my orgasm. When my legs finally stopped trembling, he smiled at me.

"Do you feel all right, sadora?"

"Better than all right."

"I should go." He kissed my collarbone. "Thank you for letting me make you come, Sabrina."

"Um, you're welcome?" I could feel my cheeks turning red. "Thank you for, uh, making me come."

"It was my pleasure." He grimaced as he shifted on the couch, and just like that, I could feel his erection against my hip.

"Quill, wait," I said before he could push into a sitting position.

"What is it?"

"What about you?" I glanced at his crotch. "You didn't get to come."

"I will take care of it when I return to my quarters."

"I could help."

Holy shit. Why the hell did I say that?

He hesitated, and I swear I felt his cock grow harder against my hip. "That is probably not a good idea, little human."

"I want to," I said. "I, um, I don't want to have sex, but I could give you a hand job."

He continued to hesitate.

"I want to," I repeated before reaching for the button on his pants.

He didn't stop me as I unbuttoned his pants. In fact, it was he who pulled the front of his pants down and tugged his cock out. My breath caught in my throat as I stared at it. The shaft was the same green as the rest of his body, but the head was a slightly darker green.

He was gripping the base, and I reached out before hesitating. He groaned under his breath, and I gave him a nervous look.

"I've never done this before. I'm sorry."

"Watch," he said.

I watched as he rubbed his dick with hard and firm strokes. He stopped at the head and circled his fingers across the top of it before rubbing the shaft again. He moaned when I put my hand over his and immediately dropped his hand. My heart thudding in my chest, I wrapped my hand around him. He was long and thick, and I bit my bottom lip as I rubbed and squeezed gently.

"Harder," he gasped out.

"I don't want to hurt you," I said.

"Krono! You will not! Please, sadora."

The pleading in his voice sent new lust through me, and I tightened my grip and pumped him with firm strokes. His dick was steel hard, but the skin was velvety soft. He thrust into my hand, making low, raspy moans that made my pussy throb. I watched in fascination as a drop of light green precum appeared at the head of his dick.

I swiped my thumb through it and, without stopping to think, licked it off my thumb. It was slightly sweet with the lingering taste of gallberries. I licked my thumb again. Christ, I was in real trouble if Quill's cum tasted like gallberries.

"Fuck, sadora!" he almost snarled as he watched me lick my thumb. He grabbed my hand and returned it to his dick.

"Rub!" He had a feral look of need on his face, and I rubbed hard, circling the head with my fingers and ignoring my urge to lick away the fresh pre-come that was spilling out. His hips were thrusting wildly now, and he cupped my naked breast, pulling at my nipple as his body stilled against mine.

He shouted harshly, and his back arched as his cock

swelled in my hand. Startled by his reaction, I tried to let go of his cock. He groaned, and his big hand covered mine. He moved his hand up and down, forcing my hand back and forth over his cock as his come splattered on my stomach. When his cock started to soften in my hand, he released me and studied the light green liquid on my stomach. Without speaking, he rubbed it into my soft skin, smearing it upwards and coating my breasts as well.

"What are you doing?" I asked.

He didn't answer, just finished spreading as much of his seed over my soft skin as he could. When he was finished, he relaxed against the couch and nuzzled my neck.

"I'm all sticky now." I wanted to sound indignant, but I mostly just sounded confused.

He laughed. "It will dry, sadora."

"Why did you do that?"

He shrugged before pressing a kiss against my collarbone. "It is late. I should go."

"We can talk a while longer." It was silly, but I didn't want him to leave me. I shook my head at my stupidity. I wanted an alien, one who wasn't my mate and never would be, to cuddle with me and tell me stuff about his life. I'd been drinking too much gallberry juice.

"I cannot," he said.

"Yeah, I know," I said. "Sorry, it was stupid of me to ask you to stay. Talking isn't exactly what you aliens are interested in when it comes to human females."

I was afraid I would sound bitter and was thankful when I sounded more resigned. I wasn't bitter. I knew exactly what Quill wanted from me, and there was no point in wishing for more.

He studied me for a moment before rubbing his thumb across my cheekbone. "I would enjoy learning more about you, little human, and that is the truth. But I cannot stay because if I do, I will try to fuck you."

Liquid lightning zipped through my veins. "Oh."

He kissed my throat before sitting me up. I reached for my shirt, and he shook his head. "No, let me see those magnificent breasts until I walk out the door."

I blushed and fought the urge to cover my tits as he gave them an appreciative look. I didn't think they were all that magnificent, and they weren't nearly as perky as I would have liked, but there was no denying the lust in Quill's face when he brushed his thumb over one nipple. It hardened, and he smiled with satisfaction before tucking his cock back into his pants. We stood, and he did up his pants before taking my hand. I walked with him to the door, and he kissed me thoroughly as he cupped my right breast and teased my nipple.

"Do not bathe before you go to bed tonight, Sabrina," he murmured against my lips.

"Why not?"

"I like knowing you are covered in my seed while you sleep."

Was it weird that I was immediately turned on?

Yeah, it was weird, I decided.

"Do you promise not to bathe?" He nipped my neck, and I shivered in delight.

"I promise," I whispered.

"Good girl, sadora." He kissed me again and opened the door.

"Quill? What does sadora mean?"

He looked away. "It is just another Draax word for human. Goodnight, Sabrina."

"Good night, Quill."

# CHAPTER 8

*Quillan*

I knocked on the door of the human's quarters and waited with barely concealed impatience for her to open it. I'd spent most of the morning with Roden reviewing the soil samples he had created. Three of them had tiny plants sprouting out of them – Roden said they were a food the humans called potatoes – and the head gardener was both excited and proud of his experiments.

The afternoon was spent with Galan, watching and reviewing the newest recruits who had joined the king's guard as they went through their training practices. I didn't technically need to be there, but I missed my old duties. Watching the new ones train and giving them advice was a reprieve I sorely needed. One that Galan understood and granted me.

I meant to have dinner with the little human, but Teo invited me to join him in his quarters, and I could think of no reason to say no. He didn't like that I was spending time with Sabrina, and while I understood why he believed I should avoid her, I couldn't. I wanted – no, *needed* – to fix my mistake with her.

*Is that all it is? You act almost as though she is your mate. You have never denied Galan the chance to fuck a woman with you. Why is it different with this human?*

The door opened, and I smiled at Sabrina.

"Good evening, little human."

She wore those delightful tight, stretchy pants again and a thin shirt. Her dark hair was braided and hung to the middle of her back. I had a sudden urge to unbraid it and run my fingers through all that silky softness.

"Hello, my king." She curtseyed clumsily and then wrinkled her nose at me when I grinned. "I didn't exactly need to learn to curtsey on earth."

I stepped into her quarters and resisted my desire to kiss her. "What did you do today?"

"Nothing," she replied. "Well, I made some more origami animals from the paper Teo gave me." She pointed to the new row of paper creatures sitting on the table. She followed me to the table and watched as I picked one up.

"What is this one?"

"It's an elephant," she said.

"May I have it?"

She nodded, and I pocketed it to join the other two sitting on my bedside table. "Did you eat today?"

"Yes. Faro brought me my meals, but he didn't stay or anything. I've been alone all day."

I cringed, but truthfully, the little human didn't sound accusatory or angry. Still, I said, "I am sorry, human. I was very busy today."

She gave me a look of surprise. "I know. You don't need to apologize to me. You're the king, Quill. I can only imagine the responsibilities you have. I understand that you can't spend time with me every day. I was just..."

She trailed off and cupped her elbows before turning away.

"You just what?"

"I miss my sister a lot today." Her voice was shaky, and I immediately rushed forward and turned her around before slipping my arms around her waist. She wasn't crying, but her face was drawn, and her eyes watered.

"As soon as the storm ends, you can hologram chat with your sister." I wiped away the tear sliding down her cheek with my thumb. "I promise."

"Thank you. I'm sorry."

"For what?"

"I shouldn't be talking about this with you. It's not your problem that I miss my sister."

I frowned. "I do not mind."

She smiled a little. "Sure, you don't. Anyway, I know you're busy, but could you take your temporary pet for a quick walk?"

"You are not a pet," I said more harshly than intended.

She flinched, and I rubbed her back immediately. "I am sorry."

"No, I am." She rubbed at her forehead. "I'm being a jerk for no reason."

"Come, I have a surprise for you," I said.

"You do?" Her face lit up, and I couldn't resist pressing a kiss against her mouth.

"I do." I took her hand and led her out of her quarters and down the hallway. It was late, and no other males were around, but I wound my tail around her waist anyway. She didn't object, and I pulled her closer so her hip brushed against me with every step. I led her to the west side of the palace. We walked by my private quarters, and for a moment, I was tempted to open the door and lead her inside. Now that I was close to her, now that my tail was hooked around her waist, and she appeared in every way to belong to me, I wanted to take her to my bed and bury my cock deep inside of her.

I shook off my temptation and kept a steady pace past the door. She didn't want me to fuck her. She needed more assurance that I wouldn't hurt her again and that I wanted only to please her. Tonight, I would do just that.

"I've never been in this section before, have I?" she said.

I shook my head. "No, you have not."

She made a face at me. "I'm terrible with directions. I would forever be getting lost if I tried to go by myself. Although, I might be able to find my way to the garden now."

"You will get used to the palace layout with time," I said without thinking.

She gave me an odd look. "The storm will end, and I will be gone before I learn my way around the palace."

My tail flicked angrily at the thought of her leaving, and she winced when it snapped against her thigh.

"I am sorry." I gave her an anxious look as I relaxed my tail. "I did not mean to hurt you."

"I know," she said. "And I know that first night was an accident as well. You need to stop beating yourself up over it, okay?"

"What do you mean beating myself up?" I asked.

She thought for a moment. "It means you keep feeling bad and punishing yourself emotionally for what happened. You need to stop doing that."

"It is my fault," I said. "But I will fix what I have done, I promise."

She squeezed my hand but didn't reply. I sighed inwardly

and took a left down the hallway before stopping in front of the last door. I opened it and guided her inside. Her gasp of surprise and the look of pure delight on her face made me smile.

"The pool!"

"Do you like it?" I murmured into her ear.

"It looks amazing!"

"Good." I couldn't resist nipping at her earlobe as I stepped behind her and nestled my cock against her soft ass.

I splayed my hand across her round belly and kissed her neck. "Would you like to swim, sadora?"

"Yes," she moaned as she turned her head to give me better access to her throat. "What will I have to give you for it?"

"Kissing." I grasped her chin and turned her face to mine. I kissed her hard, sliding my tongue between her lips so I could taste her sweetness. My cock was hardening, and she rubbed her ass against it. I pulled my mouth away and smiled at her whimper of protest.

"Touching." I cupped both her breasts through her shirt. She moaned and arched her back. I gripped her full hip as I rubbed my cock against her ass.

"Open your legs for me, sadora." I was delighted when she immediately did what I asked. I slipped my hand into her pants and cupped her pussy through her panties. The crotch was already starting to dampen.

"Tasting." I sucked on her earlobe.

"T-tasting? Tasting what?"

I smiled at her innocence and squeezed her pussy. "Your sweet pussy, my sadora. I wish to taste it."

"Why?"

"Why did you taste my seed from your thumb?" I asked.

"I don't know," she admitted.

I kissed her throat again. "It would bring me great pleasure to taste your pussy. Do you wish to swim, Sabrina?"

"Yes," she whispered.

"I will allow you to swim if you allow me to eat your pussy tonight. Do we have an agreement?"

"Yes," she said quickly. "We have an agreement."

I rubbed her clit through her panties as a reward, and she moaned again before arching against me. "Maybe - maybe we should do the pussy eating first?"

My low laugh made her blush, and I gave her clit a final stroke before removing my hand from her pants. "Go and enjoy your swim, my sadora. I will eat your pussy later."

"Do you promise?" She asked.

"Yes." I squeezed her breast and kissed her mouth. "I promise."

"Are you swimming?"

I shook my head and pointed to the water in a separate, smaller pool. "I will relax in there. Join me when you tire of your swim."

She hesitated. "I don't have my swimsuit."

"Do you need it?"

"I can't swim naked," she said. "What if someone else comes in to use the pool?"

"I have locked the door. No one else will join us."

"I'll swim in my bra and panties."

"Whatever you want, sadora," I said.

---

SHE DIDN'T SWIM FOR AS LONG AS I THOUGHT SHE WOULD. THE water had turned her bra and panties translucent, and I deliberately avoided looking at the way her nipples had hardened and how her panties clung to her sex. She joined me in the warming pool, sitting across from me and smiling happily.

"It's like a hot tub without the jets."

I arched an eyebrow at her, and she said, "We have these things called hot tubs with jets of water that – oh!"

I'd pushed a button on a panel embedded in the floor next to the warming pool. The water bubbled, and she shifted so that one of the jets pressed against her back. "This is nice."

"I am glad you are enjoying it. Did you like the pool?"

"So much. Did you know that humans used to use a chemical called chlorine in their pools? Have you ever heard of anything so ridiculous?"

I laughed. "The humans do many things that seem ridiculous to the Draax."

"Yes, I suppose we do."

We sat in comfortable silence for a while. I was intensely curious about her life and couldn't resist asking about it. "Do you have other siblings?"

"No, it's just me and my sister. My parents were killed in an accident when I was nineteen. I left school and returned home to care for my sister."

"She could not care for herself?" I asked.

"My sister is," she paused, "fragile."

"What did you study in school?"

"I was going to be a doctor."

I didn't reply, and she said, "It's a person who heals the sick and -"

"I know what it is," I said. "We have healers on Draax. They are called kadanas."

"Why?" She asked. "Doesn't the gallberry juice heal everything?"

I nodded. "Yes, but our kadanas diagnose the ill and administer the gallberry juice. They help deliver our young and guide our elderly to the other side when the gallberry no longer heals."

"Oh," she said. "Anyway, once my parents died and I had to take care of Carrie, I couldn't go to school anymore. So, I took a job as a nanny."

"You are fond of children then?"

She nodded. "I am. I always knew I wanted lots of kids."

"You could be a healer here," I said casually.

She stared at me, and I tried to sound indifferent. "You could train under our palace kadana once your nanny employment ends and then find work here on Draax."

"If I stay on Draax, I won't see my sister," she said.

"You can go back and visit, or your sister can come to the planet."

She laughed. "It costs a great deal of money for space travel."

"I would cover the costs," I said.

"Why would you do that?"

"Does it matter?"

"It matters if you require something in return."

I flushed. It didn't serve me well to forget how clever Sabrina was. I was ashamed to admit it, but the truth was I only offered her this opportunity because I did want something. Her. She could not bear me children like my actual mate Evelyn, but it didn't mean we couldn't fuck once or twice a week.

*You would treat Sabrina like a common earth whore? You may not have known her long, but you already know she would never agree to it if you were mated to another. Besides, she deserves better than that.*

My inner voice was right, and my shame grew. I wasn't thinking of Sabrina or Evelyn or of my kingdom. My people didn't want a king who did not treat his queen with the respect she deserved. I needed to remember that once I had shown Sabrina that sex would not always be painful, we would be finished. I would have no need to see her again.

"My king?" Sabrina said.

"What is it?" I said gruffly.

"Would you require something in return?" she repeated.

"No. Forget what I said," I replied. "You cannot be that far from your sister, and you will need a human male to give you children."

My stomach burned at the thought of her mating with another man, and I stood up abruptly. I was naked, and Sabrina's face flamed red as she stared at my cock. I stepped out of the warm pool and dried off with a towel before yanking on my pants and shirt.

Sabrina had climbed out and wrapped a towel around her wet body. She touched her wet braid a bit nervously as I took her hand.

"I'm not dressed," she said.

"You are covered well enough," I replied. "Come, little human."

She gathered her clothes in one hand and took my hand with her other. I wrapped my tail around her towel-covered waist and led her out of the pool room.

---

*Sabrina*

QUILL WAS ANGRY WITH ME. I DIDN'T KNOW WHY, BUT IT WAS easy enough to see in the stiff way he walked next to me. He didn't say a word as we returned to my small apartment. He opened the door for me and dropped his tail from my waist. I stepped inside, but he remained in the doorway. I gave him a look of confusion.

"Are you not coming in, my king?" It felt strange to call him that, but calling him Quill when he was angry with me seemed wrong.

"No," he said shortly.

My stomach dropped, and I tried to hide my disappointment. "But we had an agreement."

He didn't reply and pulled back when I tried to take his hand. "My king, we had an agreement, remember?"

"Yes, but I have changed my mind."

"Tell me what I've done wrong." I was starting to be angry about his sudden change in heart. We had an agreement, and it wasn't right that he could just change his mind.

"You have not done anything wrong," he said.

"Then why are you breaking our agreement?"

"I am your king. Do not ask me to explain myself."

"I deserve an explanation."

"Go to bed," he said. "We will talk tomorrow."

"Will we talk, or will you eat my pussy?" I said crudely.

He flushed, and his gaze dipped to my crotch. "Enough, little human."

"We had an agreement," I repeated.

"You will do as I say and go to your bed." He shut the door in my face.

"You asshole! You promised!" I shouted before slamming my fists on the door. It hurt my hands, and I cursed again before stomping into the small living room. I stormed back and forth in front of the couch.

"Asshole," I muttered again. "He thinks he can just offer to eat my -"

The door opened, and Quill strode into the room. He shut the door and stalked toward me. I should have been afraid, but all I could feel was lust and need. I didn't object when he lifted me and tossed me over his shoulder like I weighed nothing. His big hand squeezed and caressed my ass as he carried me into the bedroom.

He set me on my feet and pulled the towel away before kissing me hard on the mouth. His hands flicked open my bra, and he yanked it away and dropped it to the floor. I returned his kiss and pulled at his shirt. He pulled it off, and it joined my bra on the floor. I traced my hands over his chest and then his abdomen, running my fingers over each hard ridge of muscle.

He kissed me again, cupping the back of my skull and squeezing my breast with one hand until I gasped.

"I am sorry," he whispered against my mouth. "I am sorry, my sadora."

"It's fine."

"I should never have spoken so cruelly to you."

I wrinkled my nose at him. "You weren't cruel, just a little cranky."

He sucked on my bottom lip before squeezing my ass through my wet panties. "Will you still allow me to taste your pussy?"

"Yes," I said. "I want you to."

"I want it too," he whispered.

We kissed again, slow, deep kisses that heated my blood and made me rub my pelvis against him. He groaned when my fingers dug into his back. He reached for my panties. I helped him slide them down my legs and stepped out of them as he touched the dark curls at the top of my pussy.

"I cannot wait to taste you, sadora."

We fell onto the bed in a tangle of limbs, and I lay quietly as he took out the elastic at the end of my hair and unbraided it.

"Your hair is pretty." He gently combed out the tangles with his fingers.

"Thank you."

"It is soft and smells good." He inhaled deeply, and I tugged on his short, dark hair.

"Not that I don't love the compliments, my king, but you promised to eat my pussy."

"Quill," he said. "You will call me Quill when you are in my bed."

"Technically, we're in my bed." I pointed out.

He laughed, and my chest tightened. God, I loved his laugh.

"Quill. Say it," he demanded.

"Quill," I whispered.

He bent his head and sucked on my nipple until it was a tight little bud, and my back was arching.

"Oh please, Quill," I moaned.

"Patience, my little sadora," he murmured against my breast.

He spent what felt like hours licking and kissing and sucking at my breasts. My nipples were hard as glass, and each brush of his tongue made my back arch helplessly. By the time he pressed a warm kiss against my abdomen, I was already feeling nearly insane with need. I yanked at his hair when he licked around my belly button.

"Enough teasing!"

He smiled up at me. "My sadora is impatient, is she not?"

"Yes," I said. "Do what you promised, Quill."

"Whatever you want, little human." He nudged at my thigh with his shoulder, and I spread my legs with a shameful eagerness as he stretched out between them. He kissed and licked my inner thighs teasingly, and I squeezed them around his head.

"Please!" I shouted when he licked the crease of my thigh.

His warm breath washed over my pussy, and I couldn't hold back my hoarse shout when he licked the lips of my pussy.

He lifted his head and smiled at me. "You taste delicious, sadora."

I pushed on his head. "I want more."

He pressed a kiss at the top of my pussy before licking my pussy lips again. I was soaking wet. I could feel liquid dripping out of my pussy and slipping down my inner thighs, but I didn't feel any shame. Not even when Quill cleaned my thighs with his tongue before delving back into my pussy. My clit was so swollen that it peeked out from between my lips, but Quill deliberately avoided it as he kissed and licked.

"Quill! Please!" I had never had my pussy eaten before, had never even had a man touch my clit until Quill. But after only a few minutes of having his warm wet tongue tasting me, I was very confident if he didn't lick my clit, I would die. The tension in my belly was too much to take, the pressure nearly pain, as I clutched helplessly at his head and tried to guide him where I wanted him to go. "Please, Quill! I can't take it. Please!"

His warm, wet tongue brushed across my clit with a firm stroke. He'd gotten me so hot, so worked up and needy that the single brush of his tongue was enough. I screamed, my pelvis arching as pleasure flooded through my body, lighting up every single nerve ending. Quill's big hands clamped down on my hips, holding me steady as I writhed and screamed again. His tongue was still on my clit, and the light strokes he made across it increased the intensity of my orgasm. I screamed a third time and collapsed against the bed as Quill pushed into a kneeling position between my legs. He fumbled at his pants, tearing them open and pulling his cock out. He rubbed it hard, staring at my breasts as he moaned.

"Stop!" I gasped out.

The look of agony on his face was evident. He stopped rubbing but kept his hand around his cock before pleading, "My sadora, please. Do not make me stop. I need my relief just as much as you."

"I know," I said. "I want to have sex with you."

His body froze, and he released his cock before leaning back. "What did you say?"

"I want to try having sex with you."

"Are you certain?"

"Yes. But if I ask you to stop, will you?"

"Yes," he said immediately.

"*Can* you stop?" I hated the doubt in my voice, but I needed to know.

He rubbed my thigh. "Yes, my sadora. I can. I will never hurt you again, I promise."

"Okay," I said.

He stayed where he was as if he couldn't quite believe what I was saying.

"Quill, I'm ready."

Precum leaked from the head of his cock and dripped onto my thigh. He stared at it for a moment before shifting his gaze to me. "I – thank you, sadora."

He shoved his pants down his thick thighs, and I tried not to giggle when he nearly fell off the bed, yanking them off his feet. He squeezed my knee. "You will be on top. You can control the pace and how much you take, and if it becomes too much -"

"No, I want you on top."

He hesitated, and I spread my legs wide and held out my hands toward him. "I trust you, Quill."

Something flickered in his lovely, silver eyes, too quick for me to understand what emotion it was. He lowered his gaze to my pussy before he cupped my ass and lifted it so that his tail could wrap around my waist. I gave him a questioning look. He hadn't wrapped his tail around me before when we were intimate.

He either didn't see my look or purposely ignored it as he positioned his heavy body above mine and propped himself up on his hands. He leaned down to kiss me. I returned his kiss as I arched my back and rubbed my hard nipples against his chest.

He made a guttural moan of need and nipped my bottom lip. I squeezed my hands around his narrow waist and licked his throat. He moaned again, and I tried not to stiffen when I felt the head of his cock brush against my pussy. He reached between us and guided the head to my wet entrance.

He studied my face intently before kissing me. "I will not hurt you, sadora."

"I know," I said. "I know you won't."

He nuzzled my throat and made a gentle push. The head of his cock breached my entrance, and I released my breath in a harsh rush.

"All right?" he whispered.

"Yes. It doesn't hurt."

"Good." He pushed again, sliding in a little further before pulling back.

"Still good." I clutched at his waist.

He smiled at me, and I watched his face as he used the same slow, gentle thrust and retreat motion until he was fully sheathed within me. He held perfectly still, a muscle ticking in his jaw and a vein throbbing in his temple, as I took a deep breath. I was stuffed full of his cock, and my inner walls worked to stretch around the unexpected invasion. It was slightly uncomfortable and a little strange feeling, but after a few minutes, the discomfort disappeared. I shifted beneath him, and Quill released his breath in a hiss.

"Are you all right, sadora?"

I stared at the vein that pulsed in his temple and the way he seemed to be almost in agony. "Yes. Are *you*?"

"You are very tight," he groaned. "I – I must move. Please."

I arched my hips against his, and his warm breath washed over my face as he made a low groan before making three long and slow strokes. It didn't hurt, and I gave him an encouraging smile. "That's good, Quill."

He closed his eyes, and I watched his face in fascination as he moved a little faster. I braced my feet on the bed and tried to meet each of his thrusts. His tail squeezed tighter around my waist, and I could swear it was helping me find his rhythm. Tugging and releasing with each of Quill's strokes.

"Krono! I am not going to last!" Quill muttered. "I cannot…"

He trailed off and made one final hard thrust that actually did hurt a little before his big body arched, and he groaned in pleasure. He shook as he made a few more short and hard thrusts. He was panting heavily, and when he collapsed against me, I pushed at his shoulders. "Air! I need air!"

He withdrew and rolled off of me. My pussy was aching pleasantly, and I didn't object when Quill cupped my pussy and rubbed lightly. When he withdrew his hand, his fingers were covered in his seed, and I watched as he smeared it into my lower belly.

"Why do you do that?" I asked.

He just shrugged and kissed my breast. "Turn on your side, Sabrina."

I turned on my side, and he spooned me, cupping my

breast and kissing the back of my shoulder as his tail curled around to rest on my hip.

"I am sorry," he said.

"For what?"

"I should have made you come again while I fucked you."

"It's fine," I said. "I didn't expect more than one orgasm."

He grunted in irritation. "Krono, that makes me feel even worse."

I laughed and squeezed his hand. "I'm not sure what you want me to say. You gave me the best orgasm of my life, and it didn't hurt when we had sex. You singlehandedly changed my mind about never having sex again. That's a good thing, Quill."

His hand tightened on my breast for a moment. "That makes me happy."

"You don't sound happy."

He didn't reply, and I tried not to sound resentful when I said, "This is it for us, isn't it?"

He sighed heavily and kissed the back of my shoulder. "We are not mates, Sabrina."

"I know," I said. "And I know you only did this because you feel bad about what happened earlier."

"It was not just that," he said. "I wanted you, little human."

"But now that you've," I paused, "had me, you don't want me anymore?"

"Does it matter?" he asked a little harshly. "There is no point in continuing. You are not my mate, and when the storm ends, you will go to your employer."

"No, it doesn't matter. You're right about everything." I lifted his hand from my breast and kissed the palm. "You should go, Quill."

His tail flicked in agitation. "I can spend the night with you."

I sat up and smiled at him. "I appreciate the offer, but it's probably best if you don't. I could get used to you in my bed too easily, my king."

He gave me a guilty look. "I only wanted to show you how good it could be, sadora. I did not mean to upset you."

"You haven't," I said. "You haven't done anything wrong, and I appreciate what you did for me. But it's not a good idea for you to spend the night in my bed."

He continued to stare guiltily at me, and I made myself smile at him before leaning forward and pecking him on the cheek. "Stop looking at me like that. I understand, and I'm not upset. I promise."

"Sabrina -"

I slid out of the bed, grabbed my nightshirt, and pulled it on quickly. "It's late, Quill."

He sighed and got out of bed before dressing. I followed him to the door and pasted another smile on my face when he turned and pulled me into his embrace. He pressed a light kiss on my mouth.

"Thank you, little human."

"I should be the one thanking you, remember?" I was impressed at how cheerful I sounded. I smiled even wider until my cheeks ached. "It was awesome, Quill. Evelyn is a lucky woman."

His green skin darkened, and he gave me such a miserable look that I immediately regretted my flippant remark.

I squeezed his waist and kissed his broad chest through his shirt. "I'll see you tomorrow, okay? Maybe we can walk in the garden if you have time in the evening."

He cleared his throat. "Perhaps. Good night, Sabrina."

When he stepped back, I dropped my arms from around his waist and ignored my stupid urge to beg him to come back to my bed. He left my apartment, shutting the door behind him with a soft click. My smile dropped, and I wiped away the tears immediately streaming down my cheeks.

"You idiot," I whispered. "You should have let him stay the night."

I sighed and walked to the kitchen. There was a jug of gallberry juice in their version of a fridge and I poured myself a glass before drinking it in three big gulps. I stared at the bottom of the glass. It was better that I didn't let Quill stay the night. I was already dangerously close to feeling something I shouldn't for him. Spending the night with him, sleeping with him again, was a dangerous idea. The storm would end eventually, and I had a contract to fulfill.

*You could sleep with him until the storm ends*, my inner voice whispered persuasively. *There's no harm in that. Just keep your emotions out of it.*

Keep my emotions out of it. Could I do that, I wondered? I knew Quill wasn't mine. Even if I didn't have a work contract, I was breeding incompatible, and Quill needed an heir. There was no future for us, and if I kept that in mind, then why couldn't I have sex with him? I already craved more of the pleasure Quill had given me tonight. There was so much more we could do. I hadn't even tried sucking his dick. I bet if I asked Quill to let me practice on him, he'd be more than agreeable to it.

I rinsed the glass and put it in the sink before returning to the bed. The sheets smelled like Quill, and I buried my face in them and inhaled deeply. I would ask him tomorrow if he wanted to keep having sex. I could keep my emotions out of this. No problem.

# CHAPTER 9

*Sabrina*

"You need to eat your dinner, human."

"I'm not hungry." I pushed my plate away and stared defiantly at Teo.

The old Draax sighed and picked up my plate. "You cannot starve yourself to get his attention, human."

"I'm not," I snapped at him. "I'm just not hungry."

I wasn't lying. It took three days of no contact from Quill to finally get through my thick skull that I was getting the Draax version of ghosting. When I finally realized it wasn't work keeping him away, my appetite disappeared as easily as he had. Even worse, I was no longer allowed to walk around the palace with Galan or anyone else. Teo or Faro delivered my meals, and they didn't stay with me while I ate. Tonight, when Teo returned, I hadn't touched any of the food.

"He is not your mate, human," Teo said gently.

"I *know*," I said. "My lack of appetite has nothing to do with him. I'm bored and going out of my mind. I get that your king is done with me, but why can't I at least go for walks in the garden or around the palace with Galan?"

Teo glanced uncomfortably at the floor. "The king has insisted that you stay in your quarters."

"Why? I won't go near him, for God's sake. I don't even know where the hell he sleeps. He can't possibly think that I'm going to find him and force him to have sex with me, does he?"

Teo's skin turned a dark green. "I cannot presume to know what my king thinks, human."

"Ask Galan to talk to him. I know Galan can convince him to at least let me go for walks in the garden."

"That is not possible." Teo carried my plate to the door and paused in the doorway. "I understand this is difficult, human, but the storm will end soon, and you will be where you are supposed to be. If you do not eat, you will be too weak to do the job your employer expects of you."

As he left my apartment, I wanted to yell at him that he could just leave me a bunch of damn groceries, and I'd cook my own meals, but I couldn't do it. Having my meals brought to me was the only time I saw anyone. I'd never lived alone before, and I was going stir-crazy.

I paced the living area for over an hour as my agitation grew. Not getting to leave my apartment was bad enough, but Quill avoiding me for the last three days was more upsetting than it should have been. I didn't mean anything to him, and it shouldn't have surprised me that he was ghosting me, but dammit it did. I really thought he would at least still want to be friends. I sighed and rubbed my forehead. God, I was so stupid.

I slapped my hands on my thighs in frustration and grimaced when my hand stuck to the gallberry juice stain on my pants. I'd been wearing the same damn pants for three days, and I hadn't even showered today. I sniffed my armpit before making a face and walking to the bathroom. I stared at myself in the mirror. I looked pale and drawn, and anger bubbled in my belly.

He had no right to keep me a prisoner. I was a grown woman, and I'd be damned if I let some stupid alien king tell me what to do. They didn't lock me in my quarters, and it was time for me to take advantage of that. I'd have a bath and do my hair and makeup and dress in something other than damn yoga pants. Then I'd take my adult self and go for a walk in the gardens.

---

*Quillan*

"My king, you must eat," Teo said.

"I am not hungry."

"You need to eat," Teo replied. "It has been three days, and you cannot -"

"Did you see her today?"

Teo hesitated before nodding. "I brought her evening meal to her."

"Did she eat it?"

"Of course, my king."

I studied Teo's face before curling my lip at him. "You are lying to me, Teo."

He sighed and sat down next to me. "She eats as little as you do, my king."

Worry gnawed at my stomach. The little human didn't carry enough meat on her bones to go without food for long.

"She needs to eat."

"I have told her that, but she is stubborn."

"Yes, she is." A smile crossed my face. My little sadora was stubborn, and I missed her stubbornness more than I thought possible in the last few days. "Take her more food and tell her I have commanded that she eat."

"I am your advisor, not your errand boy," Teo said.

I blinked at him, and a look of shame crossed Teo's face. "Forgive me, my king. I did not mean to -"

"It is fine. We are all on edge as of late, it seems," I said.

"As I grow older, the storms grow more difficult for me to bear," Teo said quietly. "But I do not think it is the storm bothering you."

"Nothing bothers me," I said.

"If you miss the human, perhaps you should talk to her," Teo said. "She is upset that she is not allowed to leave her quarters. Take her for a walk in the garden and ease both your irritation."

"I cannot," I said.

"You can. You are not busy."

I glared at him. "I cannot see the human again, Teo. Do not ask me to do so."

"Why not?" Teo asked. "I know you have shown her that fucking is pleasurable."

"How do you know that?" I snapped.

"Do you forget that my quarters are close to hers?" Teo said with a grin. "I heard her screaming the other night. I may be old, and it may have been many years since I've lain with a female, but I still remember what pleasure sounds like."

I could feel myself blushing, and the old Draax grinned again, saying, "I do not see the problem with taking the human for a walk once a day."

"She is not a pet that I must feed and water and walk!" I

snarled. "She is a human with feelings and needs and desires…"

My cock twitched in my pants. It was the little human's desires and needs that kept me away from her. If she asked me to fuck her again, I would not be able to deny her. Krono, if she even looked at me with need, I would fuck her. She was the first female I'd lain with who could take my cock in its entirety. I had spent the last three days in my private quarters thinking of nothing else but how it felt to be in her pussy.

"I have never seen you so conflicted about a female before, "Teo said.

"I am not conflicted," I said.

"She is not your mate, and she is breeding incomp -"

"I am aware of that!" I shouted. "Why do you think I avoid her now? There is no point in fucking her again!"

Breathing hard, I glared at Teo. He returned my look calmly, and I muttered a curse before standing and pacing. "I cannot see her, Teo. Do not ask me again."

"All right," he said. "But you have locked yourself away for the last three days, which will not improve your mood. Go for a walk in the garden. It will help ease your anger."

He stood and clapped me on the back. "Go, my king. Walk the garden and find peace."

"Perhaps you are right, old friend," I said. "I will do as you suggest."

I followed him out of my quarters, and we walked together in silence until we reached the entrance to the garden and said good night. I walked into the warm, quiet stillness of the garden and breathed deeply. I passed Bitta and a few others and nodded to them but did not stop. I headed toward the less desirable west side of the garden. The flowers were not as plentiful on the west side, nor was their fragrance as sweet, and most Draax in the palace avoided it. I would find the peace I needed there.

*Will you?*

I ignored my inner voice as I followed the stone path. Yes, I would. I had to. If I didn't do something, I would go mad with my need for the little human. She was all I could think about, and my desire to fuck her, to hear her soft cries of pleasure and to lie in her bed with her was overwhelming in its intensity. I had no idea what was happening to me, and I didn't like it.

I cocked my head and slowed to a stop as I heard a familiar voice. I cursed loudly before storming down the path. I rounded the corner and snarled, "What are you doing here?"

Sabrina stared wide-eyed at me. "Wh-what are you doing here?" She turned and glanced behind her at the wall of vines as I glared at her.

"It is my garden! Who brought you out of your quarters?"

"No one," she said. "I brought myself."

"You could not find the garden on your own."

She blushed and gave me a defiant look. "Well, I did."

"I heard you talking to someone, human."

"I was talking to myself."

I moved closer, and before she could step back, I snapped my tail out and wrapped it around her waist. She was wearing a dress for the first time since I met her. The bodice hugged her full breasts and showed a hint of cleavage. The dress hem ended just below her knees, and I studied her smooth calves. An image of those legs wrapped around my waist went through me, and my cock hardened. I pulled her close until her breasts brushed against my chest.

Her dark hair was loose and flowing around her shoulders. I wound my hand through the soft strands and held tightly. Krono, I had missed her scent and the feel of her soft curves. Ignoring my urge to kiss her, I rubbed my thumb across her cheekbone and then pressed my erection against her lower belly. I grinned at her low moan.

"Tell me the truth, human. Who were you speaking to?"

---

*Sabrina*

WELL, IT WAS OFFICIAL. I WAS LOST IN THE GARDEN.

I pounded my hands on my thighs in frustration before smoothing down my dress. I was standing in the middle of a cross-intersection. I'd been very proud of myself when I found the garden with no trouble, but I had quickly become lost in the maze of trees, flowers, and stone walls.

I was currently standing in a section that I was pretty sure I'd never been in before. It was no less flush with plant life, but there were more trees and bushes than flowers and no benches to sit down and enjoy the view. I reached out and traced the stone wall that lined the left side of the path. It was over ten feet tall, and I stared at the birds perched on the top. They were about the size of a sparrow but bright orange with lime-green beaks. They made a low beeping sound that intensified when I stepped toward the wall. Moving as one, they spread their wings and flew off the wall, disappearing quickly into the distance.

"Are you flying in the direction of the waterfall?" I yelled after them. "Should I follow you?"

I giggled at how stupid I sounded, yelling at a flock of birds before cocking my head and listening intently. The sound of the waterfall was very faint, but I thought it might have been coming from the left. I turned that way and walked quickly, still tracing my hand along the stone wall. The garden was massive, and with my lousy sense of direction, I could easily wander in it for weeks without finding my way out. I had a sudden and disturbingly clear image of my bloated and decomposing body being discovered by a random Draax a few weeks from now and shuddered.

"Don't be so silly," I told myself. "You won't die in the garden, for heaven's sake. You'll find your way out eventually, and if you don't, someone else will find you before you…oh shit."

I had been staring at my feet as I talked, and I looked up in time to see that the path ended in a wall of tangled vines. Thankfully, the path was a t-junction, and I hurried forward and looked to the right and then the left.

"Are you kidding me?" I groaned. Both directions were dead ends, and I muttered a curse before tentatively touching the wall of vines. Maybe I could push my way through it. I snorted loudly. Going off path was a terrible idea. I just needed to turn around and choose another direction at the cross-intersection. Easy peasy. I wouldn't die in a beautiful garden in the middle of an alien's palace. That was just silly.

"What are you doing here?"

I whirled around and stared wide-eyed at the copper-eyed alien standing behind me. "Galan, thank God. I'm lost."

"You should not be here," he said. "You are confined to your quarters. Who brought you here?"

"No one brought me here. I decided I wanted to walk in the garden, so I did. I'm not a prisoner."

He sighed and leaned against the stone wall as his gaze flickered over my body. "Sabrina, disobeying our king's orders is a terrible idea."

"He's not my king," I said. "And do you think it's fair that he's trying to keep me a prisoner?"

He hesitated before shaking his head. "No, but it is for your safety."

"It has nothing to do with that." I walked to Galan and leaned against the wall next to him. "He's acting like a spoiled little boy who keeps his favourite toy locked up so no others can play with it."

I gasped in surprise when Galan turned and pressed his hard body against mine. He lifted my arms above my head and pinned them against the wall as he stared down at me. "Does his toy wish to play with another?"

I swallowed and licked my lips. Galan's cock was hard and pushing against my stomach, and just like that, I was so turned on that my panties were wet. Shamefully, it was taking every ounce of my willpower not to rub against his dick. What was wrong with me? I was a terrible person.

I liked Galan, and I definitely lusted after him, but there were none of the butterflies in my stomach I felt whenever I was around Quill. I didn't have the urge to ask Galan everything about his life or spend time with him that didn't involve him making me climax.

I blushed furiously at my shameless, dirty thoughts and looked away. Galan cupped my face with his free hand and made me meet his gaze. "Do you wish to play with another, Sabrina?"

"I – he told me not to," I whispered. "I may want to play with another, but I won't betray Quill."

Shame flickered in Galan's eyes, and he dropped my wrists and stepped away. "Nor will I. Forgive me, human. I lost control, and it will not happen again."

"I'm sorry too, Galan." I reached out to touch him, and he moved away, shaking his head.

"No, do not touch me. I wish to obey my king, but a Draax only has so much willpower."

"I'm sorry," I said again.

He backed away until he was standing in the middle of the t-juncture and gave me a wry look. "I fear that if our king even knew I was alone with you, he would banish me from the palace. Or, perhaps he would simply take my head and be done with it."

I frowned at him. "He wouldn't. He doesn't care about me. Besides, we did nothing wrong, Galan. We were only talking."

I stiffened when I heard a familiar curse coming from behind me. I turned around and stared wide-eyed at Quill when he came around the corner.

"What are you doing here?" he snapped at me.

"Wh-what are you doing here?" I glanced nervously behind me. Galan had disappeared. He must have been standing in the dead-end path to the left or the right. Probably a smart move on his part. Quill looked angry enough to lose his shit, even on his best friend.

"It is my garden! Who brought you out of your quarters?" Quill barked.

"No one," I said. "I brought myself."

"You could not find the garden on your own."

"Well, I did."

"I heard you talking to someone, human."

"I was talking to myself." I tamped down my urge to glance behind me at the vine wall again.

He moved closer as his tail lashed out like a whip and wrapped around my waist. He pulled me close until my breasts were pressing against his chest and wrapped his hand in my hair. His gaze dropped to my mouth before he rubbed his thumb across my cheekbone. He pushed his erection against my lower belly and grinned with satisfaction when I moaned.

"Tell me the truth, human. Who were you speaking to?"

"No one. I was talking to myself."

"Why did you disobey my orders to stay in your quarters?"

"Why have you been avoiding me the last three days?" I countered.

"Answer the question. Why did you disobey me?" His big hand cupped my right breast, and I suddenly wished I wasn't wearing a bra.

"I'm not your slave," I whispered as I arched into his touch.

"No, you are not." He kissed me, pulling back when I tried to slip my tongue between his lips. "But you disobeyed me, which means I must punish you."

I wasn't sure if it was fear or excitement I was feeling. "What kind of punishment?"

He squeezed my breast before bending his head and sucking on my throat. "I've missed you, sadora."

"You're the one who's avoiding – oh!"

His hand had slipped under my dress, and his fingers stroked my leg before slipping between my legs and cupping my pussy through my panties. "I like your dress. I like how easily I can touch your pussy when you are wearing it."

He rubbed me through the wet material and made an appreciative growl. "So wet already, my sadora."

I cast a guilty look at the t-junction, and Quill's hand tightened in my hair. "Look at me."

I stared up at him obediently, and he kissed me until I was moaning softly, and my mouth was swollen and red from his kisses.

"Time for your punishment."

He led me to the stone wall and leaned back against it. I was standing in front of him, and he unwrapped his tail from my waist before pulling his shirt over his head. I stared at his broad, naked chest as he folded his shirt into a thick pad and placed it on the ground between us. My confusion was cleared up when Quill pushed on my shoulders. "On your knees, little human."

"Quill," I said as my face flamed bright red. "I've never... that is..."

Quill stroked my face. "I know, sweet sadora. On your knees."

He pushed again, and I sank to my knees, resting them on his folded-up shirt as his big hand stroked my hair. His other unbuttoned his pants, and I watched as he pulled his cock free and rubbed it with his hand.

"Open, sadora."

My gaze flickered to the t-junction again. Galan was there, no doubt listening and knowing exactly what I was about to do. Would he look, I wondered. Would he peek around that corner and watch as I sucked his king's cock?

The thought that Galan would watch sent fresh lust through me, and I squeezed my thighs together in an effort to stop the ache.

"Sabrina, obey your king and open your mouth," Quill said.

My pussy throbbing with need, I turned my gaze back to Quill and opened my mouth. He pushed the head of his cock past my lips, and I sucked tentatively at it as he stroked my hair.

"Good, sadora," he praised. "Take more."

He fed me more of his cock and cupped the back of my head with his hand. He held me firmly as he pushed his cock in and out of my mouth. His low moans and the look of delight on his face made me bold. I sucked more firmly as I wrapped my hand around the thick base and rubbed hard.

"Krono, that is good," he muttered. "Such a good sadora to suck my cock." He swept my hair into a ponytail and gripped it hard, using it to guide my mouth back and forth over his dick. I licked at the ridge as precum dripped onto my tongue, and the taste of gallberries filled my mouth.

I moaned around his cock, and he shuddered before thrusting more quickly. I sucked eagerly and cried out in disappointment when he pulled his cock from my mouth. He was staring at the t-junction, and my stomach dropped when he said, "Who is there?"

"Quill," I licked the head of his cock, "don't -"

"Show yourself," he demanded. He groaned when I sucked on the head of his cock and pushed me away again. "Be still, Sabrina."

"Quill..."

Galan appeared in the t-junction. My eyes dropped to the front of his pants. His erection was evident, and it sent a flood of wetness to my pussy.

"Forgive me, my king," Galan said in a low voice. "I should have announced my presence immediately."

Quill's nostrils flared. "Yes, you should have."

Galan's gaze dropped to me, and Quill followed it. "Sabrina," he said hoarsely, "did you know Galan was there?"

I nodded. "He found me in the garden just before you did."

"Why did you not say anything?" Quill asked.

"I didn't want him to get in trouble for speaking to me," I whispered. "And I liked that he was – was listening to us."

Quill inhaled sharply, and precum dripped from his cock. I licked it away with my tongue. Both men groaned, and without taking my eyes off Quill's face, I parted my lips and slid my mouth over his cock. I took as much as I could, which embarrassingly was only about half, but I sucked with hard enthusiasm as Quill watched me with glittering intensity.

After a few minutes, he glanced at Galan. "Watching you suck me is driving him crazy. He cannot resist touching himself. Do you like that, sadora?"

I nodded around his cock and stared at Galan. His hand was in his pants and fisting his cock.

"What do you think it would do to him to see you being fucked?" Quill asked.

My gaze snapped back to him, and I didn't object when he pulled me to my feet. He kissed me hard as his hands reached for the zipper of my dress. He yanked down the zipper and curled his fingers into my dress before tugging it down. It pooled at my feet, and he flicked open my bra and raked it from my body. He dropped it to the ground and nibbled at my earlobe as he reached for my panties.

I grabbed at his hand and gave Galan a quick, fleeting glance. "Quill, I -"

"Your body is beautiful, sadora," Quill said into my ear. "I wish for Galan to see it. Will you do that for me?"

I nodded and dropped his wrist.

"Good girl," he murmured before pulling my panties down. I stepped out of them and toed my sandals off as Quill studied my naked body.

"So beautiful," he repeated before turning me to face Galan. I automatically tried to cover my body with my arms as Quill stepped behind me. His cock brushed against the small of my back as he took my arms and held them down.

"No, let Galan look at you. You are stunning, my sadora, and he wants you very much."

I stood completely still, a flush rising in my chest as Galan stared at my naked body. When Quill cupped my breasts and pulled at my nipples with his fingers, Galan groaned, and his hand rubbed frantically in his pants.

"Do you see how beautiful he finds you, sadora?" Quill said.

I arched my back when Quill pulled on my nipples again. "Would you like to see his cock?"

I nodded, and Quill kissed my neck. "Show her your cock, Galan."

Galan immediately unbuttoned his pants and pulled his cock out. I stared wide-eyed at it as he squeezed the base. He was as long and thick as Quill, and my damn mouth watered as I stared at it.

"Do you want his cock, my sadora?

"Yes," I whispered. "Yes, please, Quill."

His low laugh made me shiver with pleasure. I parted my legs when he cupped my pussy and rubbed it.

"He is not allowed here," he said loud enough for Galan to hear. "Your pussy is for my cock and my cock only. Do you understand?"

I nodded, and he squeezed my pussy. "Say it, sadora. Say it so I know you understand exactly what I am saying."

"My pussy is only for your cock," I said. "Galan isn't allowed to fuck me."

"That is right, little human." Quill stared at Galan. "Do you understand, Galan?"

"Yes, my king," Galan gasped out as he fisted his cock. "No fucking."

"Good," Quill said.

I moaned when Quill rubbed my clit. His talented fingers stroked and petted my clit for only a few minutes, and I was already on the verge of my climax. I forgot Galan was watching and pumped my hips without shame against Quill's hand.

"Come for your king, sadora," Quill murmured. He pinched my clit, his other hand covering my mouth to muffle my scream of pleasure. I shook with the force of my orgasm as it rushed through me. His tail around my waist kept me on my feet, while his hand between my legs kept little ripples of pleasure spreading through my pussy.

"Is she not so beautiful when she comes, Galan?"

My eyes popped open, and I blushed as Galan groaned and nodded. "Very beautiful, Quill."

Quill moved his hand away and Galan groaned again when Quill showed him the wetness on his fingers. He pushed them against my lips, and I cleaned his fingers with my tongue as Galan watched with bright desperation.

"Galan will enjoy being in your mouth," Quill said, "but for tonight, he will watch as I fuck you."

He turned me in his arms and lifted me. His tail wrapped around my waist as I slung my legs around his hips and clung to him. He kissed me again before resting my back against the stone wall. He supported me against the wall with his lower body and bent his head to suck and lick at both of my nipples. I clutched his head and stared at Galan. He had moved closer, and his face was a mask of need and want as he watched Quill suck my nipples into stiff and swollen buds.

Quill lifted his head and kissed my throat. "Are you ready for my cock, Sabrina?"

"Yes," I whimpered. "Yes, I need it, Quill."

"I know." He shifted me and reached between us. I clung to his shoulders, arching against him as he guided his cock to my entrance. He pushed and half of him slid in so easily that it brought a grunt of surprise from his lips.

"So wet," he said. "You are enjoying being fucked while Galan watches."

"Yes," I admitted. "Please, I need more, Quill."

Quill pushed again, and we both moaned when he sank in to the hilt. I wiggled against the invasion, feeling that delicious burn as I stretched around him.

"Krono," Galan groaned, "she can take all of you."

"Yes," Quill gasped. "She is so tight, Galan. You cannot imagine."

"Please," I begged as I squeezed his waist with my thighs. Now that he was in me and filling that empty ache, I needed him to move. "Fuck me, Quill."

Galan made a low gasping noise of need as his hand moved faster over his cock. "For the love of Krono, fuck her. Do what your mate asks."

Quill cupped both of my thighs in his hands and held me up as he spread them wide. "I'm going to move harder this time, sadora. Tell me if it is too much."

"I will," I moaned as he moved slowly. I was worried that I would be too heavy for him to support, but his biceps barely bulged as he leaned back and watched his dick slide in and out of my wet pussy.

Galan moaned, and I turned my head to study him. His eyes were glued to my pussy, and I grew wetter when precum spilled from the tip of Galan's cock.

"Harder, Quill. Fuck her harder," Galan said in a low voice.

Quill did what he asked, sliding in and out in a hard rhythm that made my body bang against the stone wall behind me. I clutched at his shoulders, gasping and moaning and not even caring that my tits were bouncing wildly with every hard thrust that Quill made.

"Touch yourself, sadora," Quill demanded.

I reached down and rubbed at my clit. It was still sensitive from my earlier orgasm, and I was almost immediately ready to climax. Quill and Galan moaned in unison, and a little trickle of power went through me. I rubbed harder, circling my clit as they both watched. I was on the verge of coming, but Quill and Galan made harsh noises of disapproval when I tried to slow down.

"I'm close," I whispered. "I can't – I'm so close."

"Good," Quill said. "Come all over my cock, sadora. Squeeze it with your tight pussy."

I cried out and rubbed at my clit as Quill drove in and out of me. I had enough sense not to scream when I climaxed, but it was a barely won battle. Pleasure roared through me, blotting out the discomfort of the scraping of the stone against my bare back as Quill fucked me hard and rough. My pussy squeezed around him, pulling him deep inside of me and refusing to let go. He breathed my name and buried his face in my neck as he came deep inside of my pussy. Vaguely, I was aware of Galan's harsh pants and his low moan as he climaxed.

Quill held my trembling body as I slumped against him. I kissed his thick neck and glanced at Galan. He was rubbing his cock slowly as it softened, and there was a puddle of light green semen soaking into the ground in front of him.

I gave him a shy smile as Quill eased out of me and lowered me to the ground. My legs were trembling, and Quill flicked his tail around my waist, helping me to stay on my feet before pressing a kiss against my forehead. I thought I would feel embarrassed as both Quill and Galan tucked their cocks away and buttoned their pants, but I didn't. Instead, I felt sated and relaxed for the first time in three days. I leaned weakly against Quill as Galan approached us.

"Thank you, my king," he said in a low voice before smiling at me. "You are beautiful, Sabrina. Good night."

"Bye, Galan," I said.

He walked down the path and disappeared as Quill pulled his shirt on before picking up my panties. He helped me into them, and I slipped on my sandals as he handed me my bra. I winced when I tried to put it on, and it sent pain up and down my back. I touched my back tentatively as Quill picked up my dress. I could feel wetness, and I pulled my hand away and stared in surprise at the blood.

"Sadora? Why are you bleeding?" Quill grabbed my shoulders and swung me around. "Krono!"

"What's wrong with my back?" Now that the pleasure was fading, I could feel the throbbing starting in my back, and I craned my neck to try to see my back.

"It is scraped from the rock. Some of it quite badly." Quill muttered another curse and stared at the streaks of blood he could see on the rock wall. "What have I done?"

"It's fine," I said. "It was an accident."

"I said I would not hurt you again!" Quill was almost shouting, and his tail flicked back and forth so quickly that it was a blur.

"Hey," I put my arms around him and squeezed. "Don't be upset. It was an accident. I didn't even feel it when it happened, and it doesn't hurt that much now."

"I need to take you to Sigan, the kadana. He needs to clean it and -"

"Stop." I reached up and cupped his face to make him look at me. "It's not that bad. I'll clean it when I return to my quarters and drink some gallberry juice. That'll help. If it doesn't, I'll see the kadana tomorrow, okay?"

He studied me for a moment before taking my bra and stuffing it into his pocket. He helped me into my dress, easing the zipper past my scratched and bleeding back with infinite gentleness.

"Thank you," I said.

He took my hand and led me quickly to the garden entrance. I let go of his hand when we stepped into the hallway. "Thank you, Quill. I know the way to my quarters from here. Good night."

I turned and walked away. His tail wrapped around my waist almost immediately and stopped me.

"What are you doing?" I asked.

"I will return with you to your quarters and help you clean your back. As well as make sure that you eat. Teo told me you are not eating."

I shrugged. "I haven't been that hungry lately."

He scowled at me and led me toward my quarters. "You will let me clean your back, and then you will eat what I cook. Do you understand, human?"

"Yes, my king."

# CHAPTER 10

*Quillan*

I set the plate of food on the table and sat in the chair before patting my lap. "Sit down, Sabrina."

She sat in my lap without protest and ate some food. She had removed her dress so I could clean her back and was now wearing panties and a shirt that she told me was called a tank top. It was tight and hugged her large breasts in a very appealing manner. It dipped low in the front and the back, and I studied the scratches on her back with remorse before handing her a glass of gallberry juice.

"Drink."

"I've already had two glasses," she said with a hint of exasperation. "My back doesn't even hurt anymore."

I rubbed her lower back. "I am sorry I hurt you."

"It was an accident." She ate a piece of bacuri root.

I handed her a strip of grundleswat. "Eat this. The protein will also aid in healing you."

She ate it obediently and I helped myself to some food as well. Now that I had sated my hunger for Sabrina, my hunger

162

for food had returned. We ate in comfortable silence as we shared a glass of gallberry juice.

"Man, I have to meet your cook." She ate another piece of grundleswat.

"You did meet him. Jarka is the palace cook."

"But at Teo's birthday party, he just said he worked in the kitchen."

I shrugged. "He is a modest Draax."

"I didn't think a modest Draax existed," she said tartly.

I laughed and pressed a kiss against her bare shoulder. "Should I be jealous of your love of Jarka's cooking, human? I cooked your meal this evening, and you have not said a word."

"Having food delivered from the kitchen is not cooking," she laughed.

I grinned at her. "What is it you humans say? It is the thought that counts?"

She laughed again and ate a chunk of warracot. "Fine. Thank you, my king, for this amazing meal."

I stole the next chunk of warracot from her fingers and popped it into my mouth as she slapped me playfully on the chest. I kissed her soft lips and said, "Did you know that your pussy is even sweeter tasting than warracot?"

I expected her to blush, and she did, but I didn't expect her to give me a saucy grin. "Did you know your cum tastes like gallberries?"

I roared laughter and nuzzled her neck. "I did not."

"I guess it makes sense, considering how much of the juice you drink." She hesitated. "I'm not craving it as much now. I mean, I still like it a lot, but I don't have the intense craving for it."

"Good," I said, "that means whatever ailed you is better."

"I really didn't feel sick at all."

"You must drink lots tomorrow to help heal your back. If the scratches are not gone by the afternoon, you will see the kadana."

She just shrugged, and I squeezed her thigh. "You will do as your king commands, little human."

"Will you take me to see the kadana, or will you disappear again for three days?" she asked.

I flinched, and she sighed. "I'm sorry. I shouldn't have said that."

"I am sorry, Sabrina," I said. "I should not have avoided you like that, but I..."

She smiled at me. "I know why you avoided me, I do, but it isn't necessary. I'm fine with what you can offer me, Quill."

"What do you mean?"

"I thought about it after you left that night. I know I'm not your mate, and I'll be leaving soon, but I'm okay with having some fun while the storm lasts if you are. I wouldn't expect anything other than sex. I won't ask you to spend the night, and you don't have to spend time outside the bedroom with me."

I didn't reply, and she turned bright red. "Oh God, that came out sounding way more whorish than I thought it would."

"It did not," I said. "I am just surprised."

"Why?" she asked.

"I do not know." I really didn't. I had been with plenty of human females who were looking for sex and nothing more, and I thought nothing of it. It shouldn't bother me that Sabrina desired the same, but for some reason, it did.

*Not enough to decline her offer.*

Shamefully, no. There may have been a part of me that wished Sabrina wanted more from me, but it was better she didn't. Better and easier. She was offering me the chance to fuck her as much as I desired, and I would not be so foolish as to turn her down. Perhaps if I fucked her every day, my obsession with her would end when the storm did.

She was sliding from my lap, and I latched my tail around her waist to prevent her from moving. "Where are you going?"

She smiled at me. "Honestly, I'm feeling foolish. I thought you wanted to keep fucking, and it's obvious that you don't. I'm sorry for putting you on the spot like that. I didn't mean to. I understand, and I won't bother you again, but can I leave my quarters? I'm going crazy in here. I won't be any trouble. Hell, even if I could sit in the garden for a while every day, I'd be happier. What do you say?"

I cupped the back of her neck and angled my mouth over hers, licking at the seam of her lips until she opened them and granted me access to her warm, wet mouth. We kissed until my cock had stiffened, and she was rubbing her ass against it.

She blinked dazedly at me when I pulled my mouth away, and I cupped her face. "I want you very much, sadora."

"Good," she said a little breathlessly. "I want you too."

I cupped her breast and teased her nipple through the thin fabric of her shirt. "Have you eaten enough?"

She nodded, and I eased her from my lap before standing. Keeping my tail wrapped around her waist, I led her to her bedroom. I undressed quickly. Sabrina's gaze dropped to my cock as I peeled off her tank top.

"Quill, did I – I mean, was I…."

I was already cupping her breasts, my fingers teasing her nipples into hard points, but I stopped at the look on her face. "Were you what?"

Her face turned bright red, and she shook her head. "Never mind."

165

"Tell me," I insisted. I pulled her into my embrace and tilted her head up until she was looking at me. She looked nervous and uncertain, and I didn't want my mate ever to be afraid when she was with me.

*She's not your mate.*

"It's stupid," she said.

"Tell me."

"I've never given a blow job before, and I just wondered if I was... okay at it."

I couldn't stop the smile from crossing my face. She groaned and buried her face against my chest. "Oh God, I told you it was stupid. Just forget I said anything."

I bent my head and nuzzled her soft cheek before kissing my way to her ear. "It was amazing, sadora." I sucked on her earlobe and reached down to squeeze her curvy ass. "I enjoyed it very much."

"I doubt it was amazing." Her voice was muffled against my chest. "No one is amazing at something when it's their first time."

I tilted her head up again and kissed her forehead. "You did very well. But if you are concerned, I am more than happy to let you practice some more."

She laughed, and my chest tightened. Krono, I loved her laugh.

"That's very kind of you, my king."

"Quill," I reminded her. "You are to call me Quill in bed."

She hesitated before giving me a look that was both shy and seductive at the same time. It brought my desire for her up to another level, and I immediately cupped her breast, pinching her nipple as she said, "Will I practice only on you?"

I pinched her nipple again as my cock smeared precum across her belly. "You wish to have Galan's cock in your mouth?"

She didn't reply, and I bent my head and sucked on her nipple until she was making soft cries of need. I lifted my head and pushed my finger into her mouth. "Suck."

She sucked on my finger, and I groaned harshly before saying, "You must be truthful with me, Sabrina. Do you want to suck Galan's cock?"

I pulled my finger free of her warm, wet mouth. She licked her lips and whispered, "Yes."

"Then you shall have what you want," I said. "But tonight, it is only my cock you taste."

"Yes, Quill."

I reached between her legs and cupped her pussy through her panties. The fabric was soaking wet, and I smiled in satisfaction before easing them down her legs. She stepped out of them and I left them on the floor as I led her to the bed. She sat on the edge, and I pushed my way between her legs as I stroked my cock from root to tip.

"Open, sadora."

She opened her mouth immediately, and I slid my cock into her mouth, moaning with pleasure when she licked around the ridge.

"Good," I praised. "Lick just the head now."

She did as I asked before sucking firmly. My hips jerked, and I threaded my fingers through her dark hair. "Look at me while you suck."

She raised her gaze obediently, and I smoothed the strands of hair back from her face. "Perfect, little human. Take more."

She made a muffled sound of protest when I fed her more of my cock, but I shook my head and wouldn't let her pull away when she tried. "No, sadora. I won't give you too much. Relax and open your mouth wide for me."

She did what I demanded, and I petted her soft hair

before pushing a little deeper. Her lips were stretched wide around my dick, and her nostrils flared as the head of my cock pressed against the back of her throat. She tried to pull away again, but I held her hair tightly.

"No," I said. "Be my good girl, Sabrina."

I pulled back a little and let her take a few deep breaths before pushing forward again. I watched her throat work compulsively, and I pushed a little further. Her hands dug into my thighs, and I made a soothing noise under my breath as I watched more of my cock disappear into her mouth. Her eyes started to water, and I pulled out of her mouth as she took a deep breath.

Her lips were swollen and red, and precum dripped from my cock at the sight. "Lick me clean," I said.

She licked the head of my cock clean, and I moaned and tried to stay in control when she sucked on just the head again. This time I allowed her to control the pace and kept my grip loose as she bobbed her head back and forth over my cock.

I was already close to coming. Sabrina's lack of experience was a surprising turn-on, and the combination of her innocence and the eagerness with which she took my cock in her mouth made me want to see her reaction to swallowing my seed. An image of my sweet Sabrina on her hands and knees flooded through me. I would fuck her tight pussy while she sucked Galan's cock. I could easily picture the way her dark hair would look wrapped in Galan's fist, the way her mouth would stretch around his cock, and the sounds she would make as I pushed myself deep into her pussy.

My balls tightened, and I pulled out of Sabrina's mouth in a hurry. I squeezed the base of my dick, willing myself not to come as Sabrina gave me a surprised look.

"Quill? What's wrong?"

"Nothing," I gritted out. "I was just very close."

Her smug little smile made me laugh. I sat next to her and pushed my hand between her thighs. She was very wet, and I stroked her clit as she clutched at my wrist.

"Please," she moaned.

"Please, what?"

"I want you to fuck me," she whispered.

"You need to come first," I replied.

"No, I – I don't," she stuttered as I circled her clit with my finger.

"You do." I sucked on her earlobe before nipping it. "My little sadora is very tight. She will always need to have an orgasm before I will fuck her."

"Quill!" She pouted at me, and I stroked her clit again. "I don't need an orgasm first!"

"You do. I will not hurt you again, sweet sadora."

"I swear you're more – oh, oh God, that feels good – more traumatized by what happened than I am," she moaned. "It doesn't hurt now, and I want it. I *really* want it."

I grinned and pressed on her clit. "As soon as you come for me, you may have my dick."

She slapped me sharply on the chest in frustration, and I smiled again before pushing one thick finger into her tight warmth. She cried out, her thighs squeezing around my arm and her body arching up. Mindful of her injured back, I cupped the back of her neck and kept her upright when she tried to fall back on the bed.

"Is this better, sadora?" I whispered into her ear as I pushed my finger in and out of her. Her pussy tightened around my finger, trying to hold it deep inside of her. I gritted my teeth and ignored my urge to fuck her hard and rough.

"I – a little," she moaned as she rocked her pelvis against my hand. "Please, Quill, oh please."

I rubbed her clit hard. She made a breathless cry of pleasure, and her thighs clamped around my arm again. Her pussy tightened exquisitely around my finger, and there was a flood of wetness against my hand as she came with a hoarse cry. Her body shook, and she leaned against me as she panted heavily.

"That's my good girl," I whispered into her ear. I pulled my hand out from between her legs and kissed her before lying on my back on the bed. "Straddle me, sadora."

She straddled me, moaning when my cock brushed against her pussy. "Oh, Quill, please. Hurry."

She braced her hands on my chest and raised her body. I guided my cock to her entrance and pressed the head against her opening. The moment she felt my dick, she shoved her body down.

"Sadora," I said in alarm, "do not -"

She pushed again and took all of my cock in one hard thrust. I moaned, my hips bucking hard. She made a low cry, her fingers digging into my chest.

"Sabrina!" I stared anxiously at her as my fingers cupped her hips. "Sweet one, did I hurt you?"

She shook her head. "No. No, it feels really good."

"You have to take my cock more slowly. Your pussy is very small and -"

She poked my chest and gave me a look of frustration. "Oh my God, can you give me the lecture about fucking after we fuck?"

I laughed, and she moaned happily when it made me move inside of her. She braced her hands again and moved up and down. My hands tightened on her hips as my tail wrapped around her waist, and I helped her push harder and faster.

"Oh, oh my goodness..."

Her voice died off in a sweet moan. She gasped when I cupped her breasts and pulled on her nipples. Her back arched, and she squeezed around my cock as she rode me. I rubbed her clit, and she cried out and rocked against my fingertips frantically.

"Oh, oh, oh," she moaned. "Quill, I'm going to come again."

I rubbed harder, thrusting my hips back and forth as her pussy clenched around me. When she came with a soft shout, her pussy gripped me so tightly that I groaned and grabbed her hips again. I held her in a tight grip as I fucked her. Her beautiful breasts bounced, and I stared at her hard nipples as she held my forearms and rode each thrust of my pelvis.

My balls tightened, and I made my own hoarse shout of release as I climaxed deep inside of her. Panting and moaning, I thrust repeatedly as her pussy milked my cock. When my hips finally slowed, she leaned forward and rested her head against my chest.

"Am I too heavy?" she whispered.

"No. You are perfect, Sabrina."

She kissed my chest. "I'm already sleeping with you, my king. There's no need for sweet talk."

I didn't understand what she meant, so I stayed quiet and rubbed the silky smoothness of her back. She was growing sleepy. I could feel it in the way her body was sinking into mine. I shifted to my side and slipped my cock out of her but left my tail around her waist as she curled up against me. I should have been leaving. She'd made it clear earlier that she didn't want me to sleep in her bed, but I didn't want to go.

"Sadora," I murmured into her ear, "should I go?"

"No," she said sleepily before wrapping her arm around my waist. "Please stay with me, Quill. Will you?"

"Yes." I kissed her forehead. "Yes, my sweet sadora."

---

*Sabrina*

"Hello, my king." I smiled happily at Quill when I opened the door to my apartment.

"Good evening, Sabrina," he replied. "May I come in?"

I nodded and followed him into the kitchen. He carried a large tray filled with food in his hands. I hadn't seen him since he left my bed early this morning, and I sat down at the table as he opened a bottle of gallberry juice and handed it to me.

"Did you have a good day?" I took a drink of the juice.

"Busy. How was your day?"

"Good. Teo took me for a walk in the garden after breakfast, and Faro and I went for another tour of the palace after lunch. We got lost." I grinned at him, and he laughed before handing me a plate of food.

"Faro is fairly new to working and living in the palace and is not known for his sense of direction," he said. "I am sorry I could not spend more time with you today."

"That's okay," I said. "Teo told me that you were very busy today. Were you working with Roden again?"

He shook his head. "No, I was meeting with Bitta most of the day."

"Is there something wrong?" I asked. He seemed tired and a little moody.

He fidgeted in his chair before pushing his plate of food

away. "What I'm about to tell you, only myself and Bitta know."

"I won't say anything to anyone else."

"Bitta oversees our communication equipment. He keeps it in working order and sends and receives messages and holograms on behalf of the kingdom."

"Okay," I said. "So, he's like your IT guy. Got it."

"What is IT?" Quill asked.

"Information Technology. On earth, IT guys work in offices, fixing computers or hologram machines and downloading new software – things like that."

Quill nodded. "Yes, that is what Bitta does."

He drummed his fingers on the table. "During storms, Bitta is not as busy as he normally is. We cannot send or receive messages or holograms until the storm eases. Yesterday, he was doing routine maintenance work on our system and found something."

I leaned forward. "What did he find?"

"A series of encrypted messages sent to the planet of Gokmard."

My jaw dropped. "Gokmard? You're kidding me."

"I am not, little human."

I studied him for a moment. "How bad is this?"

"Very bad," he said. "After we defeated them, the Gokmards returned to their planet. They continued their practice of raiding other planets but stayed away from this star system until two moons ago."

"What happened two moons ago?"

"The Gokmard army attacked the eastern province."

"What?" I gave him a look of stunned surprise. "There wasn't anything on the news back home about Draax being attacked."

He shrugged. "Humans often cannot see past their own

noses. They are grateful to us for our protection against the Gokmards, but their obsession with gallberry juice and what it can do for them is all they care about."

I gave him a look of shame. I couldn't even argue with his logic – humans really did just want the gallberry juice and didn't give a second thought to anything else.

"I'm sorry," I said.

He reached out to squeeze my hand. "You have nothing to apologize for, Sabrina. Besides, we are not innocent in the arrangement. We use the gallberry juice to take what we need from the humans."

I must have still looked miserable about it because he reached over and urged me to sit in his lap. His tail wrapped around my waist and squeezed comfortingly as he pressed a kiss against my mouth.

"All races take what they want without much thought for other races. It is the way of the galaxy, little human."

"I guess. But if you guys talked to our government and told them that the Gokmards were attacking you, maybe they would – I don't know – send humans to help. We have armies and -"

He laughed. "Your human army is pitiful, Sabrina. You would fall quickly against the Gokmards and be more of a liability to us than useful. We are a warrior race and can handle the Gokmards."

I wondered if he even heard the arrogance in his voice. Probably not. Besides, was it arrogant if he was being truthful? I had seen how he and Galan sparred and could only imagine how fierce they were when they fought.

A shiver went through me. The thought of Quill fighting, of possibly being injured or even killed, sent dread through me, and I unconsciously leaned into him. "You aren't allowed to fight because you're the king, right?"

"Yes. But I am still a warrior and will do what is necessary to protect my people."

"But if you die without an heir, that's bad for the entire province. You can't fight anymore." My relief was quickly disappearing.

"I would not die in battle, sadora. Do not worry."

I scowled at him. "You don't know that. What if you're having an off day with sword fighting or something? You could die, and then I'll be all -"

I stopped abruptly. I was about to say I would be all alone and Jesus, could I be any more selfish? If Quill died, the Draax would lose their king. What did it matter if I was alone? Besides, Quill wasn't mine. He belonged to Evelyn, and when the storm ended, I would be alone anyway.

"Sadora? What is wrong?" Quill rubbed my lower back as the end of his tail rubbed my hip.

I made myself smile at him. "Nothing's wrong. Just worried about you fighting."

"I am the best warrior in the western province."

I couldn't help but smile. Quill's arrogance could, from time to time, be somewhat charming. "Right, I keep forgetting that. These encrypted messages – have you figured out what they say?"

"No, not yet. Bitta is working on it, but he says it will take quite some time. They are heavily encrypted."

"So, it's someone smart at computer stuff," I said thoughtfully. "Is there anyone in the palace besides Bitta who is good at that sort of thing?"

"Galan."

"You don't honestly believe it's Galan, do you?"

"No, I do not. Galan would never betray his people." His face turned a dark green, and his eyes flashed silver fire. "But when I find out who the betrayer is, Krono help them. I will show no mercy."

I shivered again, and Quill returned to rubbing my lower back. "So," I said tentatively, "is everyone in the eastern province okay?"

He grinned at me. "Yes, little human, they are fine. They destroyed the Gokmard army easily."

"Really?" I had seen the holograms of the war and watched the Draax defeat the Gokmards, but I was still a little surprised. The Gokmards were large, hulking beasts covered in thick brown fur who looked like they would be more comfortable on all fours rather than walking upright. They looked like mindless beasts and acted like mindless beasts, but they weren't. They were incredibly intelligent, and their level of technology was superior to ours.

"Why are you so surprised?" He raised his eyebrows at me, and I could hear a hint of irritation in his voice.

"Because they have guns and long glowing stick thingies that can cut a person in half, and you fight with swords."

"The energy from their rayguns can barely pierce our skin," he said with a roll of his eyes, "and they have no talent for sword fighting. Their energy blades are only dangerous if they can get past our swords, and they cannot."

He grinned at me with bloodlust in his eyes. I probably should have been nervous, I had never seen this side of Quill before, but I wasn't. Truthfully, I was a little turned on. I thought back to the way Quill had looked when he was sparring with Galan, and my damn pussy dampened.

My face burned bright red when Quill inhaled deeply. He grinned and cupped my breast through my shirt as he nuzzled my neck. "I can smell your arousal for me, little human."

"No, you can't."

"Yes, I can. Quite easily."

"The polite thing to do would be not to mention it," I said.

He laughed and reached between my legs to cup my pussy. I was wearing jeans, and he pressed the denim against my clit. "I like knowing you are so needy for me."

"I'm not that needy," I muttered. He pressed harder, and I was helpless to stop my soft moan.

"No, not at all," he said teasingly. "Why are you not wearing your thin pants? I do not like these pants." He pulled at the stiff material of my jeans. "From now on, you are to wear dresses without panties or the thin, tight pants so that I can easily access your pussy."

I laughed. "Do you really think you can tell me what to wear, and I'll just obey, my king?"

"It was worth a try, was it not?"

"Sure." I cupped his face and kissed him. We kissed deeply for long moments. When his big hand cupped my breast, I arched into his touch. He frowned and pulled at my bra strap through my shirt.

"I dislike this as well, little human. Stop wearing it."

"Not a chance. I have enough problems with gravity, thank you very much," I said. "Besides, I have a feeling that you really won't be happy unless I'm walking around naked."

His silver eyes turned slate grey, and I moaned when he bit my neck lightly. "You are a very clever little human."

"Thank you."

Quill was nipping at my neck, and his hand was under my shirt and worming its way under my bra. With a growl of impatience, he pulled my shirt over my head and flicked open my bra, then dropped it on the table. His hot tongue circled my nipple before he sucked heavily.

I cried out and clutched at his head, rocking my ass against his hard dick as he laved and licked and sucked both of my nipples until they were dark red and stiff and swollen. When he lifted his head, I moaned in disappointment.

He plucked at my nipples. "You did not eat all your dinner, sadora."

"I'm not hungry for food." I bit my bottom lip. "Please, Quill."

"What are you hungry for?" he asked.

"You."

"Be more specific, human."

I glared at him. "Oh my God, are we going to have sex or not?"

He laughed. "So impatient, little human. We will have sex when you tell me what I want to hear."

"Fine!" I huffed. "I'm hungry for your cock, all right? I want it in my pussy."

There was a knock on the door. I squeaked and automatically covered my breasts as I stared at Quill. "Who is that?"

"Answer the door and find out, sadora."

"I reached for my bra and shirt, and he shook his head. "You do not need those."

"Like hell I don't!" I tried to grab my bra, but he was faster than me and tossed it behind him to land on the floor.

"Quill!"

He handed me my shirt as there was another knock on the door. "Your modesty is very cute, little human. Go and answer the door."

I yanked my shirt over my head, huffing at him again when I slid off his lap, and he gave me a light spank on the ass. As I reached for the door, I glanced at my chest. My nipples were still rock hard and poking against my thin t-shirt. I clamped my arm over my chest and opened the door.

"Galan?" I blinked at him as he smiled politely at me.

"Good evening, Sabrina."

"Um, hi. What – what are you doing here?"

He gave me a puzzled look. "The king requested my presence in your quarters this evening."

I clutched at the door and turned my head to stare at Quill. He grinned at me, and a funny little cramp of pleasure went through my lower belly.

*Don't be silly*, my inner voice whispered. *He probably just needed to talk to Galan about something. He didn't bring his best friend to tag team you tonight.*

"Let Galan in, Sabrina," Quill said.

I turned back, and my cheeks flushed bright red when I realized I had dropped my arm. Galan was staring at my tits, at the way my nipples were visible against the material of my shirt. When he raised his gaze to my face, my mouth went dry. Fuck, his copper eyes had darkened to burnt bronze, and I could almost feel the heat of them on my skin.

I backed up, stumbling a little over my own feet and crossed my arms over my breasts. "Uh, come in, please, Galan."

My voice was little more than a whisper. Still staring at me, Galan stepped into the room and shut the door behind him.

*Don't look at his crotch. Don't look at his crotch*, I repeated inwardly in a desperate litany as my eyes wandered to his crotch. The bulge of his erection was evident against his pants, and he adjusted himself without any shame as I stared at him.

The hard warmth of Quill's body was suddenly against my back and I didn't resist when he tugged my arms to my sides. Galan immediately stared at my tits again, and Quill nuzzled my neck.

"Hello, Galan."

"Hello, my king. I am sorry I am late."

179

"You are not. We were just getting started. Were we not, little human?"

"Starting what?" I moaned when Quill cupped my breast and rubbed his thumb across my nipple.

"Bringing you pleasure," he whispered into my ear. His fingers tugged on the hem of my t-shirt. "Lift your arms, my sadora. Galan wants to taste the sweetness of your nipples."

Moaning again, I lifted my arms and allowed Quill to pull my shirt over my head. He dropped it to the floor and took my arms, pulling them back behind me until my back arched. My breasts were thrust forward on display, and Galan drank in his fill of them as Quill kissed my shoulder.

"Would you like Galan to suck on your nipples?"

"Yes."

"Yes, what?" He nipped my neck, and my hips bucked.

"Yes, please," I moaned.

"Galan, give Sabrina what she wants," Quill said.

"Yes, my king," Galan replied.

He stepped forward, and I couldn't hold back my moan when he cupped my breasts. His hands were warm and rough, and he toyed with my nipples as I gasped. Quill kissed my neck, and my hands tightened into fists when Galan leaned down and licked my right nipple. He blew on it, and it puckered into a tight little bud.

"Beautiful," he whispered before sucking my nipple into his mouth.

"Oh my God!" I arched forward, and Quill held me in a hard grip as Galan teased and licked both of my nipples. Each tug of his mouth sent a bolt of pleasure straight to my crotch, and I pumped my hips uselessly back and forth.

Quill released my arms, and I immediately clutched Galan's head, threading my fingers in his dark hair and holding on for dear life as Quill rubbed my belly and Galan sucked hard on my throbbing nipples.

"Please," I whimpered.

Quill licked my throat as his fingers unbuttoned and unzipped my jeans. He tugged my jeans and my panties down over my ass and pushed them down my legs.

"Galan," he murmured.

Galan released my breasts and crouched at my feet. I squeaked in surprise when Quill's arm slipped around my waist, and he lifted me. Galan pulled my jeans and panties off my feet and tossed them aside as Quill set me back on my feet.

Galan leaned forward and pressed a kiss against my upper thigh. I moaned and parted my legs immediately. Galan made a hoarse sound of need, and Quill cupped my pussy and rubbed it lightly.

"Galan wishes to taste your sweet pussy, sadora. Would you like that?"

"Yes," I said. "God, yes. Please."

Quill and Galan chuckled, but I felt no shame as Quill lifted me and carried me to the bedroom. He set me on the middle of the bed on my knees, but when I tried to roll onto my back, he shook his head.

"No, sadora. Stay on your knees and spread your thighs wide."

I gave him a confused look, and he kissed me hard, sucking on my tongue as I moaned and melted against him. When he released my mouth, I gave him a dazed look of need, and he smiled at me. "Do as I say and spread your legs."

I spread my legs as I felt the bed dip behind me. I jerked when Galan's warm and naked chest pressed against my spine, and his arm slipped around my waist. He had undressed while Quill and I were kissing, and I ground my ass against his cock. He groaned and cupped my face, turning it to the side so he could angle his mouth over mine. He kissed me, sliding his tongue into my mouth and tasting me with long, slow strokes as I leaned against him. Where Quill's kisses were hard and demanding, Galan's coaxed and teased. Both drove me crazy with desire. When he cupped my tits and pulled on my nipples, I reached behind me and dug my fingers into his rock-hard thighs, silently begging him for more.

He broke the kiss and smiled at me. "Such a sweet tasting human."

"Please," I whispered.

He kissed me again before sliding off the bed. I whined in disappointment, but Quill was standing next to the bed, and he reached out and stroked my breast. "Shh, sadora. We know what you need."

He was naked now, and I reached eagerly for his cock, stroking it from base to tip. He groaned and gave me a hazy look of need before pulling on my thigh. "Wider, my sadora."

I was confused, but I spread my legs even wider until I could feel the burn in my thighs. "I thought Galan was going to eat my pussy?" I was a little embarrassed by the whine in my voice.

"He is," Quill said as the bed dipped again.

My eyes widened when I felt Galan's shoulders brush against my inner legs. He was lying on his back between my legs. He wedged his upper body between my thighs, and I stared down at him in shock before automatically reaching down to cover my pussy. I was soaking wet, and I was worried that I'd drip all over his damn face.

"Move your hand," Quill said from my left.

"Quill, I don't – I mean..."

Quill pulled my hand away, and Galan wrapped his large

hands around my thighs and tugged. "Sit on my face, little human."

I shook my head vehemently. "I can't do that. I'm too heavy, and I'll suffocate you."

"You won't," Galan said with a grin.

"I will. Quill, don't make me -"

My protests cut off with a squeal when Galan made a sharp tug on my thighs and pulled me down as he lifted his head. He licked my pussy from the wet entrance to my throbbing clit, and I squealed again.

"Oh my God!"

Galan licked me again, and shamefully, that was all it took to convince me to sit on his face. I sank down and ground my pussy against his mouth as his hot, wet tongue licked at my clit with slow, firm strokes. I dug my hands into his hair and babbled incoherently. Holy mother of Mary, Galan could eat pussy like a goddamn champ.

"Sadora, look at me."

I barely heard Quill's low voice as I rubbed my pussy back and forth over Galan's mouth.

"Sadora."

I turned my head, and my mouth watered. Quill was kneeling on the bed beside us, and his hand was stroking his cock back and forth. Precum beaded out of the top, and I licked my lips as Quill's hand threaded through my hair. He pushed my head down toward his cock, and I licked away his cum before sucking on the head.

Quill groaned, his hands fisting in my hair as he pulled me further down his cock. "Take more, Sabrina."

My eyes watering, I tried to relax my throat and take more of his cock. I could barely think past the growing pleasure in my belly. I was already close to coming, and I gave Quill a desperate look of need as he guided my mouth back and forth over his cock. My cheeks bulged, and my lips stretched wide as Quill stroked my hair.

"Good girl." He glanced down at Galan. "Make her come so I can fuck her, Galan."

Galan immediately sucked my clit into his mouth. My scream of pleasure was muffled by Quill's cock, and as I climaxed all over Galan's face, Quill moaned and shoved his cock deep into my mouth. Just when I thought I would pass out from a combination of pleasure and oxygen deprivation, Quill pulled away. He caught me when I would have fallen over and lifted me enough to allow Galan to slide out from between my legs.

He was panting hard, and he wiped my juices from his face before giving Quill a desperate look of need. "Quill, for the love of Krono..."

Quill turned me sideways on the bed and stroked my lower back before pushing lightly. "On your hands and knees, my sadora."

I dropped to my hands obediently, and Quill made a low growl of approval before kneeling on the bed behind me and pushing his way between my thighs. He rubbed his cock against my pussy, and I cried out as Galan moved to the opposite side of the bed. He knelt in front of me, one hand stroking his cock as Quill slowly pushed his way into my pussy.

"Oh God! Quill, it's too big," I moaned and tried to wiggle away. In this position, Quill could go nice and deep and for a moment it felt like he would split me in two.

Quill's tail wrapped around my waist, and his hands clamped heavily on my hips. He made another low growl. "Relax, sadora. Let me in."

I took a deep breath and tried to relax as I stared at

Galan's cock. It was thick and long, and my mouth watered again as I watched him fist it slowly.

"Oh!"

Quill had made one final push, and I craned my head. "It's too much."

"Shh, sadora." He stroked my ass. "You have taken all of my cock like a good girl."

Stupidly, a little tingle of pride went through me, and I pushed my ass back. Quill made a low chuckle and rubbed my ass again. "My sadora has a very greedy little pussy."

He leaned forward. It made him sink even deeper within me, and I moaned happily. He gathered my hair in a ponytail before pulling my head back. I was face to face with Galan's cock now, and Quill cupped one breast and pinched my nipple.

"Open, sadora. Open so that Galan can fuck your mouth."

I opened my mouth immediately and Quill straightened but kept his hand wrapped in my hair. Galan slowly slid his cock into my mouth. I sucked eagerly as Quill released my hair. Galan's hands took his place, and he used my hair to guide me back and forth over his dick. I stared up at him like Quill had taught me, and his copper eyes flashed like bronze fire as he watched his cock slide in and out of my mouth.

"Such a pretty little human," he groaned as he pushed his hard length further into my mouth. My eyes were watering, and he wiped the moisture from my cheek as he allowed me to take a breath before pushing back in. Cum coated my tongue, and I moaned and sucked hard. Not surprisingly, Galan tasted faintly of gallberries as well.

Galan reached beneath me and cupped one breast, rubbing my nipple as Quill pushed gently back and forth. I moaned again, and Galan petted my hair when Quill pulled my thighs apart a little farther.

"Your mate looks very pretty with a cock in her pussy and a cock in her mouth," Galan said to Quill.

"She does," Quill agreed as he reached under and rubbed my clit. I squealed around Galan's cock, and he groaned when I sucked hard in response. Quill smiled and showed Galan his dripping thumb and fingers. "She's soaking wet."

When I felt his thumb brush across the crack of my ass, I yanked my mouth away from Galan's cock and stared at Quill over my shoulder. He pushed lightly on my hole, and I squeaked and tried to pull away. His tail wrapped around my waist and held me immobile as he pressed against my hole again.

"Quill!" I glared at him, and he gave me a wicked grin as he pushed for a third time.

"Suck on Galan's cock, sadora."

"Get your thumb out of my ass, and I will!"

He laughed as Galan's hard hand threaded through my hair and pulled my head back to face him. He rubbed his cock against my lips. "Open, little human."

I shook my head and gave him a huffy look as I tightened my ass against Quill's invasion. Behind me, I heard Quill chuckle again before his other hand slipped under me. His rough fingers rubbed my clit, and when he tugged on it and gave me two hard thrusts of his cock, I gasped and moaned. My mouth dropped open, and Galan slid his cock into my mouth like the world's neatest parlour trick. I squealed around his thick length as Quill pushed his thumb past the tight ring of muscle and deep into my ass.

"That is my good girl." Quill's tone of smug satisfaction would have made me bristle at any other time. But apparently, having a thumb in my ass, and a dick in my pussy and in my mouth had made me lose my mind. I was already starting to wiggle and moan, clenching my pussy and ass around Quill's cock and thumb in a silent appeal for more.

"Ready?" Quill murmured to Galan.

Still cupping my head and keeping his cock deep in my mouth, Galan nodded. I moaned when Quill thrust hard in and out of my pussy. Each of his movements pushed more of Galan's cock into my mouth, and Galan groaned loudly when I sucked hard in response.

"Krono, Quill – I will not last long," he gasped.

Quill grunted in reply and pumped harder as he slid his thumb in and out of my ass. I was nearly glassy-eyed with desire. I was only vaguely aware of the aliens' low grunts of pleasure, of how Galan petted my hair and Quill's tail squeezed my waist tightly. Every part of my body was tingling with a lust so intense I could barely stand it. The tight coil of need in my belly was filling me up, making it hard to breathe or think, and I began to babble incoherently around Galan's cock. I was nearly sobbing with the need for relief as both men thrust their cocks in my pussy and mouth.

I moaned, my hands fisting in the bed sheets and my back arching as Quill reached under me. His fingers found my clit, rubbed it, pulled it, and then pinched. I screamed as my orgasm exploded within me. I shook with the intensity of it, squeezing my eyes shut and screaming again as pleasure flooded through every part of my body. There was a low, hoarse shout, and then Galan's seed filled my mouth. I swallowed instinctively as Quill's thumb shoved deep into my ass, and his tail tightened painfully around my ribs. Seconds later, his hot seed splashed against my insides, coating me entirely in its warmth as his big body shook against mine.

Galan pulled away, and despite how hard I had tried to swallow everything he gave me, I could feel his cum sliding down my chin. My legs were like jelly, but before I could collapse on my face, Quill pulled out, and the two men quickly laid me down in the middle of the bed before lying on their sides on either side of me. I was still shaking and shuddering wildly, my body heaving for air. I kept my eyes closed as both aliens murmured low sounds of comfort. Galan's warm fingers brushed my chin, and I wasn't surprised when he smeared his cum across my mouth and over my cheeks.

Quill was dipping his hand between my thighs, and I made a low moan of protest. I was too sensitive, and I didn't want my clit touched.

"Shh, sadora." He took his seed that was slipping out of my body and rubbed it into my belly and breasts.

"You're making me sticky again," I complained, and both Quill and Galan laughed.

"She looks beautiful covered in our seed, does she not?" Quill said.

Galan nodded, and I sighed happily when both men pressed their hard, warm bodies against me. "I feel so good."

"I am glad, sadora," Quill said. "Sleep now."

# CHAPTER 11

*Quillan*

"**D**id you enjoy your swim, Sabrina?"

She smiled at me and took my hand, squeezing it affectionately as we walked down the hallway. "I did. Thank you, my king. I feel bad, though – I know you're busy and don't have time to spend the morning at the pool with me."

"I am less busy during the cold months," I reminded her as we turned the corner. It was true, although I probably should have spent the morning reviewing the reports Galan had emailed me about the recruits' progress. But I couldn't resist spending the morning with Sabrina. Galan had left before she woke, and I had spent more time than I cared to admit just studying her face and holding her in my arms.

When she'd finally awoken, she immediately wanted to shower. I followed her to the shower. After she had protested vigorously that I wasn't strong enough to lift her and fuck her against the shower wall, I lifted her, pinned her against the wall, and proved to her how wrong she was with a very hard and thorough fucking. I could still hear her cries as she clung to me, the warm water cascading over her lovely pale skin as I fucked two body-shuddering orgasms from her before letting myself climax. I had filled her full of my seed, then washed her hair and her curvy body for her.

We ate breakfast together, and when we were finished, I told myself to say goodbye to her and return to my private chambers to work. Instead, I asked her if she wanted to go for a swim. The way her eyes lit up made any doubts I might have had disappear instantly.

"What will you do after you drop me off at my apartment?" she asked as we turned another corner. My private quarters were just ahead on the left, and I slowed down as she gave me a curious look. "What?"

"Come with me." I opened the door to my private quarters, and Sabrina followed me in. Her jaw dropped.

"Holy crap. This is really nice."

"It is my personal quarters," I said. "I do not allow anyone but Teo, Galan and Krey into my private quarters."

It was ridiculous, but I needed her to know what allowing her access to my private quarters meant. How special it made her to me.

She studied me briefly before saying, "Thank you for bringing me here."

She walked through the large kitchen and into the attached living area. It was decorated in dark greys and rich burgundies, and she ran her hand over the couch. "Wow. This looks a lot like houses of the uppers on Earth."

"Most of it comes from Earth," I admitted.

She grinned at me. "I knew you stole our decorating ideas." She pointed at the dark burgundy curtains. "Is that a window behind those curtains?"

I nodded, and she hurried over and yanked them open to reveal the massive window hidden behind them.

"Oh my God," she whispered.

I stood behind her and wrapped my tail around her waist before tugging her back against my chest. We stared at the falling snow together, and she shivered when a gust of wind rattled the window.

"You weren't kidding when you said the storm was bad. I can't see two feet in front of me."

I didn't reply. Truthfully, the worst of the storm was already over, and there was a noticeable difference in how much snow was falling. In a week or so, the storm would end, Sabrina would be on her way to her farmer, and I would never see her again.

The thought made me angry, and she tugged on my tail when it squeezed around her. "Too tight, Quill."

"Sorry." I pressed a kiss against her temple.

"How cold is it out there?"

"I'm not sure of the conversion between Earth's temperature measurements and ours," I said. "I could ask Galan. He knows more about earth conversions than I do."

"That's okay," she said. "I just wondered if you would freeze to death the second you stepped outside or what. When I first arrived, I found it cold, and it had barely started storming yet."

"If you wore warm clothing and kept moving, you would perhaps survive for an hour or so before you froze."

She shuddered all over and stared up at me. "How often do people die in the storms?"

"Not very often," I assured her. "The Draax are used to the storms, remember? They know to be prepared in the cold months."

"Some places on Earth get very cold in the winter, and many of the lowers freeze to death," Sabrina said. "The uppers don't do anything about it. They consider it an effective culling method to keep the lowers population down."

"Uppers and lowers refer to your social status, right?" I said hesitantly. I was suddenly wishing I had paid closer attention during my studies of Earth. But I had never thought I would be king, had never thought I would be mated to a human for life.

"Yes. We have three – uppers, middles, and lowers."

"Were you an upper?"

She laughed. "No, definitely not. The uppers are all politicians, celebrities and people lucky enough to be born into wealth. I'm a middle leaning more toward lower than I would have liked. The nanny job I took after my parents died kept a roof over our head and groceries on the table, but that was about it."

"Did your sister not work?" I asked.

She shook her head. "No, Carrie is very fragile. She was my parents' favourite, and they babied her a little too much. She never had to work, and after they died, she was too heartbroken to do anything."

"So, you work and take care of her?" I said.

"Yes."

"Who takes care of you?"

She gave me a startled look. "What do you mean?"

"Who takes care of you?" I repeated.

"I – well, no one. I take care of myself," she said.

I scowled, and she said hurriedly, "I don't mind taking care of Carrie, and besides, I don't need to take care of her anymore. She has Josh, and he loves her very much. He has a good job, too, and can provide for her and any babies they may have. I was just about to move out and start my life when Carrie got sick."

I pulled her closer as she stared out the window at the

blowing snow. "Is that why you were an innocent? You were too busy caring for your sister to mate with males?"

"I suppose. Well, that, and I'm not considered beautiful to human guys. They weren't exactly beating down my door to have sex with me or anything."

I snorted in derision. "They are fools."

She giggled. "Yeah, they are. I'm all that and a bag of chips."

"What do you mean?"

Her giggle turned into her warm, throaty laugh that automatically made my cock harden. "It's an old saying from Earth. It just means that I'm awesome."

"You are." I nuzzled her neck affectionately and pressed my cock against her curvy ass. She rubbed against me as I cupped her breasts. "So, you gave up another three years of your life to save your sister?"

She frowned up at me. "It was worth it to me, Quill. I would do it again without any hesitation. I love my sister."

"I know," I said. "I did not mean to imply that you did not."

She sighed and stared out the window again. "I guess a part of me is sad about leaving my home for three years, but I try to think of it as an adventure. Besides, it's only three years. That's not that long."

"What will you do when your contract is up?"

"Return to Earth. Find another nanny job and get a small apartment. Learn what it's like to live on my own."

I swallowed down my disappointment. What was I expecting her to say? That she would return to the palace so we could continue fucking? I would be mated to Evelyn and undoubtedly have one or two children by then.

Depression flooded through me, and my tail flicked agitatedly against Sabrina's hip. Two weeks ago, the thought of being a father had filled me with excitement and joy. Now, it brought on nothing but dread. I didn't want this Evelyn to be the mother to my children. I wanted it to be the woman in my arms. My sweet sadora.

"What's wrong?" she asked.

For a moment, I was tempted to ask her – no, beg her – to stay with me even though I would be mated to another. Self-loathing immediately filled me. Even though Draax males enjoyed sharing their women occasionally, they were always loyal to their chosen mate. Galan had told me once that it was a common occurrence on Earth for mated males to have second mates on the side – he said they were called mistresses – but that many humans looked down on it, and it was considered disgraceful to their first mates.

I instinctively knew that Sabrina would never agree to be my mistress. Besides, she deserved better than that. She deserved a mate who could give her children and spend the rest of his life worshiping her.

*You would not be happy with her as your mistress, anyway. You want her and only her. You love her.*

I jerked all over, my tail squeezing Sabrina so hard that she squeaked in pain before pulling at it.

"Quill, ouch!"

"Sorry, sweet sadora." I loosened my grip on her.

"That's okay," she said. "Tell me what's wrong?"

I almost laughed. What was wrong? Only everything. I was in love with a woman I could never have. I owed it to my people to give them an heir, and Sabrina would never carry my child in her belly.

My hand dipped down and cupped the curve of her belly. I rubbed it as she gave me an anxious look. "Tell me what's wrong, Quill."

"Nothing," I said hoarsely. "Nothing is wrong."

"You're lying. Please don't lie to me."

I picked her up and carried her toward my bedroom. I set her on her feet next to the bed and pulled her shirt over her head as she squeezed my arms.

"Quill, talk to me."

"Please, sadora," I rasped. "Please, I need you."

She hesitated, and I kissed her hard on the mouth, desperate to show her just how much I needed her. She didn't respond, and my stomach churned. She was with Galan and me last night, and it was obvious that she enjoyed it. Did she expect Galan to always be with us now? I had shared many women with Galan in the past and enjoyed sharing Sabrina with him last night, but for the first time, I had no wish for it to be a common occurrence. I only had a limited time with my sadora, and I wanted her to myself, but if she wished for Galan to join us, I would not deny her what she wanted.

"Do you need Galan to join us?" I tried not to sound bitter.

She blinked at me and took a step back. I curled my tail around her hips and immediately pulled her back against me before cupping her face. "I know you enjoyed having Galan join us. Do you want him again?"

She stared silently at me, and I squeezed her waist. "Tell me the truth."

"I did enjoy last night," she said slowly. "I liked it very much, and I'm grateful you gave me that experience because it was something I wanted. I know the Draax like to share women, but I…"

I stroked my thumb over her cheekbone. "But what?"

"I would prefer just to be with you," she whispered. "We do not have much time together and I would rather spend it with only you in my bed."

Relief flooded through me as she gave me an anxious look. "But I know you, uh, like threesomes, so if you want Galan to join us -"

"I do not."

"Are you sure?"

"Yes," I replied. "I am. I want you all to myself, my sadora."

She stood on her tiptoes and pressed her mouth against mine. "Then take me, my king."

---

*Sabrina*

I STRETCHED LAZILY AND THREW BACK THE COVERS ON QUILL'S bed. I was alone in the bedroom, but I knew Quill would be sitting at the desk tucked in the corner of his living room. I had no idea what time it was as I yawned and slid out of bed. I padded naked to the bathroom that was attached to Quill's bedroom.

I'd spent the day in Quill's private quarters alternating between napping and fucking Quill. We would have sex, Quill would leave me completely sated and as relaxed as a kitten in his bed while he worked, and I fell asleep. He'd wake me a few hours later and fuck me again. We had repeated the cycle all damn day with a couple of breaks for food. I rubbed my sore thighs before flushing the toilet and washing my hands.

I yawned again. Despite how much I slept today, I was weirdly tired, but I chalked it up to all the exercise I was getting. I returned to the bedroom and caught sight of myself in the mirror on the wall. I frowned and stepped closer to the mirror before turning sideways. My breasts looked fuller somehow, and even my nipples seemed larger. Probably just swollen, I decided. They were very sensitive, and Quill delighted in spending a lot of time sucking and licking on them until I was begging for him to fuck me.

My pussy throbbed, and I rolled my eyes. God, Quill was turning me into a nympho. I was already thinking about fucking him again and –

I cocked my head and stared at my belly before running my hand over it. Jesus, was I getting fatter? How was that possible? I knew I was eating more than usual, but the food here was delicious. Still, I was also doing way more physical exercise than usual. Shouldn't that have evened it out?

Maybe the gallberry juice had a lot of calories, I mused. I grabbed one of Quill's shirts and pulled it over my head, hiding my suddenly curvier body. Quill was constantly plying me with it. My mouth watered, and I had an urge for the juice that was so strong my belly cramped. My craving for it had returned with a vengeance, and I wondered if my sore thighs and – admittedly, slightly sore pussy – had something to do with that. Quill had said that when you were injured, your body craved it more. I decided I didn't care why I was craving it, only that I needed some.

I walked out of Quill's bedroom. "Hey, Quill? I'm stealing some of your gallberry juice, then you'll take a break from work, and I'll ride you like a pony."

I giggled and grabbed juice from the fridge before taking a big swig. It tasted sinful, and I moaned with happiness before wiping my mouth. "What do you think of that, big guy? Think you can handle round – hell, what round are we on anyway, seven? I know I can, but you might have to take it a little easier on my poor pussy. She's a teeny bit sore from your giant dick, and I'm not sure that even gallberry juice is going to heal her fast enough."

There was no reply and I glanced at his desk. "Quill? Are you tapping out on me already – oh shit."

"Hello, human." Teo stood beside Quill's desk, giving me a polite smile as my face turned a scorching shade of red.

"Uh, hi, Teo. Where, um, where is Quill?"

"Our meeting was interrupted. Bitta asked to speak to him in private. He is meeting with him on the other side of the palace but will return soon."

"Oh."

There was a moment of awkward silence that Teo broke. "I am surprised to see you in the king's private quarters."

"He brought me here."

Teo smiled. "Yes, I assumed that."

"Is it a problem?" I asked defensively.

"Yes," Teo replied.

"Why?"

"The king grows too fond of you. He does not usually allow others into his private space."

I didn't reply, and Teo sighed. "You are not his mate, human."

"I know."

"Do you?" he asked.

"Yes."

"You cannot bear his children, and it is imperative that Quill produces an heir."

"I know," I repeated. "I'm not stupid."

"No, you are not," Teo said, "but you are in love with our king."

"I – I'm…"

I wanted desperately to say I wasn't, but I couldn't get the words out. I gave Teo a miserable look as he sighed again.

"You should start to distance yourself from Quill," he said not unkindly. "The storm will end within the week, and you will leave the palace, and the king's true mate will take your place."

I winced like he had physically hit me, and Teo gave me a sympathetic look. "I am sorry, human. Truly, I am. I know you care for him, and Quill cares for you. I have not seen him so happy since his brother died. But you cannot be together."

"Yeah, I know."

"You should return to your quarters before Quill comes back. Staying with him in his private quarters is not a wise idea. When he returns, I will speak with him about leaving you alone."

"Right," I said. "I'll just, uh, get dressed and go."

"I will call Faro and ask him to return you to your quarters," Teo said. "You will get lost."

I laughed a little bitterly. "Yeah, probably."

"I am sorry, human," Teo repeated.

"Me too."

---

I BARELY HAD TIME TO FINISH MY BATH AND PUT MY nightdress on before Quill stormed into my apartment. He slammed my door so hard it shuddered in the frame, and I stared in surprise at him from the small kitchen.

"Quill, what -"

His tail flicking rapidly, he stalked over and glared at me. His nostrils flared, and he yanked me into his embrace, winding his hand through my hair and pulling my head back until I stared at him.

"I did not give you permission to leave my quarters, little human."

I blinked at him. "I wasn't aware that I needed permission to – son of a bitch!"

Quill had scooped me up and heaved me over his shoulder like I was a side of beef. He started toward the door, and I whacked him on the back as his tail flicked past me, barely avoiding smacking me in the face.

"Put me down, you – you, big green caveman!" I wiggled violently and grabbed his madly-waving tail before pulling hard on it.

"Hush, sadora." He spanked me on my upturned ass, and I yelped in surprise from the stinging pain.

"That hurt!"

"It was meant to." He strode out into the hallway. "Perhaps next time you will not disobey me."

He spanked my other cheek, and I yelped again before biting him hard on the back. He grunted with pain, and I received a third spanking for my impudence.

"You are in so much trouble when you put me down!" I threatened.

He laughed and, this time, rubbed my ass in a gentle caress as he walked through the maze of hallways. "You are too tiny to harm me, but you are welcome to try, sweet sadora."

He slipped his hand under my nightgown and stroked my naked, burning ass. "Your ass is nice and warm from my hand. Perhaps when we return to my quarters, I will put you over my knee and spank you until it is covered in my handprints."

"You wouldn't dare!"

He laughed and squeezed my ass cheek. "Keep provoking me, little sadora, and I will."

"I am not a child!" I seethed. "You can't…oh God!"

His hand had slipped between my thighs, and he rubbed my pussy before withdrawing his hand from under my nightdress. "You are very wet, little human. I think you like the idea of being spanked by me."

"Like hell, I do!" I protested vehemently. Christ, I would never admit that he was right. The minute he had started spanking me, my pussy had responded with a goddamn flood. I was a damn pervert.

"Perhaps we will find out," he said. "Good evening, Henden."

I squeaked in humiliation as a Draax passed us and gave me a curious look before bowing slightly. "Good evening, my king."

"Put me down!" I said in a fierce whisper.

"So you can run back to your quarters?" Quill said. "I think not, little human."

"Quill!"

"Quiet, sadora or I will put you over my knee right here and let every Draax who walks by watch me turn your delightfully pale ass a bright red."

God help me. The mental image from Quill's words sent a lightning bolt of need from my pussy all the way down to my toes. I squeezed my thighs together and tried not to whimper with need when Quill rubbed my ass through my nightdress again. Fuck, forget pervert – I was a sexual deviant.

It didn't take long for us to reach Quill's private quarters. He carried me into the bedroom and set me beside the bed. He turned me until I was facing the bed and pulled my nightdress over my head before cupping my naked breasts and kneading them roughly. He used one thick thigh to push mine apart before placing his big hand in the middle of my back and forcing me down until I was bent over the bed. My heated cheek rested against the bedcovers, and my ass was raised high in the air. It was the perfect position for spanking, and I squirmed with both need and a little bit of embarrassment as evidence of my arousal dripped down my inner thighs.

"Do not move, sadora." Quill stepped back.

I should have moved. I should have stood up and turned around and punched him right in the face for being such a Neanderthal, but I remained where I was. Bent over his bed, legs spread wide and my quivering pussy on full view for him.

"So pretty," he murmured.

I heard the rustle of his clothing as he removed it, and I twitched wildly when his big hand smoothed over my ass. I waited with breathless anticipation for his spank and, when it didn't happen, said, "Are you going to spank me?"

Fuck, did I have to sound so needy? So eager?

His low chuckle made me blush, and I buried my face in the bed. It muffled my squeal of surprise when I felt Quill's warm breath on my pussy and then his wet, hot tongue slicking across my slit.

"Oh my God!" I raised my head and clutched at the bedcovers. Quill held my thighs as he leaned in and licked me again. "Oh fuck!"

"I've decided on a different punishment for your disobedience, sadora," Quill said.

"Ooh!" I squealed with pleasure when he tongued my clit. "Oh, I like pussy eating as a punishment."

He laughed again, and I pushed back eagerly against his mouth when he parted my swollen wet pussy lips with his thumbs and sucked on my hard clit. My legs began to shake, and I was on the verge of my orgasm when Quill pulled back.

"No! No!" I stared desperately at him over my shoulder. "Don't stop!"

He just grinned at me, and my eyes widened with sudden understanding. "Make me come, Quill."

He massaged my inner thighs, holding me firmly when I tried to wiggle away. "Quill, goddammit, make me come!"

"Yes, sadora."

My moan of relief soon turned to desperate need as he repeatedly brought me to the brink of climax and then denied me. After nearly half an hour, I was a moaning, shivering, begging mess.

Quill stood and grabbed my hips, pulling them up until his cock lined up neatly at my pussy entrance. I clutched at the bedcovers and stared at him.

"Please," I moaned.

"Will you leave my quarters again without my permission, my mate?" His voice was stern.

"Teo told me to leave," I whimpered.

He pressed the head of his cock against my entrance but held me still when I tried to push my body back to take more. "Is Teo your king?"

"No," I moaned.

"Who is your king?"

"You!" I cried. "You're my king."

"And will you do what your king tells you to from now on?" He pressed forward until the head of his dick was snug in my pussy.

"Oh fuck, oh God, yes! Yes!" I panted as my fingers pulled at the bedcovers. "I'll do what you say. Just fuck me."

I was nearly delirious with need and barely heard Quill's smug little whisper. "That's my good mate."

He pushed his dick deep into my pussy, and I screamed my pleasure as he took my arms and lifted my upper body off the bed. He held them tightly, and my back arched. He fucked me hard and deep as I screamed again.

"Good, sweet sadora. Let everyone hear how your mate pleases you."

He pumped in and out, each slide of his thick cock brushing against my inner walls. I squeezed compulsively around him as his long, slow strokes turned short and furious. I had never come without touching my clit before, so when my orgasm hit me, hard and intense and completely unexpected, I screamed so loudly my voice cracked.

The pleasure soared through me, and I bucked wildly against Quill's grip. He thrust hard and climaxed deep inside of me. Warmth flooded through me and set off another equally intense orgasm. I screamed again as my pussy spasmed wildly around his cock. He groaned and continued to fuck me with slow strokes until he had softened completely.

He pulled out and released my arms. I fell to the mattress like a boneless kitten. I turned my head and gasped in breaths of air as Quill rubbed my pussy before climbing into the bed. He pulled me close and turned me on my side with my spine against his chest before hooking my top leg over his hip. He pushed his hand between my legs and rubbed my clit.

"No!" I cried. "No, I can't have another one."

"Yes, you can. Be my good mate and come for me right now."

"I can't." I tried to wiggle away, but his other hand cupped my throat and held me still as his fingers rubbed my clit. "Oh, oh my God!"

My voice was hoarse, and I cried out when he pinched my clit. His other hand drifted from my throat to my breast, and when he pinched one swollen, hard nipple and my clit again at the same time, it sent a third orgasm roaring through me. I screamed for a record fourth time, and I was pretty sure I came close to blacking out as Quill rubbed my clit and whispered in my ear.

I could barely hear him over the blood roaring in my ears. I drew in breath after breath of desperately needed oxygen as Quill petted my thighs, belly, and breasts.

"That's my good mate," he crooned into my ear. "I'm so happy with my pretty, clever little mate. What a good girl you are to come for me so many times. Good mate, sadora."

Suddenly, desperately tired, I fell asleep with his warm hand rubbing my belly and his low voice telling me repeatedly that I was his good mate.

# CHAPTER 12

*Sabrina*

"Sit up and drink, my mate."

I sat up and drank the gallberry juice obediently before lying back on the bed. I watched as Quill walked out of the bedroom with the empty glass before staring up at the ceiling. It had been nearly a week since Quill carried me from my quarters to his. He'd had my things brought here, and I'd spent every night in his bed. Hell, most of the days, too.

For the last six days, I had done nothing but swim, walk in the garden, eat, drink gallberry juice, and fuck Quill. I stretched lazily and yawned before burrowing deeper under the covers. I was like a contented little house cat, I thought with a slight giggle. Never in my life had I been so spoiled, and I could easily get used to being Quill's mate.

*Not his mate. Stop thinking that way.*

My good mood was dispelled almost instantly, and I stared at the ceiling again. Every time we slept together now, Quill called me his mate. He didn't do it outside of the bed and we never talked about the fact that he called me his mate. We both knew it wasn't true, but being called his mate made me feel good. I couldn't bring myself to say it to him, though. I wanted to, but I couldn't.

I supposed part of it was because I knew it wasn't real, but there was also Evelyn to consider. I grimaced. I didn't understand why I was worrying about the feelings of a woman I had met only once. But as the days passed, I thought more and more about her and compared myself to her. How would I feel if the situation was reversed? How hurtful would it be to be mated for life to an alien who would always love another?

I blinked rapidly as hot tears threatened. Quill did love me. I wasn't stupid. I could see it when he looked at me, feel it in his warm touch and how he whispered the sweetest endearments in my ear when we made love. I asked Galan one day when he was visiting, and Quill was out of the room, what sadora meant. I could barely contain my tears when he told me it was a pet name that a Draax gave to the one he loved.

Most nights after the lovemaking was over, Quill coaxed secrets and truths from me that I never thought I would tell anyone. He hadn't judged me when I admitted tearfully that while I loved Carrie, I was, in fact, a little resentful that I'd had to quit medical school to take care of her. I'd felt awful the moment I said it, but Quill had soothed me quickly and assured me it was normal to feel that way. I'd told him about my childhood and parents and how much I still missed them.

He had also told me about his childhood and how important Galan and Krey were to him. The only part of his life he didn't share was how his brother had died. I hadn't pushed him to talk about it. I had come dangerously close to losing my sister, and I couldn't imagine how painful it was for Quill.

Quill hadn't invited Galan to join us in bed again, although Galan had spent a couple of evenings with us. I thought it would be awkward as hell, but surprisingly it wasn't. Galan and Quill were so close, and the lack of awkwardness between them had quickly made any of mine disappear.

I sighed and rolled to my side. I should have been pulling away like Teo said. I had, at most, a few days left with Quill before the storm ended, and I would never see him again. My stomach churned. Yeah, I really should have put some distance between us, but I couldn't do it. Not when this was my last chance to be with him. I would never see him again, and I'd spend the rest of my life alone and mourning my love for him.

*Fuck! Stop thinking that way!*

My inner voice was right. I needed to stop thinking about it and enjoy my time with Quill while it lasted. I would be alone soon enough and have plenty of time to cry then.

When Quill returned to the bedroom, there was no trace of tears on my face, and I smiled happily at him. "Hey there."

"Hello, sadora. I am sorry. Bitta called and needed to speak with me."

"That's okay. Has he figured out what the encrypted emails say?"

He shook his head, and I could see the frustration on his face as he slid into bed beside me. He relaxed on his back and put his arm around me. I rested my arms on his chest and studied his face. "Is he any closer?"

"He says he is, but I am starting not to believe him," Quill grumbled. He rubbed his hand over his face, and I could feel his tail curving around to thump against my thigh under the covers. "I spoke to Galan and Teo about it two days ago, hoping they might have an idea of who is sending the emails, but they can not think of anyone either."

I rubbed his chest as his tail flicked more rapidly. "Hey, it's okay. You're doing your best."

He shook his head. "There is a very real threat to my people, and I am failing them as their king."

"No, you're not. You're a good king, Quill."

"My brother was a good king," he said moodily. "I am a good warrior."

"Do you like being king?" I asked.

He shrugged. "It is my obligation to my people, and I will do it."

"But you find it stressful."

"A little," he admitted. "It is more stressful as of late."

"You'll figure out who is sending the emails to the Gokmards," I said confidently.

"Yes." His gaze slid away from mine.

"That isn't what's making it so stressful, is it?" Guilt flooded through me. I was making Quill's job as king more difficult. I was demanding too much of his time and gave him a look of shame. "I'm sorry. I shouldn't be taking up so much of your time."

He shook his head and pressed a kiss against my forehead. "No, sadora, that is not it. It is more stressful because I suddenly want something I can never have, but if I were not king, it would not matter. I could have what I wanted."

I swallowed past the lump in my throat. What he said was sweet, and I loved him for it, but we had spoken about his desire for children. Even if he wasn't king, I could never be his mate. He wanted children desperately, and I could never give him what he wanted.

I made my voice gentle. "You need a mate who can give you children, whether you are king or not, Quill."

"I would be happy without children," he said stubbornly.

I smiled at him and kissed his broad chest. "No, my king, you would not."

He just gave me a moody look, and anxious not to ruin our last few days together, I changed the subject. "Were you close to your brother?"

"Not as close as you and your sister," he said. "He was over a decade older than me, and I was more of a nuisance to him growing up."

I smiled as he stared at the ceiling. "I admired him, though. He was very clever and well respected by our people. He was my father's favourite, but I did not resent him for it."

"Was your mom around?" I asked.

"She died giving birth to my sister," he replied. "She lost too much blood, and not even the gallberry juice could heal her in time."

I gave him a look of surprise. "You have a sister?"

"She died shortly after birth."

"I'm so sorry," I said before kissing his chest again. "I'm so sorry, honey."

"Thank you, sadora." He rubbed my back. "It was a long time ago."

"Will you tell me how your brother died?"

"He was visiting the Delorth planet to negotiate a trade agreement. On the return trip home, his ship malfunctioned, and they crash landed. No one on board survived the impact."

"Oh, honey," I whispered. He spoke stoically, but I could see the pain in his eyes. I hugged him and kissed his chest again as his tail wrapped around my waist.

"Teo was the one who told me. I did not believe him at

first. I – I screamed at him and called him a liar. He brought Galan and Krey into the room, and they convinced me of the truth. Galan and Krey were the," he paused, and I heard his throat click as he swallowed, "the ones who arrived at the ship first."

I rubbed his chest as he sighed. "I was crowned king the next day, and Galan was named head of the king's guard."

"You miss it," I said.

"Very much. But my duty is to my people."

"Why wasn't your brother mated?"

"He was searching for a mate when he died. He waited in hopes of finding a Draax female. He wanted a pureborn Draax as his heir, but he had underestimated how few Draax females of breeding age were left. Teo was beginning the process of finding him a human when his ship crashed."

"Do you believe your people want a pure Draax as an heir?"

He shook his head. "No, they do not care. They only want an heir. My brother's death made them nervous, and my lack of children is a worry for them."

"What would happen if, uh, you died without having children?" Even thinking about Quill dying made me feel sick to my stomach.

"Most likely, Eastolf would claim it as his own. He is the King of the Eastern Province," he said before I could ask.

"Is he a good king?" I asked.

"He is not as concerned about his people's needs and wants," Quill said. "He rules differently than my brother did, or I do, and it makes some Draax unhappy."

"Oh," I replied.

We lay quietly in the dark for a few moments before Quill cupped my breast and teased my nipple into a hard point. "Are you too sore to make love, sadora?"

I shook my head. "No."

"Are you certain? You have been craving more gallberry juice the last few days."

"I'm positive. I want you, Quill."

He rolled to face me and kissed me sweetly. "I want you too, my mate."

---

*Quillan*

She still slept when I slipped out of bed early the following day. Not used to our planet, the sudden silence that indicated the storm's end hadn't awoken her. I had roused immediately and, with dread in my belly, dressed quickly and left.

By the time I found Teo, he'd already contacted Earth and found the name of Sabrina's new employer. He'd also sent the Draax, a farmer named Brandel, an email.

"What was his reply?" I asked.

"He has not replied," Teo said, "but that is not unusual. No doubt the signal is not viable yet in his area. It always takes a day or two for it to work outside of the city after a storm."

"We should wait until he does."

"What for?" Teo gave me a puzzled look. "I sent the message only as a courtesy. Does it matter if he knows we are coming or not? No doubt he will be very pleased to finally have the correct human, and he is only a few hours away by land vehicle."

"We should wait," I said stubbornly.

Teo sighed. "My king, it is best to take the human today. I know you care deeply for her, and I am sorry you must give her up, but your responsibility to your kingdom comes first."

"I know!" I snapped. "I am not a fool, Teo."

"No, you are not," he said patiently. "But you are in love with the little human and wish to do whatever you can to keep her with you. It is not possible, my king."

He placed his hand on my arm and stared at me. "I am sorry, Quill. But you must give her up, and you must do it today. The sooner you breed with your actual mate and fill her belly with a child, the better for the kingdom."

My stomach rolled at the thought of sleeping with someone other than Sabrina, and Teo gave me a look of alarm. "Quill? Are you all right?"

"Fine." I shook loose of his grip. "I have to go."

"Will you get the human ready for transport this afternoon?" He called as I stalked toward the door.

"Yes." I slammed the door shut behind me. I walked to my quarters and opened the door. Sabrina was standing in the kitchen wearing my shirt and drinking a glass of gallberry juice. Her smile of greeting died on her lips.

"Honey? What's wrong?"

"The storm ended."

Her face paled, and she set the glass on the counter before walking to the window. She drew back the curtains and held up her hand when the bright light streamed in. I joined her as she stared silently out the window.

"There are more buildings than I expected," she finally said.

"The palace overlooks the biggest city in the western province."

"Oh," she said. "Did you find out who my employer is?"

"Yes. Teo has already contacted him."

"Of course he has."

The despair in her voice made my chest hurt, and I wrapped my tail around her waist. "My mate -"

"No," she said quickly. "Please don't call me that, Quill. Not now."

"I am sorry."

"Me too." She studied the cold landscape. "When do I leave?"

"This afternoon."

She jerked in surprise but leaned away when I tried to pull her into my embrace. Only my tail touched her, and I resisted my urge to tug her closer.

"Could I hologram my sister before I leave?" she asked.

"Of course," I replied. "Sadora, please look at me."

"No," she whispered. "Don't make me."

"Please," I pleaded.

With a low sigh, she turned her head as tears slipped down her cheeks. For the first time since she arrived, the sun touched her face. It made her silky dark hair gleam, and I blinked in surprise when I studied her eyes. I had thought her eyes to be blue, but the bright light revealed a lovely purple tint to them that reminded me of the colour of our females. I stepped closer and bent to study her eyes more closely.

"Why are you looking at me like that?" She blinked, and the purple was gone.

"I wish it were different, sadora," I said.

She smiled and began to cry in earnest. I pulled her into my arms and hugged her tightly, pressing kisses against her face. "Please do not cry, my mate. Please."

She wiped her face and gave me a shaky smile. "I am not your mate, Quill. Evelyn is. I wish to God I was your mate, but I'm not."

"I wish for that too." I stared helplessly at her. "But my duty to my people -"

"I know. The stupid thing is, I admire you so much for doing the right thing even though it isn't what you want."

"It is not," I said raggedly as I kissed her again. "I want to be with you, sadora."

"We don't always get what we want," she whispered.

"Come to bed," I said. "We have time before -"

"No, I'm sorry, I can't." Fresh tears spilled down her cheeks. "I just - I can't. It'll make it so much harder to leave. Do you understand?"

"Yes," I said, even though I didn't.

"Will you help me hologram my sister?"

"Yes."

---

### Sabrina

"SABRINA! OH MY GOD! OH, SABRINA!" CARRIE'S PALE FACE was flushed with colour, and she leaned forward as she studied me. "I was so afraid. Are you all right? Why haven't you contacted me? It's been nearly a month. I called the agency, but they wouldn't tell me anything."

"I'm sorry." I stared at the slender figure of my sister. Quill helped me place the call before leaving his quarters to give me some privacy. "There was a storm when we landed, and it knocked out all of the Draax communication."

"You keep blipping in and out," Carrie said.

"The signal probably isn't great yet. The storm only ended this morning."

"It lasted all month?"

"Yes."

"Weird. How do you like your new employer?" Carrie asked. "Is he nice?"

"Actually, there was a bit of a mix-up, and I ended up being sent to the king of the western province."

Carrie blinked at me. I might have been fuzzy and blipping in and out to her, but she was crystal clear on my end. I had to bite back my urge to try to hug her.

"The king?"

"Yes. They implanted me with the wrong identification chip."

"Oh my gosh. What happened?"

"Uh, nothing. I've just been hanging out here at the palace and waiting for the storm to end."

"Did you meet the king?" Carrie asked.

I nodded. "Yeah."

"That's kind of cool."

"Sure. Anyway, I just wanted to let you know that I'm okay and leaving for my employer's home this afternoon. It's the cold season here, and they get quite a few storms. I might not be able to email you daily like I promised."

Carrie pouted unhappily. "But I miss you."

"I miss you too," I said. "How's Josh?"

"He's good. He's at work right now."

"How are you feeling?" I asked a bit anxiously.

"Perfect. At my last doctor's appointment, the tumour was completely gone."

"That's wonderful," I said. "You look really good. You've gained back some weight."

She smiled at me and rubbed her belly. "Actually, there's another reason why I'm gaining weight."

My heart dropped into my stomach, but I forced myself to smile at her. "What's that?"

"I'm pregnant!" She gave me a gleeful look. "Josh and I are having a baby, Sabrina. Isn't that amazing?"

"It is." I blinked rapidly to keep the tears from falling. "It's wonderful."

"I'm just under a month along," she said. "I wouldn't have even known, except the doctor discovered it when he was doing the scan for the tumour. I'm so happy, and Josh is over the moon about it. He's already planning out the nursery and picking out baby names."

My stomach was churning, and I was incredibly close to vomiting, but I forced another smile. "That's so lovely, Carrie. Congratulations."

"Thank you. I need you here, though. Do you think your employer will give you a few weeks off to come and take care of me when the baby is born? You know I'll need help."

I swallowed down my bitterness. "Uh, I'm not sure about that. I can ask, but a few weeks is a long time."

"I know, but I'm your sister. I need you, Sabrina," Carrie said pleadingly. "Just ask him for me, okay?"

"Okay. Listen, I have to go. I'm leaving the palace soon and still need to pack."

"But I haven't talked to you for so long. Just a little longer?"

"I can't. I'll call you again in a couple of days once I'm settled in the new place. Okay?"

"Sabrina…"

"I love you, Carrie. Talk soon!" I made a kissing noise and quickly shut the hologram off before Carrie could say anything. The moment she disappeared, I jumped up and ran to the bathroom. I threw up everything in my stomach, it was mostly gallberry juice, before rinsing my mouth and staggering to Quill's bedroom. I collapsed on the bed and sobbed bitterly as I buried my face in Quill's pillow.

## *Quillan*

"I AM GOING WITH YOU!" I SNARLED AT TEO.

He shook his head as I paced like an angry pike bull in the palace's great hall. The front door opened, and Faro, his green skin dark from the cold, swept in. Beyond him, I could see the land vehicle with Sabrina's trunk sitting in the snow beside it. The door shut, and Faro gave me a nervous look when I glared at him as he stomped the snow from his boots.

"You should not go, my king," Teo said. "It will not do for your real mate to see how you look at the Sabrina human."

"I do not care!" I shouted at him. "I do not care what she thinks or what she -"

"Quill."

Sabrina's soft voice had me whirling around. She was standing next to Galan, and her face was ashen. I strode forward and pulled her into my arms before stroking her dark hair back from her face.

"You are pale." I pulled the flask of gallberry juice from the inside pocket of my travelling cloak and opened it before holding it to her mouth. "Drink, sadora."

She drank obediently, and I watched as a flush of colour returned to her cheeks. I tucked the flask back into my pocket. "Better?"

"Yes, thank you. Teo's right. You can't go with us."

I glared at her as hurt rippled through me. "You do not want me to go with you?"

She shook her head. "It'll just make it more difficult."

"I do not care what this Evelyn thinks when she sees me with you. I do not -"

"Not on Evelyn, on me. I don't want to see you with her. I know that sounds ridiculous, but I – I don't. I can't. It'll," she paused, "it'll hurt me badly, Quill."

My anger dissipated immediately when the tears welled up in her eyes. That beautiful purple tint was back, caught in the light gleaming in the windows. Not caring that Teo or Faro was there, I bent my head and kissed her deeply. She returned my kiss with a sweetness that made my throat ache.

"We must go," Teo said from behind me.

I growled at him as Sabrina cupped my face and smiled at me. "It'll be okay. Faro and Galan are with me."

"Galan," I said hoarsely, "guard her with your life."

"I will, my king," Galan replied.

I took my cloak off and wrapped it around her before pulling the hood up to cover her head. "You are not dressed warmly enough for the cold."

Sabrina rubbed her fingers along my jaw. "Thank you, Quill. Thank you for everything."

I couldn't reply as she stood on her tiptoes and brushed her soft lips against my cheek before whispering into my ear. "You're an amazing king and mate, and you'll be an even better father. I love you."

She pulled away and walked rapidly across the great hall to the door. Galan followed her, and Faro opened the door. She stepped into the cold, and I rasped, "Sadora!"

She turned, and we stared silently at each other for a moment before she curtseyed gracefully and said, "My king,"

She turned and walked away without looking back.

# CHAPTER 13

*Sabrina*

We were only an hour into our journey when I finally grew tired of Teo's nervous chattering next to me.

"Teo," I said wearily as I stared out the window, "don't take this the wrong way, but could you please shut up?"

He stopped talking and cleared his throat. There was silence for a moment, and then he said, "I know this is difficult for you, human, but -"

"No, you have no idea how difficult it is, so could you just shut up for the love of God?"

I was stupidly close to tears, and I was suddenly feeling very nauseous. As my stomach roiled, I said, "Galan, stop!"

He turned to look at me. "What?"

"Stop! Please stop, I'm going to throw up."

He pulled the vehicle over immediately, and I clawed the door open before sliding out. The vehicle was equipped with massive tires with treads nearly as deep as my hand, and it was a long drop to the ground. I sank to my knees in the deep snow and, holding my hand over my mouth, struggled through the snow for a few feet before I bent over and vomited. It was bright pink from the gallberry juice, and I whispered, "Ugh," before wiping my mouth with a trembling hand.

I could hear someone coming up behind me, and I kicked snow over the vomit before backing up. I stared blankly at the trees. It had taken only half an hour to get out of the city, and now the road was winding through a vast forest.

"Sabrina? Are you all right?"

"Fine, Galan. Just a bit of an upset stomach."

His warm hand dropped onto my shoulder, and I had to fight my urge to turn and bury my head in his chest and cry like a big baby.

"I am sorry, little human."

"Yeah, me too." I was starting to shiver despite Quill's heavy cloak, and I didn't resist when Galan picked me up and carried me back to the land vehicle. His kindness made me weepy, and I wiped at the tears streaming down my face. Teo and Faro had gotten out and stood beside the vehicle, their breath steaming in the cold air.

"Human, what is wrong?" Teo asked.

"Nothing," I muttered as Galan set me on my feet before the old Draax. "Just a bit of an upset stomach."

I was standing in a ray of light that had filtered through the trees, and I blinked rapidly before staring at Teo. "I'm ready to go."

Teo grabbed my chin, lifting my face to the light. I tried to pull free, and he tightened his grip. "Ouch! What the hell, Teo?"

He stepped closer. Galan took his arm and said, "Let go of her, Teo."

"It is impossible," he muttered as he bent and stared into my eyes. "It cannot be."

"Teo," Galan said warningly.

"She is breeding incompatible," Teo said in a low voice, "but her eyes…"

"What about my eyes?" I said.

He ignored me and stared at Galan. "Galan, what colour are the human's eyes?"

Galan turned my face toward his. "Purple."

"They're blue," I replied.

Galan took a second look before shaking his head. "No, they are purple."

"My eyes are blue," I said in exasperation.

"Faro!" Teo waved the Draax over. "What colour are her eyes?"

"For the love of Pete, they're blue," I said.

Faro studied my eyes. "Purple."

"Are you all colour blind?" I asked as Galan stared into my eyes again.

My sorrow turned into confusion, and it only deepened when Galan suddenly said, "No, wait. They are blue. But I swear they were purple only a few seconds ago."

Teo's wrinkled face broke out into a wide grin. "The human is pregnant."

My mouth dropped open, and Faro and Galan wore identical looks of shock. I nudged Galan. "He's gone crazy, right?"

"Teo," Galan said cautiously, "Sabrina cannot be pregnant. She is breeding incompatible."

"She is not," Teo said. "Her eyes are purple."

"One, my eyes are blue, and two, I am breeding incompatible. I saw the test results. I don't carry the gene."

"You must," he said. "You carry Quill's baby in your belly, human."

He reached out with a trembling hand and rested it against my belly. "We have an heir to the throne." He gave

Galan a triumphant smile. "We have an heir to the throne, Galan!"

"Teo!" I said sharply. "Snap out of it. I can't be pregnant."

He shrugged. "It has to be. We need to get you back to the palace kadana, and have him do testing on you right away. Perhaps the human testing procedure for the gene was incorrect."

"They don't make mistakes with that sort of thing," I said.

"Like they don't mistakenly implant the incorrect identification chip?" he said.

"Point taken. But explain this purple thing to me." I glanced at Galan. "Do you know what he's talking about?"

Galan shook his head. "I do not."

Teo made an impatient snort. "You and Faro are too young to remember, but I remember when we had female Draax in the western province. When they were pregnant, one of the first indications was an eye colour change when they were feeling," he waved his hand in the air, "emotional. Most of the time, it was only noticed by their mate, but in some cases, the colour change was more obvious. I have heard from other Draax with human mates that the colour change can be quite visible."

"Whoa," I said, "I've never heard of this before, and I did a lot of studying on the Draax before I came here. I didn't read anything that said our eyes changed colour when we were knocked up with a little alien baby."

Teo shrugged. "We do not share information that is not relevant to humans."

"Of course you don't." I rolled my eyes.

Teo studied my body hidden under Quill's cloak. "Are your breasts bigger, human? More sensitive?"

"I'm sorry?" I said.

"Are your breasts fuller?" he asked impatiently.

"Uh…"

"They are bigger." Galan grinned at me.

I blushed, and he laughed as Teo raised his eyebrow at me. "More sensitive?"

I thought back to two nights ago when Quill had made me come just by sucking on my nipples. "Uh, yeah."

"Another indication," Teo said with satisfaction. "And if I remember correctly, vomiting is a sign of pregnancy in a human. Is it not?"

"Well, yes, but…" I gave Galan a blank look.

He grinned at me. "You carry Quill's baby, Sabrina."

"Holy shit," I whispered. "I – I'm pregnant."

"Come, we must get you back to the palace immediately," Galan said.

He turned, and his body stiffened as he made a low groan.

"Galan? What's wrong?"

"Faro?" He whispered as Faro stepped away from him. He was holding a dagger, the blade covered in a dark green liquid.

"Galan?" My eyes widened when Galan fell to his knees before toppling forward. "Galan!"

I dropped to my knees beside him and heaved him onto his back. Dark green blood was pouring out of a deep stab wound just above his ribcage on the right side. Panicked, I pressed my hand against it, trying to stop the flow of blood.

"What did you do?" I stared in shock at Faro.

There was a low growl of rage, and Teo attacked Faro. He was no match for the younger Draax's strength, and I cringed when Faro tossed him against the land vehicle. Teo's head smashed into the corner of the open door, and his eyes rolled up in his head as a dark bruise immediately appeared on his temple. He crumpled into the snow as Galan made a low gasping noise.

"What are you doing, Faro?" I said.

"I am sorry, human," Faro licked his lips nervously, "but you must come with me right now."

"No. No, I won't."

"You must. Get into the vehicle."

"I'm not leaving Teo and Galan. They need medical help."

Faro shook his head. "If you do not get into the vehicle right now, I will kill both of them. I swear it."

I swallowed my sob of fear and tucked my hand inside my cloak as I bent over Galan. "Galan, can you hear me?"

"I am sorry, Sabrina. I have failed you and my king," he whispered.

"No, you haven't." I smoothed my hand over his forehead. "Stay alive, all right? Quill will find you. He knows Faro is a betrayer."

"He does not," Faro said anxiously. "Move, human."

"Stay alive," I whispered again before pressing my mouth against Galan's. "Quill will be here soon."

I stood and studied Teo's prone body for a moment. I could see his chest moving, and I breathed a sigh of relief as Faro dragged his body away from the vehicle. "Get in."

He boosted me into the front seat. I didn't protest when he pulled out a pair of steel cuffs and placed them around my wrists before he cuffed my hands to the inside of the door and slammed it shut.

I stared out the window at Galan as Faro climbed behind the wheel and drove away. My heart thudding like a frightened rabbit, I prayed that Quill would find Galan and Teo before it was too late.

*Quillan*

"My king!"

I didn't turn at the sound of my childhood friend's voice. I continued to stare at the city below me as Krey clapped me on the back.

"Quill?"

"Welcome home, Krey."

"What is wrong?"

"Nothing."

"Where is Galan?"

"Returning Sabrina to her employer."

My voice was like my training sword. Dull, heavy, flat.

"Who is Sabrina?" Krey asked.

"My mate."

"Your mate? Quill, look at me. What in Krono's name is going on?"

I ignored both his question and the knock at the door. After a moment, Krey opened the door. "Hello, Bitta."

"Krey, when did you get back?" Bitta's face smoothed into a smile.

"Only just now."

"Is the king here? I must speak with him."

"He is." Krey's voice couldn't conceal his puzzlement.

"What is it?" I asked.

When Bitta glanced at Krey, I waved my hand with a weighted weariness. "Whatever you have to say, you can say it in front of Krey."

"I have broken the encryption on the messages."

"Have you?" My voice was apathetic at best. "That is good."

I couldn't care less who betrayed me. What did it matter when I didn't have Sabrina by my side?

"My king," Bitta said, "it is Faro who betrays you."

Molten fear bubbled, boiled, burned in my chest, drenching my lungs. A feeling I'd never had.

I couldn't catch my breath.

I was drowning.

I wanted to flay Faro alive. I wanted Gokmard heads to hang in the halls of my home. I wanted to burn their bones until they were nothing but ash.

Krey's heavy hand on my shoulder grounded me. A blood war with the Gokmards could set my people on a path of chaos and carnage.

"Quill? Are you all right?"

I needed to focus. I was a leader, a warrior, a king.

The fear faded, and I finally caught my breath. I had one goal, one mission, one purpose.

Rescue my mate.

"Why?" The word fell from my mouth like a heavy stone.

"He has made a deal with the Gokmards to deliver your mate to them once she is pregnant with your child," Bitta said.

"Sabrina." Saying her name out loud almost rekindled the liquid fear still simmering at the bottom of my lungs.

Almost.

"I am sure she is not in danger." Bitta's voice was maddening in its carelessness. "She is not your mate, nor is she pregnant. It is Evelyn who will be in danger once she carries your child. When they come back, we will arrest Faro."

I ignored him and ran to the hologram machine. I punched in Galan's code. Impatience rattled through my veins. There was no answer, so I turned to Krey. "Galan and Teo took my mate to her employer. Faro is with them and he has betrayed me. Gather ten of the king's guard and meet me in the great hall."

A true warrior, Krey didn't question my rambling explanation. He turned and ran from the room as I pulled my sword from the wall. I strapped the sheath around my waist, and Bitta said, "She is in no danger, my king. It is better to wait until Faro returns with your true mate and arrest him then."

"No. Sabrina is my true mate, and she needs me."

I pushed past Bitta and strode toward the great hall.

---

"So, Evelyn is your true mate, but you are in love with Sabrina," Krey said as he drove recklessly down the road. I had tried to explain as best I could as we drove toward the farmer's home.

"Yes. I love her, Krey. She is breeding incompatible, but I do not care. I will give up the throne for her."

"Quill," Krey gave me a cautious look before glancing in the rear-view mirror. A second land vehicle rumbled behind us and carried five other members of the king's guard. "I understand you have feelings for this human, but do not act so hastily. You are the king. You cannot simply give up the throne for love."

"I can, and I will," I said. "It was a mistake to – Krono!"

Krey slammed on the brakes as we crested a hill. Ice was under the snow, and we slid a few feet down the hill. I was opening the door and leaping out before the vehicle had come to a full stop. I waded through the deep snow and knelt beside Galan as Krey shut off the vehicle and hurried to Teo.

"Galan! Galan, open your eyes!"

He groaned as I glanced at Krey. "Is Teo alive?"

"Yes, but he is unconscious."

"Galan, look at me." Blood covered the front of his cloak,

and I eased it back. There was a wound on his ribcage, and dried blood stuck to his shirt, but it wasn't actively bleeding. Krey crouched next to me as I prodded gently at the wound.

"It is healing," Krey said.

I prodded it again, and Galan groaned, "Krono, that hurts. Stop poking at it!"

"Galan, where is my mate? Where is Sabrina?" I asked when Galan squinted at me.

"Faro took her nearly twenty minutes ago."

"Fuck! I am going to kill the bastard!" The Earth's curse words sounded foreign but wholly satisfying on my tongue.

"How are you healing?" Krey asked.

Galan lifted his right arm. My flask of gallberry juice was clutched in his shaking hand. "Your clever mate managed to give this to me before Faro took her. Is Teo all right?"

"He will live. We need to get you both back to the palace before you freeze to death," Krey said.

"Where did Faro take her?" I asked.

"I do not know, my king." Galan groaned loudly, and his green skin lightened when Krey sat him up. "I am sorry. Faro took me by surprise and stabbed me. I failed you."

"You did not," I said.

"Why did Faro even take her?" Krey said. "Bitta said that he would not be interested in her because she is breeding incompatible."

"She is pregnant with Quill's baby," Galan said.

I stared blankly at him. "Did you get hit in the head as well, Galan? That is not possible."

"It is the truth," Galan said. "Teo noticed her eyes were purple when she was upset, and he said it indicated she was pregnant. She threw up as well, and he said human women do that when they are pregnant."

"It is not possible," I said. "Sabrina does not carry the gene."

"Teo thinks the humans screwed up the test," Galan said. "Your mate's breasts are fuller and more sensitive, she said so herself, and her belly is much rounder than it was even two weeks ago. We were about to return to the palace when Faro stabbed me and knocked out Teo. He took your mate, my king, because she carries your child."

I stared at him again, barely noticing the cold wind. "She carries my child."

"Yes," Galan said.

Joy and a fierce need to protect my mate and the child she carried swept through me. Feeling half-mad, I stood and paced back and forth, scrubbing my hands through my hair as panic settled around my heart. "I – I do not know how to find her. How do I find her?"

"My king."

The voice was low and weak. I ran to where Henden and Laos supported Teo.

"Teo, I am sorry."

"No, my king. I am. I should have noticed her eyes before. Should have seen the way she…"

I gripped his arm. "We will get you back to the palace and get some gallberry juice into you. You will be fine, Teo."

"Your mate," he said. "Use the identification chip to find her. It is a tracking device as well."

I took a deep breath. In my panic, I had forgotten about the identification chip. "Thank you, old friend."

I ran to the land vehicle, grabbed my tablet and punched in a number. Bitta's face appeared in front of me.

"My king?"

"I need you to find the coordinates of Sabrina's identification chip. Remember, it is Evelyn's you must look up."

"Yes, my king." The hologram of Bitta's face was already looking away as he turned to a different screen I couldn't see. After a moment, he turned back. "I have her. She's on the move. I can send the coordinates to your tablet."

"Do it," I said. "And tell the kadana that Galan and Teo are on their way to the palace, and both are injured. They will need to be examined immediately."

"Yes, my king. Should I send more men?"

"No. We can handle Faro."

I closed the hologram and turned around. My guard had already loaded Galan and Teo into the land vehicle, urging both to drink gallberry juice as they wrapped blankets around them.

"Henden, Laos, and Krey, you will come with me. The rest of you return to the palace."

Henden and Laos climbed into the back seat of the land vehicle as Krey slid behind the wheel. I sat in the front seat, my hand gripping the handle of my sword, my head buzzing with the bloodlust of impending battle.

"My king, you are forbidden to fight," Krey said.

"Is it your intention to try to stop me from going after my mate and child, old friend?" I squeezed the handle of my sword.

"No, Quill," Krey replied.

"Good. My mate is here." I showed him the coordinates, and he punched them into the tablet of the land vehicle.

"Let us go and get your mate then," Krey said with a broad grin.

---

*Sabrina*

"Where are you taking me?"

Faro didn't reply, and I glared at him. "Answer me, you chickenshit asshole."

He stiffened and gave me a dirty look. "I am not a chickenshit asshole."

"Oh, trust me, you're the very definition of a chickenshit asshole. Tell me why you kidnapped me."

"That is none of your concern, human. Now be quiet."

"No. Tell me where we're going!" I was scared to death but determined not to let him see it.

He turned right onto a barely visible road and headed into the dark forest. I looked behind us. If we went off the main road, Quill would never find us. I swallowed down my panic. Quill would find me. Galan would live, and Quill would figure out that Faro was the betrayer and save Galan, Teo, and me. He had to.

"Do you even know where you're going?" I said as Faro squinted out the windshield. "Who were you talking to before?"

About twenty minutes after Faro kidnapped me, he'd pulled the land vehicle over and stepped outside. He had made a call on his tablet as he paced back and forth in the deep snow. His voice was muffled, and I didn't understand the language he spoke, but it was clear he was excited.

"The Gokmards."

My mouth dropped open. I hadn't expected Faro to answer me. I gave him a cautious look. "It was you who was sending the encrypted messages."

He jerked, the vehicle nearly veering off the road, giving me a quick and anxious look. "How do you know about the emails?"

"Bitta found them. He told Quill. Bitta's probably cracked the encryption as we speak, and they know it's you."

"They do not." There was doubt in his voice. "No one can crack my encryption."

"Bitta is brilliant," I replied, even though I had no idea if he was.

Faro didn't answer, and I glared at him. "Why are you even talking with the Gokmards, and what the hell do you need me for?"

"You are stupid for a human," he said.

"Fuck you!"

"Watch your tongue," he advised. "The Gokmards will not like it if you speak back to them."

My blood ran cold. "You're taking me to the Gokmards?"

He nodded, and I pulled at the cuffs that bound me to the door. "Why?"

"Because Quill loves you, and you carry his child."

The anger in his voice chilled me to the bone. "Quill doesn't love me."

Faro turned to stare at me as he laughed. I cringed back at the madness that gleamed in his eyes.

"You pretty little human fool. Quill loves you, and we all know it. It will destroy him when the Gokmards kill you."

I thought I'd been scared before, but it had nothing on the fresh fear that knifed down my spine. I swallowed thickly. "Wh-what did you say?"

"I am giving you to the Gokmards," Faro said. "They will torture you until you beg for death. Eventually, they will kill you, but not until they have shown Quill how badly his mate suffers because of him."

"Why would you betray him like this?" I whispered.

"He and his family are responsible for my brother's death."

"What do you mean?"

Faro sighed and drummed his fingers on the wheel as he

peered out the windshield. "My brother was a member of the king's guard. He was on the king's ship when it crashed."

"That was an accident."

"If the king had not taken him to Delorth, my brother would not have died," Faro said with the chilling calmness of someone who had gone completely mad. "Falten is dead because of Quill. I suffered, and now he will suffer too."

"He did suffer!" I nearly shouted. "His brother died too, remember? Quill had nothing to do with this. Jesus, you're fucking crazy!"

Faro didn't reply. The road we were on was getting more and more narrow. The snow was so deep that after only a few more minutes, the land vehicle slowed to a stop. We were stuck despite the massive tires with their deep treads.

Faro muttered a curse before sliding out of the vehicle. He waded through the snow to my side and opened my door. After unlocking my cuffs, he pulled me out. I glanced at the trees on my right, wondering if I could escape and hide in the forest. The trees had massive trunks. I could easily hide behind one of them and –

Faro grabbed my wrist and twisted viciously. It brought tears to my eyes, and I glared at him as he snarled, "Do not even think of trying to escape, human. I will catch you easily."

I knew he was right. The damn snow was almost up to my hips, and Quill's cloak weighed me down. Of course, Quill's cloak was the only thing keeping me from freezing to death. My boots were fur-lined, but the snow had slipped inside them to melt against my socks. Already, my toes felt half-frozen, and my nose and fingers were numb.

Faro cuffed my hands in front of me and produced a long steel chain from inside his cloak. He attached it to the cuffs and started forward. I stumbled after him, slogging through the snow as my teeth chattered loudly. We had only been walking for about ten minutes when I realized the trees were beginning to thin. A large natural clearing was ahead of us, and my footsteps slowed. A dozen Gokmards were standing in the clearing. Their dark fur gleamed in the rays of light that filtered through the trees, and they were all at least eight feet tall.

I had stopped completely, and Faro yanked impatiently on the chain. "Move, human."

"F-f-Faro, you d-d-don't have t-t-to d-d-do this." I was so damn cold I could barely speak.

"Be quiet, human." He yanked me forward viciously.

I stumbled and fell to my knees. Faro grabbed my arm and hauled me back to my feet before half-carrying and half-dragging me into the clearing. The biggest of the Gokmards joined us, and I craned my head to stare up at him. His eyes were black and beady, and he reminded me vaguely of a bear. I took a nervous step back when he reached out and touched the hood of Quill's cloak.

He spoke to Faro in a soft and musical tone that was utterly at odds with his appearance. Faro replied, stumbling a bit over the unfamiliar words before pointing at my belly.

"A-a-asshole," I muttered.

When the Gokmard reached to touch my belly, I slapped him on his meaty arm. Despite my gloves, my hands were so numb I couldn't feel his thick fur under my hand. The Gokmard frowned, and I cried out when he slapped me hard across the face. I flew back and landed on my back in the deep, soft snow. Shaking and trying not to cry, I stared up at the trees. Faro leaned down and yanked me to my feet.

"Do not provoke them, foolish human," he said.

My body shaking so badly I could barely stand, I said, "G-g-g-give the G-o-okmard a m-m-message f-f-for me."

"What?" Faro said impatiently.

"T-t-t-tell him if he t-t-touches me again, I'll k-k-k-kill him."

Faro glared at me. "What is wrong with you?"

He dragged me to the far end of the clearing. "You are going to die, human. You are going to die a very slow and painful death, and you are not -"

One of the Gokmards whistled piercingly, and Faro stiffened before dragging me before him. He hooked his arm around my throat and pulled his sword out as all twelve of the Gokmards removed small silver tubes from belts around their waists. There was a buzzing noise, and I blinked in surprise when dark red beams of energy emerged from the tubes.

They were staring uneasily into the trees. It was obvious that they had heard something, and my heart began a crazy, chaotic beat in my chest. Quill. It had to be my mate. I stared up at Faro and gave him a ferocious grin.

"Oh, b-b-boy, you are in s-s-s-so much t-trouble now."

"Hold your tongue, human!" he snapped as a Draax stepped out of the trees and into the clearing. He held his sword at his side and smiled at Faro.

"Hello, Faro."

"How did you find us, Krey?" I could hear the fear in Faro's voice as two more Draax males stepped out of the trees to stand next to Krey.

"I simply followed the smell," Krey said with another grin. He pointed his sword at the nearest Gokmard and laughed when it bared its teeth at him. "You smell worse than a glack-enswine."

"Where is Quill?" Faro held the sword to my belly, and I tried not to flinch as fresh fear flooded through me.

"Why would he come?" Krey shrugged. "This woman is

not his mate. What does he care what happens to her? He charged me with bringing back your traitorous head, nothing more. The Gokmards can have the woman."

"She is pregnant with his child!" Faro shouted.

"Impossible," Krey said as the biggest Gokmard turned to stare at Faro. "She is breeding incompatible."

"No!" Faro snapped. "Her eyes are purple. She threw up. Teo said she was pregnant."

"Teo is a rambling old fool," Krey said.

"Not mate?" The biggest Gokmard spoke the Draax language slowly, and he had a weird accent, but what he said was clear.

"Afraid not, you big smelly glackenswine," Krey said. "His true mate is another."

"You lie to us," the Gokmard said to Faro.

"No!" Faro said. "No, I did not. She is his mate. He loves her. I swear it."

"N-n-no, I'm n-n-not," I stuttered. "I'm n-n-nothing to him."

"Enough!" Faro turned me around and shook me roughly before slapping me across the face. It made my already painful cheek burn, and I cried out and fell to my knees in the snow. I cringed when Faro leaned down and raised his hand to slap me again. There was movement to his right before he could land the blow, and a figure emerged from the trees.

"No," Faro whispered.

Quill strode easily through the deep snow. Faro backed away, the sword trembling in his hand. His silver eyes turned the colour of flint, Quill said in a low voice, "I will kill you for touching her."

Faro dropped his sword in the snow before falling to his knees. "Mercy, my king. Mercy, I beg -"

Faro abruptly stopped speaking. Quill's hand flashed out from under his cloak, and his fist rested against the bottom of Faro's chin. I stared in stupid confusion at the dark blood that streamed out of Faro's mouth and down his chin. Quill pulled his fist away. It was wrapped around the handle of a long, sharp dagger. When the blade slid out from Faro's flesh, my stomach churned at the smears of green blood on the dagger.

Faro blinked slowly, staring up at Quill as he grinned fiercely at him. "There will be no mercy for the coward who took my queen."

He released Faro, and the Draax fell sideways into the soft snow. He twitched and grew still as Quill snarled in satisfaction. A squeal of surprise made me turn sluggishly to see Krey dart forward and casually disembowel the closest Gokmard. Its intestines fell out in a gush of clear fluid and bright red blood, and the other Gokmards stared in stunned silence.

Quill's arm wrapped around my waist, and he lifted me to my feet before pressing a warm kiss against my mouth. He pulled his sword out, and I jerked against him when he shouted, "Protect your queen!"

Confused, I looked around for Evelyn. Had they already taken her from the farmer?

Moving as lightly as dancers through the deep snow, Krey and the other two Draax had joined us before the Gokmards could even move. Quill kissed me again before smiling reassuringly at me. "Be brave just a little longer, my mate."

He stepped away and turned around to face the Gokmards. I was surrounded in a tight circle by all four of the Draax, and despite my height, I couldn't see past their large, broad bodies.

"All that matters is your queen," Quill said. "Protect her at all costs. Do you understand?"

"Yes, my king," the three Draax said in unison.

I sank to my butt in the snow, barely feeling the cold creeping through Quill's cloak. I drew my knees up and wrapped my shaking arms around them as the Gokmards, bellowing loudly and continually, attacked Quill and the others.

I could only see flashes of the Gokmard's hairy legs and the splatter of their bright red blood in the snow. Screams of agony intermixed with the low buzz of their energy blades and the loud grunts of the Draax. Quill wasn't wearing a jacket, and I watched the large muscles in his back flex beneath his shirt as he swung his sword.

Despite my terror that Quill would die, I was incredibly sleepy and couldn't stop yawning. My shivering had finally stopped, and I stared blearily at Quill's back as numbness descended over my body. When the head of a Gokmard flew over Krey's shoulder and landed in front of me, I didn't even finch. I stared at its gaping mouth and the ragged and bloody stump of its neck before resting my forehead on my knees and closing my eyes. Sleep. I needed to sleep.

# CHAPTER 14

*Quillan*

The last Gokmard foolishly tried to run. As he lumbered through the snow, I turned to Henden. The big Draax nodded and, despite his size, ran nimbly after it.

"Laos? You are injured?" I could see bright blood soaking through the material of his shirt.

Laos gingerly lifted his shirt to study the gash on his ribs. "Not badly, my king. One of their blades caught me, but gall-berry juice will heal it."

"Krono, I have been gone a moon and a half and return to find you have already lost your ability to fight," Krey said teasingly as the dying scream of the runaway Gokmard echoed through the trees.

Laos rolled his eyes and lowered his shirt as I faced my queen. "My mate, you are safe and – sadora!"

Sabrina was curled into a ball in the snow, and she didn't move at the sound of my voice. Fear kept me frozen for a moment before I lunged forward and fell to my knees beside her. I gathered her into my embrace, and my heart stopped when I felt her cold body. Her skin was completely devoid of colour, and I gave Krey a look of pure panic before cupping Sabrina's face.

"Sadora, wake up! Look at me, my mate!"

Krey kicked away the head of a Gokmard before crouching next to us. His fingers pressed against her throat. "She still lives, Quill. But we must get her back to the palace and warmed up immediately."

My legs trembling from fear, I stood with Sabrina in my arms and ran through the forest to our vehicle.

---

"MY KING."

I continued sitting beside the bed, holding Sabrina's hand and studying her face. Galan squeezed my shoulder before sitting in the chair on the other side of the bed.

"How is she?" Galan asked.

"She will not wake up." Even I could hear the plaintive sound in my voice, but I was powerless to control it. "Why will she not wake up, Galan?"

"It has only been a couple of hours, Quill. The humans are weaker than us. She needs time to heal."

I studied the bag of pink liquid hooked up to Sabrina's arm. "Sigan is giving her gallberry serum. Why is it not working? He said it would, and it has not. If she dies, I will banish Sigan from the planet!"

"My king, Sigan is an excellent kadana. I am sure the serum is working," Galan said. "Her colour has returned, and her skin is warmer."

"Humans have died from hypothermia," I said.

"She is not going to die. Her heartbeat is steady, and so is the baby's. Your mate is strong. She will live."

I glanced at him. "How do you feel, Galan?"

"Completely healed, my king."

"And Teo?"

"He is almost healed as well. Sigan has allowed him to return to his own quarters. He wanted to see you and your mate, but Sigan said he needed to rest."

"I am glad to hear it." I leaned forward and brushed my lips across Sabrina's mouth before resting my forehead against hers and closing my eyes.

"I love you, sadora," I whispered. "I love you. Please wake up."

"I love you too."

Her croaked reply made me sit up in a hurry. I stared at her, and she blinked sleepily before smiling at me. "Hi."

"Sadora." I pressed my lips against hers. "How do you feel?"

"Good." She shifted under the bedcovers. "Quill, Teo said I'm pregnant. The baby…"

"The baby is fine," I said immediately. "I heard its heart-beat earlier."

"Are you sure?" She was starting to cry, and I wiped away the tears.

"Yes, my sadora. Our baby is fine."

She took a deep breath before saying, "Galan and Teo?"

"They both live. Galan is here."

I leaned back so she could see Galan. He rested his hand on her shoulder. "Hello, my queen."

"Galan, I'm sorry."

He frowned at her. "You have nothing to be sorry about. It is I who should apologize to you. I failed to keep you safe and -"

"No," Sabrina said. "You didn't know. It isn't your fault."

Galan smiled at her before kissing her forehead. "I am

glad you are awake, my queen. I will leave you alone with your mate."

He stood and left the room as Sabrina stared at her surroundings. "Where am I?"

"The infirmary," I replied. "Sigan – he is the kadana – thought it best to keep you here for now."

"Kadana – that's like a doctor, right?"

"Yes. I love you, my sadora. Are you sure you feel all right?"

"I do. All things considered, I feel pretty damn good, actually. My nausea is gone, and I feel much warmer and stronger."

"You are receiving gallberry serum directly into your system," I said.

She studied the bag hanging above her. "I thought it only came in drinkable form."

I shook my head before taking her hand and squeezing it tightly. "I love you."

She smiled at me. "You have no idea how adorable you are with your constant 'I love you's,' Quill."

I squeezed her hand again. "I should never have sent you away. I am sorry, sweet sadora."

"You didn't know I was pregnant. Hell, I didn't know, and it's my body. My cycle was a few days late, but I thought it was the stress. Honestly, I still don't know how it even happened. I don't carry the gene. I guess they could have made a mistake in the testing, but I've never heard of that happening before."

I shrugged. Honestly, I didn't care why or what had happened. My mate carried my child. That was all I cared about. "Sigan is looking into it. He took some of your blood earlier. Perhaps he will find out the reason."

"Okay." She hesitated before clearing her throat. "Quill,

you and the other Draax keep referring to me as your queen. Does that mean..."

I rubbed my thumb over the palm of her hand. "You are my mate. As soon as you are healed, we will perform the mating ritual, and you will become queen of the western province."

"That's really sweet, but you're forgetting about Evelyn and my nanny contract," she said. "If I break the contract, I'll be imprisoned on Earth."

"No one will take you from me ever again. You are my mate, and you belong with me."

"Again, that's very sweet," she said, "but I'm breaking a law if I stay with you."

"I am the king of the western province. What I say is law. I will tell the farmer you belong to me, and that is that. I am his king. He will obey me."

"Quill, that isn't -"

"I will arrange for him to have a new nanny. Do not worry, my sadora."

"What about Evelyn?" she asked. "She is expecting to be mated to you."

I shrugged carelessly. "I will find her a new mate, or I will give her a lifetime supply of gallberry juice and let her return to Earth. Whatever she wants."

"I think we should wait to get married," Sabrina said.

Panic tinged with anger coursed through me. "No! You are my mate, and you carry my child. You will do what I say and be mated to me, little human."

My fear diminished a bit when Sabrina rolled her eyes and gave me the look of exasperation I had admittedly grown to love. "Cool it, honey. I didn't say I wasn't going to marry you. I just said I think we should wait until after we talk to Evelyn."

"There is no need," I said. "She is not my mate. You are. She does not carry my child. You do."

"I know." Sabrina squeezed my hand reassuringly. "But Evelyn is expecting to be your queen. It doesn't feel right to me to show up and be all, 'Oh, hey, sorry, but I'm his queen now, not you.'"

"But you are my queen," I said. "Talking to Evelyn will not change that."

"I know," she repeated. "It's hard to explain, honey. I would feel better if we waited until after we talked to Evelyn. Okay?"

"I love you, and you will be mated to me, no matter what happens with this Evelyn. But if you wish to wait, we will wait."

"Thank you." She yawned, and I leaned forward and kissed her.

"You need more rest, sadora. I will leave and -"

"No," she said. "Don't leave me. Crawl into the bed with me, please?"

I immediately kicked off my boots and removed my pants and shirt before climbing in behind her. It was a tight fit – infirmary beds were meant for one – but I could not deny my mate anything she wanted.

I curled up behind her and put my arm around her, cupping her breast before kissing the back of her neck. "Sleep, my sadora. I love you."

"I love you too, Quill."

---

*Sabrina*

"GOOD MORNING, MY QUEEN. HOW ARE YOU FEELING?"

"Hello, Sigan. Much better, thank you." I was dressed and sitting on the hospital bed, impatiently swinging my legs as I waited for Quill to return. "Um, I'm not your queen, though."

"You will be soon enough," Sigan said absently. He took my wrist and felt my pulse. Despite having an IV in my hand yesterday, there was no mark or bruise on my hand. Probably because after removing the IV last night, Sigan had made me drink what felt like a gallon of gallberry juice. Not that I minded. My craving for it was back.

"Sigan? I'm craving the gallberry juice. Is that normal?"

"Yes. It is because you carry the king's baby. When our human females are pregnant, they require a great deal of gallberry juice to keep them healthy enough to carry the baby."

I gave him a startled look. "Is this considered a high-risk pregnancy?"

"No, my queen." He dropped my wrist and patted my arm. "Human females do just fine carrying our babies, as long as they drink the gallberry juice. It is harder on their systems to carry our young than the young of their own species, but there are usually no problems."

"Usually," I said.

He patted my arm again. "We will monitor you very closely during the entire pregnancy. You are young and strong and very healthy, my queen. I do not anticipate any problems with you carrying the king's baby."

"Do you even know how this is possible?" I asked as the door opened, and Quill walked into the room.

Sigan bowed, and Quill clapped him on the back before standing beside me. He kissed me and stroked my dark hair. "How do you feel, my mate? Is there something wrong? I should not have left you."

246

He gave Sigan an anxious look as I said, "I'm fine, honey. You've only been gone half an hour."

"Your queen is right," Sigan said. "She is very healthy. I was just about to explain how it is possible that she carries your child."

Quill put his arm around me, and I leaned against his solid warmth before saying, "Let me guess - mistake in the testing?"

"No," Sigan said, "I repeated the gene testing yesterday, and the humans did not make an error during the testing process. As you know, a human female must carry a certain gene that allows her to become pregnant with a Draax baby."

"Right," I said, "and I don't carry that gene."

"Actually, you do," Sigan said. "Only, it is a different genetic variant of the gene. The test we use looks for the actual gene sequence. Because you have a variant of it, the normal test came back negative. I could not understand why you were pregnant, but there was no denying that you were, is there?"

I shook my head as Sigan gave Quill an excited look. "I thought about it for a while and came up with the theory that perhaps she carried a gene variant. I adjusted the test and discovered I was correct. Your queen carries a variant of the gene – one that allows her to become pregnant with your baby."

"Well done, Sigan," Quill said.

"Thank you, my king."

"Wait, does that mean other women who tested incompatible might be compatible?" I asked.

"I am not certain, my queen. I will share news of my discovery with the humans, and they will adjust their testing methods. With your permission, of course, my king."

Quill nodded, and Sigan walked to the door. "Excellent."

"Sigan, can the queen travel?" Quill asked.

Sigan paused at the door. "Yes, but take plenty of gall-berry juice with you. It will help combat the nausea and weariness she will be feeling."

As the kadana left the room, Quill kissed me again before helping me off the bed. "Come, my mate. We leave for the farmer's home immediately."

"Have you heard from him?" I asked as we left the hospital ward. Quill wrapped his tail around my waist as he moved me quickly down the hallways.

"No," he said.

"That's weird, right?" I said. "The storm ended yesterday morning. The transmission would have gone through by now."

"Perhaps," Quill replied as we turned another corner.

"So, why hasn't he replied?"

Quill shrugged. "I do not know."

"You are being really blasé about this," I said.

"What does blasé mean?" he asked curiously.

"Not worried."

"Why would I be worried?" He asked as we walked into the great hall. "You are my mate, and you carry my child. The farmer cannot have you."

I stopped and stared in disbelief at the dozen Draax in the foyer. Galan and the three who had protected me from the Gokmards yesterday were among them.

"If you're not worried, why so many men?" I asked.

"It is not the farmer I'm worried about, but the Gokmards. In fact, I would feel much better, sadora, if you stayed here in the palace where you are safe."

I shook my head as Galan and another Draax walked toward us. "No. I'm going with you, Quill. I need to talk to Evelyn and try to explain. Besides, I'm safest with you."

I smiled my thanks at Galan when he wrapped a heavy cloak around me before stepping back. "My queen, this is Krey."

The Draax standing with him bowed before smiling at me. "It is an honour to meet you, my queen."

I stared up at him. I hadn't gotten a good look at him yesterday, but I supposed dying of hypothermia made a person a little less observant. His skin was the same shade of green as the other Draax, but his eyes were a shockingly light blue. I had never seen a Draax with light blue eyes before, they were either copper or silver or a very dark brown, and I blushed a little when Krey gave me a small grin.

"Sorry," I said. "I'm being rude. I have never seen a Draax with blue eyes before."

"It is rare, my queen," Krey said.

"It's very nice to meet you. Thank you for saving my life yesterday."

He bowed again. "My life is yours, my queen."

I glanced at Quill, who leaned down and pressed a kiss against my head. "All of the king's guard have sworn an oath to protect you with their lives."

"They know that we're not mated yet, right?" I said.

"They know. But they also know you are my queen," he said dismissively. "Come, let us go to this farmer's home and inform him that you are mine."

He picked me up and carried me outside. Three large land vehicles, their tires taller than me, were parked in a row, and the Draax divided themselves equally among the vehicles as Quill carried me to the middle vehicle. Krey climbed into the driver's seat as another Draax joined him on the passenger's side. Galan had hurried ahead of us and was already in the back seat.

"I can climb in," I protested when Galan leaned down and held out his arms.

Quill ignored me and set me on my feet before cupping my waist through the cloak. He lifted me, and Galan hooked his hands under my armpits and boosted me into the vehicle. He sat me in the middle of the seat as Quill climbed in nimbly and slammed the door shut.

"Ready, my king?"

"Yes," Quill said.

The Draax in the passenger seat turned and made a somewhat awkward bow. "My queen, I am Laos."

"Hello, Laos," I said. "You were there yesterday with the Gokmards."

"I was."

"Thank you for helping me."

"My life is yours, my queen," he replied before swinging around to face the front.

Quill put his arm around me, and I snuggled up against him. I felt unbelievably safe and protected between him and Galan. Despite what had happened yesterday, I didn't feel any fear of the Gokmards. Even if more showed up, they didn't stand a chance against my king and his warriors.

The land vehicles rumbled to life. As we drove through the city, Quill pointed out different buildings and landmarks to me, but I was barely listening. My stomach was a little nauseous, and I couldn't stop worrying about what would happen when we arrived at my actual employer's. What if he insisted that I fulfill my contract? What if he tried to take me from Quill? I didn't want anyone dying or getting hurt because of me, but I knew without a doubt that Quill would kill the farmer if he tried to take me.

I swallowed heavily and must have looked pale because

Quill was suddenly nudging a flask into my hand. "Drink, my sadora."

I drank nearly half of the gallberry juice before returning it to Quill. "Thank you."

"Better?"

"Yes, much better." The juice had taken away my nausea but hadn't done much for my emotional state. "Quill, promise me that no one will get hurt."

He gave me a puzzled look. "Why would anyone be hurt, sadora? I am the king, and the farmer is bound by law to do as I command." He leaned down and nuzzled my throat. "Be calm, my mate. There is nothing to worry about, I promise."

I leaned against him and looked out the window as his big hand rubbed my thigh. After half an hour, we were at the city's edge, and I tensed a little when we drove down the same road we had driven the previous day.

"Do not fear, sadora," Quill said. "You are safe with me."

"I know." I put my arm around him and leaned my head against his chest. I stared out the window again and tried not to worry. It took another hour to get to the farmer's home, and surprisingly, I was almost dozing when the vehicle slowed to a stop.

"We are here, Quill," Krey said.

I sat up in a hurry, blinking away the sleepiness as Krey shut off the vehicle. I peered out the window. There was a large stone home in front of us. If I hadn't just spent the last month living in a freaking palace, the farmer's house would have seemed like a mansion to me after living in the tiny two-bedroom apartment with Carrie and Josh. There was a slightly smaller building made of wood about a hundred feet behind the stone home, with a path shoveled in the snow between them. A land vehicle was parked next to the wooden building but was nearly buried under the snow.

"Come, my mate." Quill opened the door and jumped down. I slid to the edge, and Galan lowered me into Quill's arms.

"Put me down," I said when Quill continued to hold me. "I can walk, Quill."

He frowned at me, and I poked him lightly in the chest. "I don't want to be carried."

He sighed but set me on my feet. He held my hand tightly as the rest of the Draax jumped out of the vehicles. Galan stood on my other side, and Krey stood next to him as Laos moved into position next to Quill. The others stood closely behind us.

"Isn't this a little overkill?" I muttered as we walked toward the front door of the home.

All the Draax had drawn their swords, and I squeezed Quill's hand. "I don't want anyone to get hurt, Quill. Okay? Promise me that -"

The door to the home opened, and two Draax stepped out. They wore heavy fur cloaks and stared silently at Quill before glancing at each other. They both bowed, and Quill nodded to them as my stomach churned with nerves.

"My king," the one on the left said. His dark hair was on the curly side and brushed against his shoulders, and he had the same copper coloured eyes as Galan.

"You are Brandel?" Quill said.

The second Draax stepped forward. His hair was cut short like Quill's, and he had dark brown eyes. "No, I am."

Quill studied him, and I squeezed his hand again. He gave me a brief look before turning back to the two Draax. "Where is the human named Evelyn?"

Neither Draax replied, and Krey scowled at them. "Your king has asked you a question."

They still didn't answer, and I made a high-pitched sound of anxiety when Krey stepped forward and raised his sword. "Answer your king or -"

"Here, I'm right here." Evelyn pushed her way past the two Draax. She wore a cloak that was too big for her. A toddler, her tiny body dressed in warm layers, was on her hip. The little girl was a beautiful shade of purple, and her long, dark hair was in a neat braid. She clung to Evelyn's neck and stared wide-eyed at us as Evelyn stopped. She was a little shorter than I was, and she was dwarfed by the two Draax standing behind her.

Licking her lips nervously, she took another step forward. My mouth dropped open when two tails lashed out simultaneously and wrapped around her waist. The two Draax pulled her to an abrupt halt and stood protectively next to her as Evelyn held the toddler a little closer. Quill and Galan made identical grunts of surprise and stared at each other over my head.

I stared at the tails wrapped possessively around Evelyn's waist as she looked at Brandel and then at the Draax to her left. My heart drummed rapidly, and the churning in my stomach faded away. I recognized the look on her face - it was the same one that appeared on mine whenever I looked at Quill.

"Quill," I said in a low voice, "she loves them."

I glanced up at my mate. He was staring at how the Draax had wrapped their tails around Evelyn's waist. I almost giggled at his look of pure and unexpected delight when he grinned down at me. "I told you there was nothing to fear, my mate. I love you."

"I love you too," I said as Quill's tail wrapped around my waist. "Always."

Keep reading for an excerpt from the second book in the series, "Rule".

# RULE EXCERPT

## (THE DRAAX SERIES BOOK TWO)

Copyright © 2018 Elizabeth Kelly

*Evelyn*

"Congratulations, we've found you a mate."

I stared at the blonde woman sitting behind the desk. "You're kidding."

The woman laughed before leaning forward and tapping her pen against the shiny surface of her desk. "I assure you, Ms. Fisher, that I'm not. We have matched you with a Draax, and you'll be leaving for the Draax planet the day after tomorrow."

"I didn't expect it to be so quick," I said. "I just had the genetic testing last week and only found out three days ago that I carried the gene for breeding with the Draax. I haven't even looked through the database yet."

The woman shrugged. "We pride ourselves here at the agency on our efficiency." She hesitated and, this time, tapped the end of her pencil against her teeth. "Honestly, we rarely have breeding compatible women who sign up for the lifetime program, so we tend to fast-track their applications."

I swallowed heavily as the woman said, "Mind you, most of the women we send to the Draax planet to breed never come back."

She paused, realized how that sounded and said hurriedly, "Because they're very happy with their new life and the Draax they are mated with. Not because they're forced to stay."

"I know," I said. "I did some research before applying for the program."

The woman gave me a fleeting look, and I tried not to blush. The woman sitting across from me was a middle, and the shirt she wore probably cost more than my entire wardrobe. I pulled at my too-tight shirt. I was so poor I couldn't even afford decent clothing for the breeding program meeting. I'd had to borrow a top and skirt from my neighbour, Candy, and both items of clothing were too small.

"Oh, I didn't realize you had a tablet. Most of the lowers don't," the woman said.

I squirmed in my seat. Like most middles and uppers, the woman didn't have a clue about lowers. "I don't. But the library has them."

The woman gave me a blank look – I had an idea that she had never once set foot in a public library – before nodding. "Oh, right, of course. The library."

She glanced at the tablet on the desk before me as a rush of uncustomary anger flooded me. I tamped it down immediately. It wasn't the woman's fault that I was a lower. It wasn't her fault that she didn't know what it was like to be hungry, cold, or on the verge of being kicked out of her home. It did no good to be angry with her just because she'd never laid awake at night in a closet of a bedroom, clutching a knife to her chest and hoping that her step-brother and his friends didn't get drunk enough to try to rape her.

My stomach clenched, and I took a shaky breath. The woman glanced up from the tablet and frowned. "Ms. Fisher, are you all right? You're very pale."

"I'm fine. What is the name of the Draax I'm, um, mated to?"

I supposed it was strange to ask the name of the alien I was about to be mated to for the rest of my life. In the old fairy tales my mother read to me as a child, the girl married her Prince Charming. He was handsome and rich and madly in love with her. He certainly didn't have green skin or a tail and was only interested in knocking her up with a baby. My stomach clenched again at the thought of having sex with an alien. What if he was rough with me?

*He won't be. Candy has nothing but good things to say about the Draax aliens she slept with, remember? Besides, it's better than what will happen to you if you stay.*

I shuddered all over and closed my eyes. My inner voice was right. In fact, I should be celebrating the fact that the agency had found a match for me so quickly, not worrying about how rough alien sex would be. Even if the alien didn't take his time or didn't care about my pleasure, it would still be better than being married to that scumbag Troy. Just the thought of sleeping with Troy made me want to vomit.

I realized the woman from the agency was speaking, and I said, "I'm sorry, what did you say?"

"I said I had even better news about who you were matched to for mating. You have been matched with a Draax named Quillan, and he," the woman gave me a look of breathless anticipation, "is the king of the western province of the Odias continent."

"I – what?" I said faintly. Did the woman just say I was matched to a king?

The woman nodded. "It's true. You're our number one match for him."

"Are you sure?"

"Positive. You've tested higher than any other human for breeding compatibility. You're a - what we like to call in the business - guaranteed breeder. You'll likely become pregnant on the first try. Because of this, we pull you from the general breeding database and match you with higher ranking Draax who are in the program, and you can't get much higher than a king. We like to give these," she paused, "Draax special treatment so we match them with the guaranteed breeders rather than making them wait to be chosen, but you didn't hear that from me."

"Right," I said.

The woman smiled at me. "And with you signing up for the lifetime program, it makes you extra valuable. The king is apparently very anxious for an heir."

"Right, of course," I said. "Um, he knows I'm a lower, right?"

"We have passed on all of your information but, frankly, the Draax don't care what class you are. They just want you to be healthy and able to breed. Now, you can, of course, say no to mating with the king and choose your mate from the breeding program, but I highly encourage you not to do that. You'll be a queen, afterall."

"I didn't care about being a queen. I just cared about getting the hell off of Earth. But I smiled at the woman and said, "I'm happy to be matched with the king."

"Excellent," she said happily. "Your payment of gallberry juice is waiting for you in the front room."

The woman pushed a few buttons on her tablet and then

frowned. "This can't be right. It says you'll receive only a gallon of juice for a lifetime of service. Oh, for the love of God, the juice guys can't get anything right. I just knew they would screw this up some -"

"It's right. I only need a gallon."

The woman gave me a suddenly anxious look before speaking very slowly and clearly. "Ms. Fisher, you understand you have signed up for the lifetime program, correct?"

"Yes."

"You will never be able to return to Earth unless your mate allows it. You will become the queen of the western province and will most likely bear the king more than one child."

"I get it," I said.

"But you only asked for one gallon of juice."

"That's all I need."

The woman hesitated. "It's for the rest of your life, Ms. Fisher."

"I'm aware."

"Very well. You are to be at the docking bay at eight-thirty Tuesday morning. We'll have someone from the agency pick you up at your apartment at eight to escort you to the loading dock. Please be ready to go by eight. The pilots don't like it when the cargo is late."

"I won't be late," I said.

The woman pushed the tablet toward me. "Your signature is required on the bottom line. Did you read over the terms of the contract like I asked?"

"Yes, I read it after I tested positive for breeding."

"Good. By signing, you agree to the terms of the contract. Breaking them is considered a first-class felony, and you'll be sentenced to at least twenty-five years in prison. Is that clear?"

"Yes."

"You will go to prison, Evelyn," the woman said. "There is no getting out of it once you sign the contract. Be very certain you wish to do this."

"I'm certain." I signed across the line with the tip of my finger and only felt a moment of panic before it subsided. I sat back in my seat as euphoria washed over me. I was free of him. By this time next week, I would be on a new planet, and my stepbrother would never be able to hurt me again.

*You still need to get to the docking bay without him noticing. You're not free yet, and he's dangerous and unpredictable. Don't ever forget that*, my inner voice cautioned.

"A copy of the contract will be sent to the email address you provided. Unless you have more questions, we're finished here," the woman said.

She stood and smoothed down her skirt as I stumbled to my feet. I hesitated and then held out my hand. The woman glanced at it before giving it a brief shake. "Nice to meet you, Ms. Fisher. Enjoy your new life. Don't forget to pick up your juice at the front desk."

"Yeah, I won't forget." Did the woman think I was that stupid? I could hear the disdain in my voice, and I automatically cringed. At home, that tone would get me a punch to the face if I were lucky or a kick to the kidneys if I wasn't.

The woman gave me a strange look before pointing to the door. "The reception is to the right. Goodbye, Ms. Fisher."

"Goodbye." I hurried out of the woman's office and down the hallway. At the front desk, I picked up the gallberry juice and tucked it into the backpack I had brought for that very purpose. I couldn't very well walk through my neighbourhood carrying a gallon of gallberry juice. My throat would be slit in the first two minutes.

I rode the elevator down to the front lobby and walked

outside. I breathed in the warm air and the smell of the flowers planted in front of the office building before slinging the pack over my back and tightening the straps. An airtrain roared overhead, blotting out the sun momentarily and sending a gust of warm air over me. I studied its silver underbelly as it flew by, wondering for a moment what it would be like to travel in the air like that.

*You'll find out in two days.*

A little sprinkle of excitement bloomed in my belly. Yes, I would. In two days, I would fly in a spaceship to another planet, and my life on Earth would be a distant memory. I took another deep breath and started the long walk toward home.

# ABOUT THE AUTHOR

Elizabeth Kelly was born and raised in Ontario, Canada. She moved west as a teenager and now lives in Alberta with her husband and a menagerie of pets. She firmly believes that a person can survive solely on sushi and coffee, and only her husband's mad cooking skills prevents her from proving that theory.

For more information about Elizabeth, check out her website at

## www.elizabethkelly.ca

f facebook.com/EKellyBooks
instagram.com/elizabethkelly_author
a amazon.com/Elizabeth-Kelly/e/B00EOHZ0MS
BB bookbub.com/authors/elizabeth-kelly

# ALSO BY ELIZABETH KELLY

**Tempted Series**

Tempted

Twice Tempted

Forever Tempted

Breathless

Tempted Trilogy (Books 1-3)

**Red Moon Series**

Red Moon

Red Moon Rising

Dark Moon

Alpha Moon

Pale Moon

**The Recruit Series**

The Recruit (Book One)

The Recruit (Book Two)

The Recruit (Book Three)

The Recruit (Book Four)

The Recruit (Book Five)

The Recruit (Book Six)

**The Shifters Series**

Willow and the Wolf (Book One)

Ava and the Bear (Book Two)

Place Your Trust in Me (Book Three)

**Individual Books**

The Necessary Engagement

Amelia's Touch

The Rancher's Daughter

Healing Gabriel

The Contract

A Home for Lily

Saving Charlotte

Shameless

The Fairy Tales Collection

Broken

An Unlikely Seduction

**Holiday Romance**

The Christmas Wife

The Christmas Rescue

The Christmas Nanny

The Christmas Boss

Sordid Games

www.ingramcontent.com/pod-product-compliance
Lightning Source LLC
Chambersburg PA
CBHW050657290626
47170CB00015B/1050

* 9 7 8 1 9 8 8 8 2 6 2 4 0 *